For the real Lillian and Albert

LUCKY COWBOY

A MEN OF STONE RIDGE NOVEL

HEATHERLY BELL

PROLOGUE

*L*et me make one thing perfectly clear. Far too many of you make fun of our acronym. But no, we do not call ourselves the ladies of SORROW because we're *sad*. Far from it. We are the Society of Reasonable, Respectable, and Organized Women. We are a society, one of reasonable women, and...sure, okay, it's too long to say the entire name. There.

We're simply everything the name of our society itself indicates. Respectable women, who appreciate the position we're in. I'll let you in on a little secret, dear: we run this town. Sure, sure. We're in the minority but that has mostly worked out to be an advantage. Who wouldn't love to be one of the few? The proud? Oh, wait. Never mind.

For decades, Stone Ridge, Texas has been a town filled with a majority of men. We're not exactly sure how this happened, but let's begin with the fact that we're a ranching town. Think cowboys. Cows. Lots of lakes for fishing and hunting. In other words, it's like a huge man cave.

But honestly, our lack of women also has something to do

with the lack of jobs and services for us. We don't even have a hairdresser in town for the love of Pete. My new daughter-in-law does my hair in her home every other Tuesday. But I digress.

What we *do* have is a great deal of eligible young men around marrying age.

I myself had seven suitors before I chose to wed my sainted husband, Lloyd. This is the place to be if a woman wants to feel special. We're like Alaska, but warmer.

Yes, thank you, I will get to the point. We need more women in our quaint town because we do have the men. Oh, do we have the *men*! Rodeo cowboys, ranchers, construction workers. Hard bodies, chiseled jaws, and all those things the young'uns like. So, of course, when the subject of a local primary school came up, as it does once every five or so years, Sadie Stephens was the *first* woman I thought of. Uh-huh.

She left town for Baylor University a few years ago to get her degree in education. After graduation, for some reason unknown to me, she settled in the metropolis of San Antonio. Can you believe it? San Antonio! Sometimes, there's just no accounting for taste.

Honestly, she's the *sweetest* girl in the world. Close to her family and her older brother, Beau. Never has a bad word to say about anyone. A pretty and petite blond with hazel eyes. No, I'm not giving you her measurements. By the way, there's a rumor that her college boyfriend broke her heart, and she's been a little shy of love ever since then.

Suffice it to say, the men of Stone Ridge are above reproach. They know better than to hurt a woman's feelings. Why, they'd rather break their own leg than any woman's heart. We're glad to have Sadie back. That's right, she's agreed to take the position as our new school's first teacher.

Yes, men of Stone Ridge. You are welcome. Sadie Stephens is back in town, and she's single.

Let the games begin!

~ Beulah Hayes, acting President of the Society of Reasonable, Respectable and Organized Women (SORROW), and author of The Men of Stone Ridge, tenth edition~

CHAPTER 1

No other twenty-eight-year-old woman in Stone Ridge, Texas could say this, but Sadie Stephens started the Tuesday after Labor Day with circle time.

She stood in the old building that long ago served its purpose as the town's original church. An old white clapboard building, with a steeple and a tone-less, broken belfry. It had seen better days, on or around the turn of the century. As long as Sadie could remember, everyone had worshiped at Trinity Church in the center of town.

This morning, a small group of children ages five to eight sat in a circle inside of the old but newly cleaned and painted church. All the pews and the baptismal font were removed, and there remained one large room with a strip of carpet in the center over the hardwood floors. Small desks and chairs were flanked in groups around the room. In her class were fifteen boys and five girls. The classroom's mix of boys to girls was just about right for Stone Ridge, Texas's demographics, where men outnumbered women by about five to one.

And Sadie would be the first teacher at Stone Ridge Elementary.

"Boys and girls, you probably already know that my name is Sadie Stephens, but y'all can call me Miss Sadie." She turned to write her name in large letters on the white board in bold black marker.

Something tapped the side of Sadie's head and she turned to see a paper plane at her feet.

"He did it!" Ellie Monroe, one of her Kindergartners, pointed to Jimmy Ray, an eight-year-old.

Sadie bent to pick it up from the floor. She didn't want to start their day off in a negative way, so she turned it over in her hands and admired it for a moment.

"Why, what a wonderful piece of engineering."

"You're pretty," said Jimmy Ray.

How adorable. The cute kid grinned, showing two missing front teeth.

"Ew," said Bobby Joe. "She's old."

"Is not!" Ellie scrunched up her little face.

This brought about a general discussion between the boys and girls regarding who was old, such as one's grandmother, but Miss Sadie was simply a grown-up. Ellie won the round with her impressive logic.

"You guys are so *smart!*" Sadie took back control of the conversation. "What a lively discussion. Yes, Jimmy Ray, I'm twenty-eight, a bit old for you. But thank you for saying that I'm pretty."

"When's snack time?" Bobby Joe raised his hand. "My mom said y'all would give me snacks if I'm good. I'm bein' good. Where's my snack?"

"That's a great question! We will have our snack soon. Ellie's mom volunteered to bring it today. But I'm sure you just ate a big breakfast."

"I have a hollow leg," Bobby Joe said with conviction.

"Does not!" Ellie said, who would obviously become the classroom's fact checker.

"All right." Sadie took a deep and steadying breath. "We're going to get to know each other a little bit first. Some of you already know how to read, and others are just learning, so I need to find out more about you. This is going to be so interesting! I can't wait to find out who can already read."

Nearly every hand raised, all except for Ellie, who pouted and crossed her arms.

Oh, dear. Sadie probably shouldn't have said that. "Wait. I didn't ask you to raise your hands."

Little hands lowered.

"The point is, soon you will *all* be reading."

Sadie ended circle time after each child said their name out loud and she'd pointed them to their assigned desk with their decorated name card. She could hardly contain her excitement and nearly rubbed her hands together. She would finally *teach*, and mold little minds.

She'd dreamed about this day and it was finally here. And in her hometown, no less! How wonderful to influence the future generation of both the women and men of Stone Ridge. She would have a challenge, teaching the first class at different levels, but she'd created a plan.

Until recently many parents of grade school children homeschooled since Stone Ridge was a small remote town deep in Texas Hill Country. Older children were usually sent on a bus to the neighboring town of Kerrville, a forty-minute ride reach way. A long bus ride, one Sadie remembered well. She, her brother, Beau, and all their friends rode the bus for years. But now, local parents would have options.

Thanks to Beulah Hayes's efforts, they'd began the search for a location and a plan to raise funds last year, and wrangled support from the town's residents. There would still be many fundraisers ahead of them to fully fund the effort.

Because they didn't yet have all their district certifications, they'd applied for a charter, and received some money from the state. They'd raised enough through Beulah's pet organization, the ladies of SORROW, to pay for a year of Sadie's abysmal salary.

And while the ladies scouted for another, better location, they'd provided the old church so that Sadie could begin teaching this fall.

Two hours into the school day, Sadie counted ten times she'd returned Jimmy Ray's shoe to him, because he kept throwing it. She talked to him, but he didn't seem to think he was doing anything wrong. On the eleventh time, she got wise and put it in her desk drawer, telling him he'd get it back at the end of the day.

He then hopped around the classroom for a few minutes on one foot, earning lots of laughs. Sadie asked him to sit down, then handed out reading books, and while some of the kids took to reading them quietly, others fought over them.

Ellie wanted *Black Beauty* because of the horse on the cover, but Jimmy Ray reminded her that she couldn't read so she should go ahead and take the "baby book."

Ellie burst into tears. Sadie gathered the little girl into her arms and considered joining her. This day was not going well so far. She'd pictured an entirely different kind of experience, with well-behaved children eager to read a book and learn.

"Jimmy Ray, I'm going to need you to apologize to Ellie. There's no such thing in my class as a *baby* book."

"Baby, baby, baby!" Jimmy Ray laughed as again he hopped around on one foot.

And Sadie could take no more. She rarely lost her temper and *never* with a child. But Jimmy Ray had just stepped on her last nerve. She would never tolerate cruelty among her children.

"Jimmy Ray! How many times have I told you? Sit *down*. I mean it now," Sadie said, and stomped her foot in emphasis.

And went right through the bottom of the wooden floor.

"TERMITES CAN DO a hell of a lot of damage," said Riggs Henderson. "I've seen entire beams fall."

A local rancher, Riggs was also a foreman and worked odd construction jobs here and there. He managed the occasional renovation in town and sometimes worked with Sadie's father. He'd been driving by in his truck when he saw the commotion gathered outside the old church.

Many of the men who gathered stood eyeing the floor and the foot of crawl space under it. There were plenty of head shakes as an entire crew arrived and got to work. In their town residents came together in times of need. It took one call to the phone tree, started by Beulah Hayes herself this time, who'd walked over from the General Store nearby, which was owned by her husband.

Sadie sat with the children outside on the porch steps, out of the way of danger until their parents could arrive. To say the children were fascinated was an understatement. Suddenly no one talked about snacks or reading levels. They'd just seen their teacher's feet go through a supposedly solid wood floor.

Jimmy Ray simply stared in horror when Sadie's first foot went through the floor. He must have thought her to be "incredible cartoonish" mad. Not the case, but either she'd gained too much weight this summer, or these termites had feasted. For decades.

Beulah Hayes shook her finger. "The inspector said it was fine. We tented for termites weeks ago."

"Who did you use?" Riggs asked.

"I'll have to look through my paperwork," Beulah huffed. "But he came from Kerrville. Gave me a decent rate."

A general groan of consensus came out of the men, as if the good people of Kerrville couldn't be trusted to know a termite infestation from a scorpion one.

"Are you sure you don't need a trip to the hospital, missy?" This was directed to Sadie from Lenny, one of their volunteer firefighters, a man about her father's age.

"It's not like I fell far. My boot took the worst of it," Sadie said. "I'm fine, but thanks."

"Miss Sadie went through the floor," Ellie said. "I'm scared. There's a monster down there."

"No monster," Lenny said, bending. "It's a teeny tiny little bug, you see, so small no one can even see it."

"You're not helping," Sadie warned.

"Oh, they don't eat children," Lenny said with a chuckle and a wave. "But they eat through wood like a sumabitch."

"Lenny!"

"My house is made of wood," Ellie said with a hitch in her breath. "Will they eat my house, Miss Sadie?"

"No, no, sweetie," Sadie said, glaring at Lenny. "I'm sure they won't."

A bevy of pickup trucks arrived one after the other, their tires crunching into the gravel as they pulled into the church parking lot. This would be the second wave of men, arriving to help, meaning they would have dropped everything they were doing on the ranch.

Life wasn't easy in Stone Ridge, as services were few and residents were forced to rely on each other. The fire department, for instance, all volunteer. As a former EMT, Sadie took her turn, too. They currently didn't have a doctor or clinic, and no police, relying on the County Sheriff an hour away.

There was no hairdresser in town, no clothing stores, no

coffee shop, no movie theater, and spotty cell service and Wi-Fi. They did, however, have rolling hills, trees, rivers, lakes, and lots of great fishing. There was Trinity Church, a veterinary clinic (there were more animals in town than people), the General Store, and the Shady Grind, a bar and grill.

But the best part of her hometown was the way the men of Stone Ridge revered their few women. They were held in high regard. Protected. This was just one of the reasons Sadie came home after getting her teaching degree. Here, she'd have a better than average chance of finding a husband.

In fact, he could be here right now, wondering if he'd ever find a woman in this woman-scarcity town. Maybe he'd even bring his niece or nephew to the school one day for drop off or pick up. Ada Armstrong's nephew was coming to visit, and she couldn't talk enough about him. But Sadie wasn't too excited because he sounded so desperate for a wife. In any case, with the right man, their gazes would meet across the tops of the children's heads.

She'd feel that little zip and zing. The jolt and kablammy that her best friend Eve Iglesias talked about. Sadie's pupils would dilate, and bam! She'd fall in love. Once, she'd felt that zip and zing, and thought she knew just the right man for her. But that was years ago. She'd given up on *him*.

As the trucks filed in one after another, Sadie noticed her older brother Beau's truck, Wade Cruz, two more of the Henderson brothers, and of course, Lincoln Carver.

Lincoln Carver.

The man she'd wanted since she could remember having the slightest interest in boys. The one she'd finally given up on. A few years ago, Lincoln stopped speaking to Sadie and even though everyone else moved on from the feud that caused this, Lincoln still remained civil. But nothing more than civil. Then again, he was a loyal sort, one of his most attractive qualities.

Followed closely by the long, brawny body, strong arms, chiseled jaw, and dimples. Sigh.

He and the rest of the men went to work as if they did this every day, gathering tools and supplies from their truck beds.

Lincoln walked by her first, nodding and tipping his Stetson. "Sadie."

"Hey there, Lincoln." Her heart rate spiked the way it always did when he appeared anywhere near her vicinity.

"Hey, sis," Beau said, as he walked up the steps next. "You okay there?"

"I'm fine. Sorry to be so much trouble."

"What a first day, right?" Beau said and turned to the first crew of men. "What do we have goin' on here? How can we help?"

"We're goin' to need to move them to another location," Riggs Henderson advised. "We've got to rip out all this wood and replace it. Should take a week or more. We should do a more thorough inspection. Walls, floors, roof. I wouldn't feel comfortable having children in here otherwise."

Sadie closed her eyes and pinched the bridge of her nose. Well, there went her teaching career. Maybe she could move back to San Antonio, get her old job, and come back and try this again next fall.

"Now, now," Beulah said as though reading Sadie's mind. "I am sorry about all this, but don't you despair. We'll find another location for y'all right quick."

Except a centrally located empty building in the middle of town didn't exist.

The parents began to arrive for their children and were informed. They appeared well rested, even after the short school day. But Sadie had probably aged ten years in the last five minutes.

Because it was still early in the day, she left the men to it, and headed two blocks down to the veterinary clinic where Eve worked as a veterinarian. Most of the time Eve was out on a large animal call, but Sadie caught sight of her old blue beat-up truck parked outside. She opened the door to an empty waiting room where Eve sat behind the receptionist desk. She and the other vet, Annabeth, couldn't afford to hire an admin yet.

"Hey," Eve said, coming around from the desk to give Sadie a hug. "I heard."

By now, everyone would have. "I don't know what we're going to do."

"How did it go, otherwise?"

"You know what it's like when you see a dress you love online? And then you see that it's on sale! The last one in your size. When you place the order, it turns out you get an additional discount at check out. You can't believe your good luck. The dress arrives, free shipping of course, and when you take it out of the package and try it on, it fits just like it was made for you?"

Eve nodded, smiling in anticipation.

"Well, today was *nothing* like that." Sadie collapsed on one of the empty waiting chairs. "It was a disaster. I don't think I taught them a single thing, except that I'm a pushover."

Eve sat beside Sadie. "Oh, hon. Well, it will get better."

"I thought it would be different. I was so excited about my lesson plan, but I couldn't keep their attention. Until I went through the floor, of course. Then no one would take their eyes off me."

"Don't be so hard on yourself. You're doing something that's never been done before here."

"And maybe there was a reason for that."

"Yes. We didn't have Sadie Stephens, teacher extraordinaire."

Sadie allowed the thought to cheer her a little bit. "The point is, I was excited about teaching them. They're not quite as excited to learn. And now I don't know how they will until the termite damage is repaired."

"Don't you worry. I'm sure Beulah is on this like a bean in caffeine."

"Even Beulah can't materialize a building out of thin air." She sighed.

"I'm sure the guys will get the work done soon."

"*I'm* not so sure."

She'd seen the expression on her brother's face. He worked in construction with their father, and he didn't look happy as he studied the eaves and beams. He shook his head far too often and once he'd said to Lincoln, "Would you take a look at this. Who would let this building pass inspection?"

"Who's your favorite student?" Eve said.

"Well, a teacher shouldn't *have* favorites, but if I did, it would be Ellie Monroe."

"Aw, yeah, she's a cutie. She and her mom come around every now and then to check on our rescues. They've adopted nearly every cat we've rescued. Ellie names them after the months of the year." Eve chuckled. "She's up to May."

Sadie sighed. "Yeah, and because of me, now every kid in class knows she can't read."

"She's only five, isn't she?" Eve cocked her head.

"That's not the point. She cried when another kid took a higher-level book away from her because she can't read."

Eve frowned. Only she would know the significance of that for Sadie. She couldn't help having such a tender heart. Eve had a huge heart for animals of all types. Sadie, a heart for books, followed closely by children. All of them on Earth.

But she would have to toughen up to be a teacher. Otherwise, her students would smell her weakness the way sharks smelled blood.

"Maybe I *should* have become a paramedic. Or just stayed as an EMT," Sadie said.

Her position after getting her degree was as both a public-school teacher and an emergency medical technician in San Antonio. With the pay so poor, she'd needed two jobs to make ends meet in a bigger city. But teaching remained her first love. She'd been an adequate EMT. Mostly, she'd been a glorified taxi from hospital to convalescent home and back. Giving comfort and aide to people at the end of their lives made Sadie realize she had a lot more living to do.

She'd been about to enroll in courses to become a paramedic and increase her pay, when on a visit to her parents, Beulah again brought up the subject of a school. Sadie wanted to move back to Stone Ridge, like her best friend Eve. And Sadie missed her quirky town.

Eve stood. "Wait right here. I've got something for you."

When Eve returned from the back rooms, she carried a furry little creature in her arms. A rabbit.

"This little guy is so soft. Someone brought him in after finding him injured a couple of weeks ago. He's fully recovered and I'm ready to set him free again. There's no way you can hold him and not feel better about your day."

"Eve, I'm sorry. This must all seem so silly to you."

"Of course not. I didn't have the best first day, either."

Sadie winced. "I remember. You put a horse down."

And Eve had been through the ringer in the past few years, beginning with her last-minute decision not to show up on her wedding day to Jackson, Lincoln's younger brother. That awful day caused a feud between the two families, and of course, Sadie, also a loyal sort, took Eve's side.

Eve's problems were real, but Sadie just had a bad day.

15

Okay, a horrible day.

"I love you, little one." Sadie cuddled the rabbit, gray and white and soft as silk. "You're right. I feel better already."

No one ever said teaching would be easy, after all, but simply that it *could* be rewarding. Just because she'd lost control of her classroom today didn't mean it would happen again. She'd just have to kindly exert her authority. Kill them with kindness. Or give them a motivation that didn't involve a sugary snack for a reward.

"Maybe when we get back, I could make this little guy our class pet. Rabbits are always good for that aren't they? The kids could learn responsibility and it could be a positive behavior modifier."

"Sure," Eve said. "Although, rabbits are sensitive to loud noises. I'm close if you change your mind. I'll just come get him."

Sadie sat up straighter, inspired. "I've tried to think outside the box but some of the old tried and true methods might work also."

"Why not?" Eve said. "And don't forget show and tell. Or career day. I could come and talk to the kids about being a vet."

"Would you? That would be amazing! The girls would love that."

"And you should get Lincoln to come and show the boys how to rope. There's nothing boys love more than a rodeo champ."

Even the sound of his name sometimes landed her with a sucker punch. But despite the fact Jackson had been engaged to Eve, it always seemed that Lincoln didn't remember Sadie. But of course, he did. The few women in this town hardly faded into the background. And Sadie was Beau's sister, who happened to be one of Lincoln's close friends. He did *know* her. He just didn't much seem to care.

"That's...that's a wonderful idea, too." She continued to pet the puffy piece of silk. "I should think about asking him. Maybe."

Eve laughed. "Don't be shy about it. If you want, I can put a bug in Mima's ear. I've been spending some time up at the ranch lately, helping out with the grooming for some extra cash."

"Lincoln hasn't really talked to me since...well, you know."

"He doesn't talk much to me, either, but this might be a good opportunity. I mean, the rest of us have moved on. It's his turn."

"He's really loyal to his brother." Seeing the pained look on Eve's face, Sadie changed the subject. "And anyway, isn't Lincoln really busy?"

To hear Beau tell it, Lincoln practically ran that cattle ranch. He and his father Hank, on their own, since Jackson took off for Nashville a few years ago. During the rodeo season Lincoln tended to be gone for weeks at a time. He'd turned pro a couple of years ago and every once in a while, she'd see him at the Shady Grind, having a beer with the boys, showing off that shiny belt buckle to eager women.

He was tall with long legs, built like a running back, but despite his size carried himself with ease and grace. Hair always on the wrong side of a cut, a shiny copper brown, and his eyes...they were the deepest shade of blue she'd ever seen. And they crinkled when he smiled.

"He's not too busy to help out a friend."

"Fine," Sadie said, ready to end this topic. "I'll ask him."

"Are you going straight home? If not, I could use a little company while I straighten out the surgery suite before it gets returned."

"All I have waitin' at home is Ben & Jerry's."

Eve took the bunny back from Sadie and put it in his little cage in the back.

Sadie followed Eve through the back of the clinic, to where the trailer she and Annabeth occasionally rented sat parked. Eve called it a hospital on wheels. It looked like a fifth wheel from the outside. Some surgeries were performed in the trailer, as well as x-rays of large animals. Eve often towed it to horse and cattle ranches in the area. As Sadie stepped inside behind Eve, she noted all the space inside the trailer. The amount of room caught her by surprise.

Eve gloved up and began tidying the counters. "So, did Lincoln come out to help today?"

"You know he did," Sadie said. "All the men showed up to help poor Sadie who went straight through the wood floor on her first day of class."

"You make it sound like somehow that's *your* fault."

"No, it's just my lousy luck." She hated being rescued. This time, it couldn't be helped.

"Or Beulah, trying to save a penny and rush things. She's been wantin' this school to open since forever."

"I wish I didn't get my hopes up."

"How is Lincoln, anyway? Haven't seen him for a while."

"Still just as handsome a cuss as ever."

"Still just as single as ever." Eve smiled, wiping the counter.

"Stop. I gave up on him a long time ago."

"Yeah? If I recall, you *gave* up after my weddin' day fail. And I've told you before, because Jackson and I didn't work doesn't mean you can't wind up with Lincoln someday."

But Sadie's mind was suddenly elsewhere. Her father owned portables bigger than this trailer that he hauled from one job to another. Once a job was complete, the portable moved to the next location. And in some large cities, portables were a way of increasing student enrollment without having to budget for the costs of building, which could be astronomical.

"Oh my Lord!" Sadie jumped up, clapping her hands, as the idea became fully formed.

"What? What is it?"

"I love you! Thanks to you, I think I just figured out a way to save our school year!"

CHAPTER 2

*L*incoln began his day being kicked in the ass by a pissed off bull and ended it by tearing down termite-infested beams from the rafters of the old church. All in all, a pretty violent Tuesday for him.

"Hey, y'all!" Beau called out. "Let's head on over to the Shady Grind. We'll pick this back up tomorrow."

Knowing Beau, he'd assign some of the men who worked for his father's construction company to help, too. Lincoln would fit the work in whenever he could, but he would do his part. Thankfully there were enough men to get the job done. Manpower was never a problem in Stone Ridge. The materials were another issue entirely, but he assumed Beulah was at this moment planning yet another bake sale or knit-a-thon. He still remembered the day he'd been informed that money could be raised by knitting, of all things. Who knew?

Lincoln parked his truck and went inside just as a group of ranch hands were walking into the bar. Usually not much but cowboys in this bar and grill, one owned and operated by Priscilla, a real throwback to the seventies. She wore her big platinum blond hair teased out to the sides. That hair of hers had its own zip code.

The bar itself was old-school with a jukebox in the back that played ancient tunes and the original polished wood bar. Stools were lined up at the bar, but some tables and chairs were available for the grill in the back that served a decent "Shady burger."

"Hey, boys," Priscilla said as the men filled in all the empty seats at the bar. "What's doin'?"

"Just got back from the latest town project," Riggs said.

Lincoln ordered a beer and Priscilla slid it over to him. "How's our boy doin'?"

"Writin' songs for Keith Urban and Luke Bryan."

"Whowee, you name dropper!"

Lincoln smiled. Priscilla always needed to know the latest on Jackson's quest for superstardom.

"Heard you won yourself another buckle. Ropin' again?"

He nodded. "Yep."

The circuit could be a fun life, and he'd been at it on and off for years now, going from one event to the other, accumulating buckles. A few buckle bunnies along the way, too, though those never lasted. Between championships and qualifying events, he stayed close to home and the ranch. Lately, he'd been feeling out of sorts wondering how much longer he could keep up the punishing pace of ranch life where shit tended to go south more often than not. Sooner or later, he'd have to give one of them up.

Laying eyes on Sadie Stephens today was that bright light in one otherwise dull week. She looked like every single one of his teacher fantasies rolled into one. Lincoln and Beau were friends for a long time, and he could still recall passing through their house, overhearing ten-year-old Sadie as she presided above her classroom of teddy bears and dolls.

She'd looked beautiful and sweet sitting on the porch

21

steps with her class, keeping them close and calm, her boots a little dirty and scuffed from going through the floor. Her cheeks a little pink. Even now the thought of her made him smile. Her reputation as a klutz went right along with falling through a floor. She'd never been the most graceful girl, once actually tripping over her own two feet right in front of him. He'd caught her before she hit the ground. Jackson suggested that Sadie was so in love with Lincoln she couldn't manage to see straight, much less walk straight around him. Yeah, right. Funny.

The crush obviously faded to gray in the years after Jackson and Eve's wedding fiasco. For a while, the Iglesias and Carver families hadn't spoken to each other except when necessary. Runaway brides usually meant cutting ties with a family forever. Considering both he and Sadie were loyal to their opposite sides, it meant that they didn't speak for years.

Maybe it wasn't fair, but Lincoln told himself that Sadie could have stopped Eve from running. Could have, should have, talked some sense into her. Instead, she'd covered for Eve and actually driven her home from the church, leaving his poor brother heartbroken. To this day, he didn't understand.

Eve went off to college, and Jackson to Nashville. Sadie also left for college and returned for the occasional visit. He hadn't seen much of her since she'd been back, but Sadie wasn't exactly the type to hang out at the Shady Grind. Neither was Eve. Because Sadie was a sweet woman. Wholesome. No rodeo queen, but everyone's friend, and the girl next door. And now the town's first teacher, in case she had to further cement her candidacy for sainthood.

One of the many reasons he stayed away, in case her being friends with the enemy wasn't reason enough.

"All right, so how are we goin' to do this?" Riggs Henderson unfolded a paper napkin and started drawing up lines. "We need a plan of attack. Don't know about y'all but I sure have my share of work at the ranch. We need a schedule."

About ten years older than most of the men here tonight, Riggs occasionally served as their conscience and older brother. As the oldest Henderson brother, he alone mostly took care of his family's ranch. He'd been a widow for ten years and seemed in no hurry to rectify that situation.

"I can do Thursdays," Wade volunteered.

"Put me in for Wednesdays," Lincoln said.

"Beau?" Riggs asked.

"Aw, shit fire, Tuesdays, I guess. Might as well make it a thing."

Before long, a schedule was created. Riggs said he would talk to the older married men that weren't here about filling in where they could around their other obligations.

Beau glanced at his buzzing phone. "Ah, geez. There are advantages to lousy reception."

Downtown, phone reception was much better, though one didn't want to bet the farm on it. Heh.

"You goin' to pick that up?" Lincoln asked.

"It's Sadie," he said, finally putting the phone to his ear. "Hey. Just havin' a beer with the guys. What? Oh. I hadn't thought of that. Sure, great idea but...uh-huh. Well...sure, guess it *could* work. Temporary, right?"

He hung up and turned to the men. "Y'all, I'm goin' to need some help moving a portable tomorrow."

They all groaned and Riggs whipped out his napkin schedule.

By the time Lincoln rolled home to his own cabin on the hill he could have been juiced, but he wasn't. He'd seen first-hand what too much drinking did to a man, and he wasn't okay with that complete loss of self-control. He couldn't accept the weakness buried deep down inside a man who drank too much.

Speaking of drinking, and speaking of weakness, he should check on his father before he called it a night.

Hank was having a bad day with his back pain, so he'd stayed behind when Lincoln went to the old church. Mostly, middle-age ranchers were excused from the heavy lifting if they had sons. And Hank certainly worked that angle every chance he got. Not long ago he too was one of the many men of Stone Ridge who pitched in where needed. Now, the ranch remained his excuse for missing everything. For letting life pass him by.

No woman should have *that* much power over a man.

Most thought he still mourned over his ex-wife, but Lincoln knew better. There was a reason he'd taken Jackson and Eve's breakup so hard. Hank had a long-time thing for Brenda, Eve's mother. And that relationship would *never* happen.

Lincoln wondered what would get Hank to pull out of this funk and accept life, even if it hadn't worked out necessarily how he wanted it. A new woman in his life? Or maybe a significant emotional event, like coming close to losing the ranch. Then again, Hank was that most dangerous of men: a functioning drunk. He hid his weakness well, a part of the problem. Even Mima did not know how her only child struggled.

And Lincoln was far too loyal to rat him out.

Surprisingly, he found Hank on the wraparound porch of the main house on the hill where he lived alone. He leaned against the rail when he noticed Lincoln. *Not* surprisingly, he held a shot glass in his hand and a somewhat glassy-eyed look, all too familiar.

"Evening," Lincoln said, propping a boot on the first step.

Not a good evening, not a bad one. It was *evening*. His

main problem? He wanted to help Hank, but he also wanted him to start acting like a father and not another one of Lincoln's responsibilities.

"Where you been?"

"Just got back from the Shady Grind. Bunch of us wound up there after putting in some time at the old church. It's a termite infestation."

"All this time?" Hank scowled. "You spent half the day there."

"And so did quite a few others. It'll get done."

"It's not fair what they expect of you. Of all you men."

"You not counting yourself as a man of Stone Ridge anymore?"

"You *young* men, I mean. Not old farts like me." He tipped the shot glass to his lips and drained it.

"I don't mind."

At least it got him off the ranch, giving him contact with their community, which was important. Those connections were vital to staying human. Healthy. After all, the opposite of addiction was engagement. He'd read that somewhere. Lincoln did *not* want to wind up like Hank. It must be a lonely existence judging everybody and everything.

"If I've told you once I've told you a thousand times," Hank said. "Don't let people take advantage of your generous nature."

And another thing. So many, including his own father, were under the mistaken impression that Lincoln was kind. Good. But those same people didn't see him on the circuit, drinking occasionally, but most often cavorting with rodeo queens and the buckle bunnies who followed him from town to town. Instead of being one man among many in Stone Ridge, he'd been regarded as unique due to his championship skills. He would be ashamed to say he enjoyed that feeling of being the center of attention for a short time. For once, he wasn't just one man in the crowd.

Maybe he was more like his brother than he realized.

ONE WEEK LATER, Lincoln was reminded that when something went wrong on a ranch, it would soon be followed by at least two more. He was now attempting to fix Thing 3. The broke-down tractor. Hank was again out of commission for a day because of his bad back, code for "I drank too much last night." Lincoln was down to the few ranch hands they hired, fewer this year than last.

It didn't help that they'd been blessed with another blazing hot day in September. Of course, this morning at dawn the weather was fairly freezing. He'd gone about his day, removing clothes as he went. Now, he stripped off his tee, the last item of clothing he'd remove outside. Bending over the engine, he tightened a nut, then heard the sound of tires kicking up the dirt road to the barn.

He didn't bother looking up.

One lug nut fastened, he started on the other one. Until it stripped, the force of his wrenching too much.

"Damn! Shit fire! Damn it all to hell!"

Lincoln let loose with a volley of curses since he was all alone out here. Just him and the Texas dirt. He kicked the tractor.

"Lincoln?" came a sweet voice.

He didn't immediately see the owner of that soft voice, but he'd guess she would be feminine and sexy. And he could use a pretty woman right about now. A sexy woman would get him out of this funk right quick. He could use a little relaxation. A little unwinding. Maybe he'd happened upon another rodeo buckle bunny who'd somehow found out where he lived. Wouldn't be difficult as everyone in this

26

Podunk town owned loose lips. Picking up the rag to wipe the grease from his fingers, he moved past the tractor in the direction of that sex-on-a-stick voice.

And stopped in his tracks.

Sadie Stephens.

She of the wild cascading blond waves, sensual lips, and amazing ass. The temptress who made his skin tight every time he laid eyes on her. One of the women in town he'd never dated, even before the wedding fail. Because, c'mon, she was so *sweet*. Innocent. The girl next door with no idea of the effect she had on men.

Occasionally he caught a glance of her with the children, coming in and out of the portable which he'd helped set up in the parking lot of the old church. Renovations came to a screeching halt when someone accidentally hit a plumbing line. Safe to say there were a few more fundraisers ahead of them.

"Hey," Lincoln said, clearing his throat, and walking over to the fence line.

She'd propped her booted feet on one rail of the fence and clung with both hands. "I can see you're busy, but this won't take too much time."

Most women wore Wranglers, boots, T-shirts and flannel, but Sadie always wore dresses. Short casual dresses, mostly, like today. This one hit right above the knee.

He swallowed. "What can I do for you?"

"I just finished my first full week of teaching and it's going much better. Eve came to career day and talked about being a vet. The kids loved it."

He just looked at her quizzically with no idea why any of this involved him.

She smiled but wouldn't meet his eyes. "And…I thought… well. Eve suggested, actually, and I agree. Maybe you…I thought that maybe...um, could you come and talk to the kids about being a rodeo champ?"

He froze. There was a small fact he didn't much like to advertise but he didn't like children. Yeah, yeah. He *should* like children. I mean, who didn't like children? They were so *needy* and completely dependent on you. Often sticky. He'd liked his younger brother and sister fine. As the oldest, he helped raise them after their mother abandoned the family. And on the rodeo circuit, he did his share of meeting the younger fans. Taking pictures, that sort of thing. Usually over within a few minutes.

"I don't know. Pretty busy here. And the tractor broke down." He pointed in the direction of the yellow behemoth otherwise known as the bane of his existence.

"It would just take a few minutes of your time."

Her tone took on a pleading sound and he began to picture what it might sound like if she begged him to take her to bed. To give her a few hours of pleasure. She wouldn't have to beg for long.

He tried to rein in his thoughts because he must be getting desperate for a woman. But Sadie didn't look like his friend's sweet sister today. Not in that short dress. She reminded him of a woman who knew exactly what she wanted. And what *he* wanted was for her to be asking him for anything but career day at the grade school.

"What did you have in mind? A demonstration? Come show them my buckles?"

"Anything you'd like but all of that sounds good. I'm sure they would be happy just to meet you."

"Really? I already know most of these kids."

"Yes, but how many have you talked to in person about the rodeo?" She cocked her head.

She'd read his mind. He didn't talk to any of them. Just

waved hello when they were with their parents, pat a head now and again. For God's sake, he wasn't a total grump.

"You could demonstrate your roping technique, maybe?" She chewed on her lower lip and his resolve wore thinner.

But no. This had bad idea written all over it. There was already too much to do around here. And he didn't want to see her again. He wanted to stop thinking about her naked and seeing her again wouldn't help that situation.

"Tell you what." He tried a smile. "I will think about it. As soon as I finish fixing this tractor, hauling some hay, tagging the new heifers, and moving our cattle to the north pasture, I should have a *little* free time."

The tentative smile slipped off her face because Sadie heard "no" in that sentence, exactly what he wanted her to hear.

"Oh, okay." She jumped off the fence rail.

Giving up on me so easy, sweetheart? You didn't much want me to begin with, I'm guessing.

"You let me know, then." She turned one last time, her long blond hair catching a ray of sunlight.

"I will." He held up a hand in a wave. "Thanks for dropping by."

At the end of another long back-breaking day, Lincoln showered at his cabin and prepared to leave for a beer at the Shady Grind. Stopping to check in on his grandmother he found her in the kitchen. Lillian "Mima" Carver was a force of nature, but she'd helped raised him after his mother, Maggie Mae Carver, left the family high and dry. For that reason alone, he allowed that tornado to sweep over him now and again. The least he could do.

"Hey, there. Goin' out for a while. You okay?"

There were several skeins of yarn all over the kitchen table and she sat on a chair, doing her thing. Obviously, the knit-a-thon was already in full swing.

"What was that lovely Sadie doin' over here earlier today?"

"Wanted me to come to career day over at the new school." He helped himself to a bottled water from the fridge and twisted off the cap.

"That's a great idea."

"Nah, I don't have time for that."

She dropped her yarn. "Lincoln James Carver, are you turning down a resident in need?"

"This is Sadie Stephens we're talkin' about. She's Eve's best friend. Are we forgettin'? She's the one that drove Eve home when she should have been in the church, gettin' hitched to Jackson! And I've helped renovate that church into a school along with everyone else. Remember? I've already done my part."

"What will it take you? Twenty minutes, if that. Sadie needs our help, son. She's one little girl tryin' to teach some kids never even been to school before."

"Sadie is *not* a little girl and she can handle them."

"Well, that's not what I heard."

"Why? What happened?"

"Ellie Monroe cries once a day, and Jimmy Ray keeps throwin' his shoe. Lawd above knows why."

"Jimmy Ray is a brat. Just like his Daddy."

"Sadie needs people with interesting professions to come talk. She's of course got more boys than girls so I can see why you'd do well. And if you insist on risking your life with the rodeo, least you can do is show off to the children."

An interesting twist. She wanted him to be a show-off now. "I thought I was supposed to teach them something."

"Son, if you're not goin' to settle down and have your own children, least you can do is help us raise the ones in town."

He nearly spit his water out. "When did I sign up for that?"

"When you were born here. That's what we do in Stone Ridge. We help each other."

He didn't mind *helping* others. It was in his genes and was the way he'd been raised. Last week he'd helped a neighboring rancher pull a cow out of a mud hole he'd been stuck in. But sue him if there had been enough responsibility raising his siblings. It didn't seem that long ago that he drove Daisy to and from the high school forty minutes away. Listening when she cried because she didn't have a date to prom night.

For years, he'd run interference between Jackson and Hank. Those two were at odds from the minute Jackson picked up a guitar and found a talent. That talent didn't fall in line with Hank's vision for his youngest son. Jackson was off in Nashville doin' his thing and Lincoln didn't have to worry about him. Daisy graduated with honors a few years ago and worked as an auto mechanic in Kerrville.

Now, it was Lincoln's time. His obligations were only to his family and this ranch. And to the town, too, but those were on an as-needed basis. He'd never turn down someone desperately in need of a helping hand. But career day at the local school? Hard pass. They'd do fine without him.

Promising Mima he'd *consider* the idea, Lincoln left for the Shady Grind for that cold beer. He could have a beer at home, sure, but after a long day he needed to get away from the ranch. Blow off some steam. He immediately caught the eye of Jolette Marie Truehart checking him out as he walked inside and winked. In addition to being the only daughter of the Truehart Horse Ranch dynasty, she held the dubious distinction of being a three-time runaway bride. Runaway brides were not uncommon in their town, but Jolette Marie was also a bona fide buckle bunny.

They'd developed an understanding. She was discreet and neither one of them wanted anything permanent. From time to time they got together for a little no-strings fun. Because Jolette Marie could be all kinds of fun. That "fun" hadn't happened for some time, though, and he certainly wouldn't mind a repeat performance. But Lincoln would wait it out tonight. Men in this town chased women like a flea chased a horse, and he refused to be one of them. But if Jolette Marie didn't find herself interested in anyone else tonight, maybe later they would...talk.

A trill of laughter caught his attention and he turned to see Eve and Sadie surrounded by a small group of men. Unfortunately, Eve caught his eye before he looked away. Damn it.

Ten, nine, eight, seven, six...

"Hey, Lincoln," Eve said from behind him.

Naturally, due to the way he'd been raised, he was forced to turn around and smile at the woman who tore his brother's heart from his chest when she stood him up at the altar of Trinity Church seven years ago. It was in the past, sure, and they'd all moved on. The Iglesias and Carver families were on speaking terms again. Eve scored points with locals when she came back to Stone Ridge after grad school to take over a large animal veterinary practice. And Jackson was better off without her.

Still didn't make it any easier for Lincoln to forgive her.

He nodded. "How's it goin'?"

"Good. Sadie and I came out tonight." She waved Sadie over. "We're sort of celebrating her first week of teaching. And I did career day at the school today. The kids loved it."

Here it comes. "I heard."

"Anyway, it was fun. The kids are cool."

Lincoln took a pull of his beer and winced. "Even Jimmy Ray?"

Eve laughed. "Well…bless his heart."

"Yup. Just like his Daddy."

Eve waved Sadie over again, but the girl just wasn't moving. She stayed rooted to her spot, taking little swigs from her beer and trying her best not to look directly at him.

"She's not coming over," Lincoln said. "I told her I'd think about career day, but she heard no. And she's probably not very happy with me."

"No, that's silly. Sadie doesn't *get* mad."

"Yeah? Hell, then I feel special."

"Hi," said a little voice beside him. "Did you fix your tractor?"

He turned to see her shoved between him and the cowboy on the stool beside him. Small enough to fit between them, the soft bare skin of her arm briefly touched his white button-down. She noticed and pulled back.

Please do that again, sweetheart.

From this close, he caught the scent of her hair, a mild flowery scent. He noticed her hazel eyes, specks of yellow and green in them. And she wore the same short dress from earlier this afternoon. She looked so sweet she made it hard for a man to think. She'd asked him a question…or something.

"No." He cleared his throat. "Tractor's a bigger problem than I realized. Daisy is going to take a look at it."

Did he care that his little sister the mechanic might fix something he, as a big bad cowboy, couldn't? Hell, no. He'd been raised to think better than that.

"Okay." Sadie took a sip of her beer and seemed to have lost the power of speech.

Eve became involved in a conversation with the man next to her, so she was of no help at all.

"Look, I said I'd think about career day and I meant it. Just…give me a chance to clear the decks."

Boy, wasn't he a sucker for a beautiful woman? She'd clearly heard "no" and now he let her hear a big fat "maybe."

She blinked. "No, that's okay. I don't want you to feel obligated. Maybe I could ask Wade."

The last thing Lincoln wanted was for Wade to demonstrate how egotistical a rodeo cowboy could get when he regularly got thrown off a bucking horse and survived to tell it. His best friend could be an idiot sometimes.

"Wade doesn't have the time."

"Then I'll think of something else."

"You mean *someone* else?" He snorted. "Certainly have your pick of men in Stone Ridge."

Hell, he hadn't meant that to come out the way it did. He usually didn't mind being one of many. Made it easier to fly under the radar since if a woman wanted marriage, she didn't have to settle for him and could move on. Sometimes easier said than done. A couple of romantic entanglements in the past cost him when the girl claimed to be madly in love and didn't want anyone else but him. In high school, his girlfriend had a pregnancy scare, and Lincoln aged ten years in five minutes. From that point on, he'd been extremely careful.

"You're right," she said and sighed. "I guess I do."

At that point, Sean Henderson took the stool the ranch hand vacated. "Hey, there, Sadie. You busy tonight?"

Pretty bold of him but Sean was confident. Lincoln stared straight ahead while taking a pull of his beer.

"Um, I'm here with Eve. We're celebrating my first week of teaching."

"I love celebrating. And I'm good at it." He winked. "Let me get you a drink. Whatcha drinkin'?"

"It's just a beer. But I—"

"Hey, 'Cilla, let me have another beer for Sadie. We're celebrating."

Alright then. And they were off to the races. "I'm just gonna leave you two alone."

"Aw, thanks, bud!" Sean clapped Lincoln's back.

Lincoln stood and stretched, wandering over to the old-fashioned jukebox. He leaned against it, trying to be interested in the selection of old-time country classics, from Johnny Cash to Merle Haggard. He preferred the new country sound, people like Sam Hunt and Brad Paisley, but Priscilla said it was too expensive to buy those newer tunes and nearly impossible to update this hunk of junk.

Sometimes this old town grated on him. He stayed because of his family. Because of the ranch. And there were decent people here, too, real salt of the earth folks who cared about each other. But sometimes, he wished there was a movie theater in town…or something.

"Hey there," came Jolette Marie's throaty voice.

He turned to her. "Hey."

Speaking of confidence. Jolette Marie probably sweated confidence right through the pores of her skin. Of course, she was beautiful, which helped. A redhead, tall, long legs. He briefly wondered why Sadie didn't seem to have as much confidence. The men chased after her, too, like every other eligible woman. And she was beautiful. Clearly smart. He caught himself briefly gazing over the top of Jolette Marie's head to see Sadie, still talking to Sean. But she didn't look all that happy, taking small sips of her beer. She caught him staring.

He quickly looked away.

Jolette Marie noticed and laughed. "*Sadie?* She's headed to have herself a big wedding someday soon and plenty of babies."

"Yeah. I know." He squinted and took a pull of his beer. "And I'm not interested."

"Right. Well, although I'm standin' right *here* and you

looked over my head, I'm willing to let that go. I know you're worth it. You want to get out of here?"

He considered it. But for reasons he refused to examine too closely, he didn't want to leave with Jolette Marie tonight. Not while Sadie could see them. The idea didn't have the same appeal to him as when he'd walked in here tonight. He might be coming down with something. Because Jolette Marie would certainly help him unwind and relax with zero complications.

"I have a really early day, sweetheart." He winked and smiled. "Raincheck?"

"Sure thing." She stood on tiptoes and planted a big fat kiss on his lips.

Lincoln carefully extracted himself from Jolette Marie, doing everything but pat her on the head, and then he was out the door.

CHAPTER 3

*A*s she usually did on quiet calm evenings alone on the ranch, Lillian Carver gathered her pen and paper. Her hands were already weak from all the knitting today, but she settled at the antique rolltop desk in her bedroom and began another letter to her late husband, Albert.

My dearest Albert,

I'm worried about our Lincoln. Either he's off to the rodeo where he's doing God knows what with who knows who, or he's home where he spends too much time alone. Just him and Hank on the ranch, now that Jackson's gone to Nashville. And I won't lie to you. I know he does most of the work on the hill. Hank is drinking too much again. Both are too stupid to realize I know.

Lillian put the pen down and looked around the room. Her fingers were old and arthritic these days and letter writing took a lot out of her. Usually she simply started a letter and her late husband would show up, wearing his boots and spurs, ready to "fix" everything. He never did know how to simply listen. Oh, she wasn't crazy, the therapist said. Just as long as *she* realized that Albert was simply a figment of her imagination, he could be a comfort and a way of dealing with and managing her grief.

He'd been dead for five years now, of a sudden and massive heart attack, but it wasn't until recently that she'd needed him. She'd kept busy what with Hank and his three children, cooking for and serving up the hungry cowboys three meals a day. But now with Jackson off to Nashville, and Daisy working at the auto shop and rarely home, Lincoln spent most of his time up on the hill with her miserable son. Somehow, she needed a way to bring this family back together again. She would start in order, with Lincoln. Hank was sort of a lost cause, sadly, at least for now. But Lillian figured if she got Lincoln married off, everything else would slowly fall into place. There would eventually be more little Carvers running around (God help her, please, some girls would be heaven-sent).

Jackson would come home for the wedding. Nothing would stop that boy from standing up for his older brother, hero, and best friend. At that point, she could work on getting Jackson and Eve back together again. What happened there was just too sad for words. Lastly, she'd deal with her only granddaughter. The little hellion she'd raised from a toddler needed someone special. Someone strong.

Fingers aching, Lillian kept writing.

Sadie Stephens is on my mind. She's the one for my Lincoln. I suppose on some level I've always known. She has practically worshipped him for most of her life. He likes her, too. Just doesn't want to admit it yet. He blames Sadie for driving Eve home instead of coming to get Jackson, so he could talk some sense into Eve. Sadie is just like Lincoln: loyal to the core. I thought their fate was sealed when they each took sides in Eve and Jackson's breakup. But that was a while ago and we've all learned so much since then. I don't even blame Eve anymore, much less Sadie. Such a sweet girl with a big heart. I wish you could see her. She's the teacher now!

"Woman, what are you yammering on and on about now?" Albert appeared on his side of their bed, crossing his booted feet at the ankles. Arms crossed. Toothpick in his mouth.

He looked exactly the way she'd last seen him, before he'd walked to the barn and collapsed halfway there.

"Albert! Do you *enjoy* torturing my arthritic fingers? Do you? I've been writing two whole paragraphs until you finally decided to show up!"

"Sadie Stephens, huh? Well, that's a choice."

"The best one, naturally. I'm going to have to intervene, of course. As usual."

"Well, could you even stop yourself?"

"You make it sound as if things will just work out by themselves. They won't. I have to push them along. Sometimes shove."

"Whether you have to or not, you certainly do enjoy it."

"It keeps me occupied now that you're gone. And a fine mess you left me with, too. Thanks for that!"

"Hank will be fine. A little heartache never killed anyone."

But their son had nursed the pain of losing Maggie May for far too long. Something else was wrong. A mother had a sixth sense about her children.

"Anyway, back to Lincoln, old man." She waved her hand dismissively. "I'm going to get Lincoln more involved at the new school. They're in a portable now while the men fix the old church. But I need for him to be in close contact with Sadie. She'll be eternally grateful to him, and maybe finally let him know how she feels. He's not a mind reader. Actually, he's not very romantic, either. Sort of like his predecessors." At this she slid Albert a look of contempt.

Would it have killed him to bring home flowers every now and then? Albert just shrugged.

Lillian paced the floor. "The problem is Lincoln thinks he's already invested enough time in the new school. Sadie is organizing a career day event. I'm sure he's thinkin' he can't leave the hill for the twenty minutes it might take him. Or maybe he's avoiding Sadie. I know for certain he's avoiding commitment. Oh, that boy! If he wasn't so tall, I'd ring his fool neck."

"I'd offer a suggestion, but you probably won't want to hear it. You hate when I try to fix everything. I'm trying this new listening thing out."

"Oh, *now* you decide to listen? I need help here, Albert! Help from beyond."

"Well," Albert said, leaning back on the pillows. "Maybe you could just talk to Sadie on your own and sign him up. He'd be none the wiser. Then, on the day, you remind him to go. Pretend he knew about it all along and it must have slipped his mind."

Genius! Why didn't Lillian think of that? Wait. She had. Albert was just a figment of her imagination. And as if she needed further confirmation, when she turned to the bed again, he'd gone.

"See you next time, old man."

Plenty of work lay ahead. Best get busy.

A WEEK LATER, Lincoln had cleared his load. About three times. He'd get on top of the chores for a day and then chaos would hit. A fence line would break, and cattle would wander away. He and Hank would chase them down with help from their cow ponies, corral them to another pasture, and get to work on repairs. Sometimes the hay wouldn't be delivered on time and he'd have to go get it. Or Hank would drink too much and be of little use the next day. There was little free time on a working ranch. Even less when you were a good neighbor.

Today, he'd been up before dawn as usual and worked a few hours on the broken fence at the north pasture when Mima drove a late breakfast out to him. She lived down the hill in the newer family home Hank originally built for Maggie and their family. When he saw her truck pull up by the barn, he mounted his gelding and made fast tracks back from the fence line.

Mima pulled out a box for Lincoln. "You best hurry on, or you'll be late."

"Late to what? That fence is gonna take me all day." He unwrapped and took a hearty bite of an egg, bacon, and cheese burrito. "Hank's inside nursing another headache."

"You'll just have to get back to it after school then."

School.

Lincoln didn't have a good feeling about this. He swallowed and squinted at his grandmother. "*What* school?"

"Career day. You told Sadie you'd love to do it. And it's today."

He gaped. He would have remembered volunteering. "Today?"

"Don't worry, you have plenty of time to get there."

"You *volunteered* me? Why not at least give me a heads up before *today*?"

"Slipped my mind."

He didn't believe for a second this slipped Mima's mind. Her mind was a steel trap. Lincoln whipped off his Stetson and struck his leg with it. The closest he got to cursing in front of his grandmother.

"Now, now," she said, knowing exactly what he'd done. "Won't take you but a few minutes. Just take the wood steer and some rope. That's how Hank taught you. Talk to the children. Don't tell me you don't know how to do that."

"I'm gonna have to shower and shave first."

"Whatever doesn't kill ya makes you stronger." Mima smirked.

"You're hilarious." Lincoln took a last menacing bite of his burrito.

An hour later, he'd showered, shaved, packed his truck, and left for town. This was all so typical. He'd have done this career day thing, he would have, but wanted it to be on his own time. His decision. But his family was forever binding him to obligations when he wanted to be his own man.

The Double C Ranch should have been a family ranch, but only he and Hank worked it. Jackson was off trying to get famous in Nashville, and while Daisy was perfectly capable, she preferred mechanics to cattle. Her choice. That left him. And yeah, sometimes he wanted to run away and join the circus because he was so dang tired of being the grown-up.

He pulled onto the main street where a few days ago he'd been on the roof of the old church replacing shingles. Now, here he was, back with a wood steer. Because he was the nice guy. The good son.

Leaving his rope and steer outside, he made his way to the portable and opened the door. Every single eye turned to him as he walked inside. He only cared about one set of eyes. They belonged to Sadie, whose eyes were bright, her smile wide. She wore another one of those tantalizing dresses paired with her blue matching boots, her long hair pulled back into a high ponytail.

The anger and frustration rushed out of him so fast he swore he heard the sound of it.

Wooooooosh.

Sweetheart, you stop looking at me like that, or I won't be responsible for what I do.

"It's Lincoln!" one of the kids shouted.

"Is not! It's the rodeo cowboy," a little girl said.

"Big deal, my daddy says he coulda been a rodeo cowboy," Jimmy Ray said.

Little punk.

"When are we eatin'?" said another, much larger, boy.

Sadie clapped her hands to get their attention. "Boys and girls, this is Lincoln Carver, and he *is* a rodeo cowboy. A champion. He's come to show y'all how he ropes a steer."

Lincoln nodded to the kids, then walked toward the front of the room. "Brought a wood steer to demonstrate."

"Okay, but first let's talk to the children."

"You talk."

Sadie's smile got a little smaller. "We can ask you questions. But you'll have to answer them."

"Sure, why not?"

Hands were raised and the volley of questions began.

Yes, he'd been injured before, but no, he'd never been trampled by a bull. No, not a horse, either. Sure, he'd been thrown once by a pis—er, angry horse. Sometimes, yes, *some* blood (Sadie winced at that, and shook her head at him as if that wasn't appropriate) but mostly concussions. What's a concussion, the little girl named Ellie asked? He briefly explained a "brain bruise."

Another wince from Sadie. He scowled back.

"Who would like a little demonstration of Lincoln's ropin' technique?"

A cheer from the children, and Sadie led them all outside, single file.

Lincoln set up his steer at a distance and began to pull his rope. He explained slack, technique, and don't try this at home, boys and girls, earning him a little smile and nod from Sadie.

"That's lame," said Jimmy Ray. "You're gonna lasso a wood steer? It ain't even movin'."

"*Isn't* moving, Jimmy Ray," Sadie corrected.

"Either way. Why don't you lasso Miss Sadie?" he said. "Also stupid, but a little better."

The kids seemed to love this idea. Before Sadie lost complete control of her class, Lincoln became the voice of reason.

"Not a great idea, kids. Miss Sadie isn't a steer."

He expected her to pipe in, and agree that first, no she wasn't a steer. Second, the idea was ridiculous, practically a metaphor to the good ol' days when cowboy cavemen grabbed themselves a bride. If he lassoed Sadie, word would get out that they were headed to Trinity Church.

And they were not!

Instead of protesting, she smiled at the children. "Good idea, Jimmy Ray."

Good idea, Jimmy Ray?

No. Jimmy Ray was just like his daddy, who wouldn't recognize a good idea if it slapped him. Lincoln cleared his throat and beckoned Sadie to come closer. He bent low to whisper in her ear.

Dear Lord, she smelled even better than before. "*Not* a good idea."

"Why not?"

He scoffed. "Why not? Why *not*?"

"Oh, I see," she said. "You don't think you can do it. That's okay."

She was *serious*. Jesus. "Of course, I can *do* it. But you're hardly the size of a steer, if we're trying to be realistic."

"What if I stand on a chair? Would that be easier?"

"Yeah, if you want to hurt yourself. Much easier."

She crossed her arms. "I know I'm not the most graceful person alive, but even I can keep from falling off a small chair."

So, she was going to take this personally. And the kids were getting louder, always such a great sign.

"If you want to do this, fine. But not on a chair. Walk over to the other end of the marked recess area. That should be enough of a distance."

"Okay, kids!" Sadie held up the peace sign and got their attention. "Listen up. Our rodeo champ is going to lasso your teacher. Won't that be fun."

A cheer came from the kids.

Lincoln sighed. What he did for his town and its residents was practically humiliating. That does it, he told himself. This weekend he would tell Hank he was on his own for a day. He'd head out to San Antonio and find himself a buckle bunny he'd never have to see again.

He prepared his rope and did a few loops in the air to be showy. He did know how to work a crowd. The kids loved this part. He'd be home in time for lunch. Two seconds later, he'd easily lassoed Sadie to a cheer from the kids. The sweet way she smiled made him zero in on that pretty face. Those eyes. Shimmering hazel eyes.

Such a pretty girl, he noticed again. Beautiful, even. Far prettier than he remembered, since he'd sworn a vow never to give her the time of day again. Long, curvy legs and a sweet ass. She walked with a wiggle that drove him to distraction.

And she…was falling.

What?

Helpless, he watched as she tripped, and fell to the ground.

Shit fire! He knew this was a bad idea.

WHEN SADIE WOKE, she was surrounded by the Stone Ridge Volunteer Fire Department. Brad and Lenny furrowed their brows in concern. One of them reached to adjust an ice pack which seemed to be on her head.

"Miss Sadie!" Ellie cried out. "Are you dead?"

"Dude, that was *so* cool," Jimmy Ray said.

"Is there any blood?" someone else asked.

She blinked and realized…her head was in Lincoln's lap.

I must have died and gone to heaven.

If she thought he looked amazing the day she'd found him working on his ranch, *shirtless*, being this close to him even fully clothed would come in a *real* close second. Lincoln of the square jawline, and slightly crooked nose that kept him from being too pretty. Rugged. That described Lincoln Carver. Handsome and *rugged*. Definitely not a pretty boy. Oh, my.

She moved and heard him say sternly, "Don't move."

"I'm…I really think I'm okay."

"You're not," Lincoln said, sounding frustrated. His voice sounded low and deep.

"How did this happen?" Lenny asked.

"She bumped into her other foot. I saw it happen," one of her kids said.

Dear Lord above, she'd tripped over her own feet? She hadn't done that in…a few months, at least. These new boots were more of a heel than she normally wore. She'd ordered them online because they were so sexy. Worn them today because *he* was coming. And now she'd tripped, right after she'd assured Lincoln she would not fall off a *chair*. She couldn't even stay upright on her own two feet!

46

"Oh, I'm sorry, Lincoln," she said. "These are new boots and a higher heel. I must have lost my balance."

"Nothin' to be sorry about," he said gruffly.

Now he was being too kind. He must think she was dying. "But I'm really...*really* okay."

"You're going to the hospital, missy," Brad said, wagging a finger. "Need to get checked out. "

"I can't. What about my classroom?"

"We can call Ellie's mom," Lincoln said. "She used to have a home daycare. She can come take over for the rest of the afternoon. I have to agree, you're gettin' checked out. Concussions are nothing to laugh about. I should know."

"Yes, I guess you do." She sat up, earning glares from the men. "But I'm a trained EMT in case y'all forgot."

"Are you refusing medical care, young lady?" Brad turned to Lenny, hands on hips. "I think she's refusing medical care."

"Yes, I am."

"She's refusing medical care!" Lenny slapped his thigh. "If that don't beat all."

"But we have the *Hummer*. We can take you to the hospital in that," Brad said. "I've been dying to take it for a spin."

"If you won't go to the hospital with them, you're goin' with me," Lincoln said. "But you're goin'."

"Listen to your boyfriend, missy!" Brad chastised.

"I'm not her boyfriend," Lincoln interrupted.

My, my, he certainly *rushed* to correct them. Sadie pushed away from Lincoln.

"One of you two please check to see if my pupil size is equal and that my eyes are tracking or find me the mirror in my purse so I can do it myself."

"Let me do that." Lincoln squatted in front of her, tipping her chin, staring into her eyes. She forced herself to follow his finger and not gaze right back into beautiful deep blues.

"Well?" she asked.

"Looks okay," he said unhappily. "But it doesn't tell the whole story."

"Exactly." Sadie stood, noting no dizziness. She did, however, have a small headache, totally normal and expected. "The patient reports no nausea, eyesight fine, no dizziness."

"Well, I guess that's it, then," Brad said. "How about that beer, Len?'

"You're just going to let her go?" Lincoln yelled.

"They have to, legally," Sadie said. "Remember, I worked as an EMT. I know the drill. Don't worry, if I start to feel worse, I'll go."

The men were already crossing the street, headed over to the Shady Grind.

"I'm callin' Lenora," Lincoln said, walking a few feet away, phone in hand.

"Children," Sadie began. "I should go home early today and take it easy. Remember that I love you all. Will you promise to behave for Ellie's momma?"

"Miss Sadie, what happened?" Bobby Joe asked. "I saw you get lassoed and then you just fell down. Did Mr. Carver do that?"

"No, honey, he didn't. It wasn't his fault. I just…just…"

"Fell down," Lincoln completed her sentence. "And that's all there is to it."

She felt a little swell of affection that Lincoln stepped in and covered for her. "I'll be back Monday. Y'all have a good weekend and remember to read!"

"Thank you for not dying," Ellie sniffed.

The kids, with the exception of the older boys, circled Sadie and wrapped their arms around her waist, giving her a big group hug. She felt it down to the seat of her soul. In a short time, everything had changed. These were *her* kids, and they cared about their teacher. She hated that they'd seen this, but they'd also witnessed yet another occasion in which the residents of Stone Ridge helped when and where needed and took care of each other. And that sometimes, though their teacher was a Class A klutz, everything worked out in the end.

Assured that her children were safe with Ellie's mother, Lenora, Sadie walked outside, headed to the parking lot with her purse and keys, where she found Lincoln standing in front of her truck, arms crossed. He wore his Stetson tipped, and his long legs were clad in Wranglers that did all kinds of bad-ass sexy cowboy things for him. She gulped.

"Oh, hell no," he said. "You are not driving."

"Don't be silly."

She briefly considered explaining that she couldn't be lusting after him if she was truly injured. Her brain would be sending repair signals to the rest of her body and she'd slow down to the most basic and necessary nervous system functions. She'd be unable to process too many thoughts, and certainly not ones about jumping him.

Sexy times would be the *last* thing on her mind.

"I'll drive you home. You have to let me, Sadie. I'm worried."

Sadie let that knowledge slide into her, warm and sweet. Lincoln, worried about her. "That's kind of you."

He frowned. "It's not *kind*. It's logic, pure and simple. You were out cold."

"Right." She snapped to attention. "For how long?"

She'd forgotten to ask that before making her final evaluation. She reached deep into her training. Granted, she hadn't been a first responder in a while. But the length of time she'd have been out could have enormous significance. However, the facts of the matter were that if she'd been out for even five minutes, she probably wouldn't be standing upright now and able to talk.

"I didn't time it but seemed like a few minutes."

"And were probably actually seconds. You know how that goes." She considered that she'd woken to the fire department volunteers. "How fast did Lenny and Brad get here, anyway?"

"Well, they were just across the street about to head into the Shady Grind."

She smiled, satisfied. "I feel even better now."

"Sadie—"

She held up a palm. "Tell you what, I promise I'll get Eve to stay the night with me. Concussion duty. Feel better?"

"I'm still driving you home. Sorry, but I can't just lasso a woman, give her a concussion, and be on my way."

My goodness, she was stupid. Of *course*, he would feel responsible even if it hadn't been his idea and he'd argued against it. This was just Lincoln, being a stand-up guy.

"Okay, drive me home. But this wasn't your fault. If anything, consider it mine."

She followed him to his truck, and he opened the passenger door for her. He drove a nice, newer truck. A dark and sleek four-wheel drive, perfect for a man with long legs. Not so much for a small- to average-sized woman. She still drove her old green midsize pickup, low enough to be almost like driving a car. When she turned to ask for a stool to climb up, his hand was already outstretched.

"Thank you," she said and took his hand.

A little zing went through her at the touch of his large, warm, callused hand. The moment was over far too quickly. She fastened her seat belt, and so did he, the sounds of the click loud in their mutual silence. Awkward.

"I'm sorry," Lincoln said as he pulled out from the parking lot. "I shouldn't have let you talk me into that."

"Please, all my fault. You were just being accommodating."

"Regardless, I accept the blame."

She sighed. "No. I can't let you do that."

"You can't do anything about it."

"Right."

The men of Stone Ridge took responsibility for every one of their actions. Cared for their women. Lincoln seemed different to her from most of the eligible men in some ways. She got the feeling if he dated a woman, in private, the relationship would be more of a two-way street. The way *she* liked it. She didn't need a man to take care of her. Her father taught her how to change a tire, unclog a sink, and change her oil. She'd spent college summers working for his construction company putting up drywall.

She wanted honesty from a man, pure and simple. That, plus utter and complete loyalty.

"You have plenty of choices," her daddy said. "Marry a man because you love him, not because you need him."

Still her plan.

Lincoln drove them to the outskirts of town to her cabin near Lupine Lake. A few years ago, her father purchased a few acres of land and later built rows of small cabins spaced close together which he rented out. They would fund his retirement since like so many in Stone Ridge, he'd been self-employed all his life. Many of the cabins were vacation rentals for those coming out to fish and hunt. Sadie rented a cabin, and Eve one not far from hers. Beau lived in a cabin a little farther toward the lake.

Luckily, she'd tidied up this morning before leaving for school. If he got any ideas about coming inside, she certainly wouldn't discourage him. The attention, even if misguided, felt pleasant. Warm. But she'd be sure that he felt no obligation to her because she refused to be a pity case. She wanted his attention to come because he'd noticed her. Noticed that even if she wasn't as flashy and gorgeous as the women who followed rodeo cowboys, she possessed her own brand of charm and looks. She hoped.

"Which one is yours again?" Lincoln said as he pulled into the area.

"Right here." She pointed to the cabin on the corner.

Nothing special, just one large room with a bathroom and small kitchenette. A cute A-frame style cabin with a small wrap around porch and steps leading up to the front door. In a city, this would be the equivalent of a studio apartment.

"I forgot how nice it is out here," Lincoln said, leaning forward on the steering wheel, taking in the lake practically in her backyard.

"Occasionally we get a coyote out here, and lots of deer."

"Yeah, I remember. Before we started working on the old church, I hadn't seen Beau for a while. We've both been too busy, I guess."

Her brother worked with their father, so yes, he kept busy both in and out of Stone Ridge.

She followed his gaze to the lakeside he admired, and when she turned to ask if he'd like to come inside, he'd already climbed out of the truck. Opening the door, she took his hand again to help her down this giant of a truck. Geez, there went that sizzle again. He caught her eye and for a moment, just a slice of time, she imagined that he'd felt it, too.

"I'll see you to the door," Lincoln said.

"I was just about to ask if you want to come inside. I've got cold beer in the fridge. I definitely owe you." She went for lighthearted, breezy.

Come in, or don't, who cares?

"Got a few things to take care of at the ranch first, but I'll be back."

"Y-you will?" Her heart stuttered with spiraling hope.

He stood behind her as she unlocked the door. Hands were shoved in his pockets. "I meant what I said. I'm worried, and you refused medical care. I'm coming back before long to see that you're still okay."

"But—"

He met her gaze. "I'm done arguin' about this."

She sighed. "Fine."

If he wanted to come back, she should let him. He obviously felt guilty about the whole thing.

CHAPTER 4

*A*fter dropping Sadie off at her cabin, Lincoln headed back to the ranch to grab a sleeping bag, and quickly pack for an overnight. If the stubborn woman refused medical care, he'd be right in her face making sure that she didn't die of a brain bleed on *his* watch.

He caught up with Hank and let him know how far he'd gotten with the fence. His weekend plans slid swiftly into oblivion. He'd be a nurse all weekend. Guilt and worry flooded through him. If only she'd allowed him to take her to the hospital. He viciously threw his bag into the cab of the truck and climbed in the driver's side, slamming the door.

"What on earth?" Mima caught him as he headed out and waved at him to stop. "What is this mess?"

He hung out the driver's side window. "I went to the school. That's what this mess is about. Hope you're happy. I lassoed Sadie, she tripped, fell, and hurt her head. Now she's concussed but refuses to go to the hospital."

"Lord have mercy! You were supposed to use the wood steer."

"That would have been the smart thing to do." He adjusted his Stetson and scratched at his temple.

He used to be smarter than this.

"Why did you let this happen to poor, sweet Sadie?"

"I didn't let *anything* happen. She tripped over her own two feet."

"Oh, dear. She never has been the most graceful creature, bless her heart. Where on earth do you think you'll stay? She has a one-room cabin."

He hooked his thumb to the cab. "Got my sleeping bag. She has a porch and guess I'll sleep out there."

"Well, well, you are in quite the pickle." She chuckled.

"Thanks to you."

She waved him away. "You never know. This might be a story you'll be telling my great-grandchildren someday."

"Sure, as long as they're Daisy's or Jackson's children. I'll tell the story."

Grumbling, Lincoln headed back to the lakeside cabin. At least he'd be sleeping outside in one of the most beautiful parts of Stone Ridge. The fresh air away from manure and cattle would do him good. He needed to get off the ranch more often, and though he hadn't planned this, he'd roll with it. Figure he'd set his watch for an alarm every couple of hours and wake Sadie to make sure she wasn't unconscious. Maybe she was right, and she'd only been out a short time. He ought to know exactly how long, but all he could picture now, as if in slow motion, was running to Sadie as she lay there on the ground.

Everything faded to shades of muted colors and he'd simply held her against him. Soft and sweet, and far too quiet. Fear gripped him like tentacles. He hadn't been this terrified when he'd been thrown from his horse years ago in the California Circuit Finals. Back then, he'd been too young and stupid to be truly scared. But there wasn't a single scratch on him. That's when he'd earned his rodeo circuit nickname: Lucky.

He'd ordered one of the older children to go find help, and Brad and Lenny arrived within seconds. He'd been relieved to see them, but in the end, it made no difference that they'd been there. She'd diagnosed herself. And yeah, maybe she *was* going to be okay. Maybe he wasn't the only lucky one. He almost believed her. But he couldn't be certain without a hospital visit. He needed to find a way to get her there.

Before heading to Sadie's, he stopped at the General Store for some supplies. Ice packs, anti-inflammatories...what else? *What else?* At the register, he added a pack of Wintergreen gum. No idea why.

"You might want to get some chocolate, too," said Lloyd Hayes, the owner.

Lincoln stared at him blankly.

"Your girl? That time of month, is it? I'd add chocolate."

"This isn't for my *girl*," he growled. "It's for Sadie. I'm sure you've heard."

The General Store sat kitty-corner to the new school. Word traveled fast. What was it now, two hours, tops?

"Yup. Heard all about it. Thanks to Brad and Lenny lovin' themselves a beer in the middle of the day, they were for once right where they needed to be."

Lincoln paid up and gathered his purchases.

"Next time you think about lassoing a woman?" Lloyd called out with a chuckle. "First make sure she's not a klutz."

"Funny."

He threw his purchases in the truck, then he phoned Daisy at the auto repair shop. "Do me a favor? I need someone to get Sadie's truck from the new school and drive it back to her house."

"Sure thing," Daisy said. "Did it break down?"

"No," Lincoln said, pinching the bridge of his nose, squeezing his eyes shut. "Might as well let you know. You'll hear about this later."

He explained the situation to Daisy, who suddenly couldn't talk. Too busy laughing. "I'll...get...someone... don't...worry..."

Nice how everyone found this hilarious. Maybe one day he'd have a laugh about it, too. When he pulled up to Sadie's cabin, he noticed another truck parked in the driveway. A few minutes later, out walked Jeremy Bush.

"Hey, Linc! Don't worry, she's doing okay." He stopped right in front of Lincoln. "Where are your flowers?"

"*What* flowers?"

"For Sadie. She's hurt. Weren't you the one who did it?"

Your honor, her feet were to blame.

"I brought her ice packs and anti-inflammatories. Some gum." He sounded like an idiot.

"That's good, too. Practical." He shrugged and pointed to the house. "Door's open."

Lincoln walked through the opened front door and shut it. "I'm back."

Sadie was arranging a bouquet of pink roses into a vase she'd filled with water. "Hey, there."

Lincoln scanned the kitchen counter, where there appeared to be six bouquets of flowers neatly lined up. A box of candy. All to be expected and he should not be surprised. The men of Stone Ridge were taking care of one of "their" women. And some of the younger men, no doubt, were courting Sadie.

He ignored the hot flash of jealousy that spiked through him.

"I brought you some ice packs," he said. "That's going to help you far more than these flowers will."

"You're right." She smiled at him. "They'll all wither and

die within a few days. Such a waste. And if I eat all this candy, I'll be as big as my cabin and not half as fun."

She certainly didn't have to worry about being too big. He noted she'd changed into shorts and a tee, and for a petite woman, her legs went on forever. He joined her in the kitchen, threw all but one ice pack in the freezer, and handed her the bottle of anti-inflammatories.

"Might want to take one or two. Get ahead of it."

The doorbell rang, and *Yankee Doodle Dandy* played.

Sadie brushed by him. "I'm sorry, but this has been happening since you left. That's why I left the door open."

This time, Troy Mellencamp was at her door, carrying a pie. "Mama makes the best pies. This one is apple walnut."

"Oh, my. Thank her for me, sugar. That's so sweet of her."

"Well, it was my idea." His chest puffed up.

"Thank you, too, of course."

Wasn't Troy *nineteen years old*? Lincoln cleared his throat. "Hey, Troy."

"Oh, hey there, Lincoln." Troy stuck his hands in his pockets, shoulders lowered. "Guess I'll leave y'all alone."

"Thank you so much. Love y'all."

Sadie gently shut the door. She placed the pie on the counter, where she was running out of room. The phone rang and she picked it up.

"Hi, Mom. No, I'm fine. No, *please* don't change your plans and fly back early. Beulah really shouldn't have phoned you. You and daddy enjoy your cruise. I promise you, I'm fine. Yes. Uh-huh. I will. Love you. Okay, bye." She hung up and looked to Lincoln. "My parents are on vacation, but they've already heard. And you didn't have to come by. I'm doing fine."

"I had to see that for myself. Any headaches? Nausea?"

"No," she said, and somehow looked disappointed.

He hooked his thumb toward the front door. "I brought

my sleeping bag. I'll spend the night on the porch and look in on you every couple of hours during the night."

Her eyes widened. "On the porch? You're staying the…but Eve…"

"You don't need Eve. This is my responsibility."

She blew out a breath. "I don't want to *be* your responsibility."

"Well, too bad, because you are."

"I don't see it that way." She crossed her arms. "I can take care of myself. If you want to be here, fine. Otherwise, please *go*."

"Of course I want to be here." He removed his Stetson and ran a hand through his hair.

How else could he alleviate his fears?

"Okay, then." She picked up her landline phone and pressed some buttons. "Eve? I don't need you tonight. Lincoln's taking over concussion duty. Yep…that's right… will do…okay, love you, bye."

Knowing Eve, she'd be by later anyway just to have a chuckle about all this. Since she lived next door, she'd see him sleeping on the porch. A few wise cracks about sleeping on the job, she'd be satisfied and on her way.

He tossed his hat on the couch and took a seat. Might as well get comfortable until he could figure out a way to get her to the hospital.

"I'll buy you dinner, too. You shouldn't cook."

"In my *condition*? You're being ridiculous about this." She shrugged. "But…dinner would be nice."

"Though pretty soon you just might get dinner delivered. I didn't know you were so popular."

He didn't know how he felt about that. Sadie was always a part of his life, just under his nose so to speak, but also on the fringes of his world. Until recently, he'd only had G-rated thoughts about her. Now they were swiftly moving into R-

59

rated territory and he could see he was far from the only one who'd noticed her.

"Why *would* you know?" She sat beside him. "You spend so much time on the ranch and the rest of the time you're gone on the circuit."

"I come into town for a cold beer nearly three times a week."

"Guess I don't spend enough time at the Shady Grind to run into you there."

"Listen, you should know. I'm not one of these guys chasing you. I'm here just like I would be for *anyone* I'd hurt."

She blinked. "I should make sure I don't feel special?"

"Something like that."

"You're pretty full of yourself, cowboy. Why would I care?"

"Shouldn't. I wanted to put that out there."

He tensed, feeling like a jackass. What happened to the smooth rodeo cowboy?

"What I mean is, I'm the kind of man who realizes there are single, beautiful women in other towns, too. Other states, even. No need to get desperate."

Oh, Jesus. He may have winced.

She crossed her arms. "Thanks. Message received loud and clear. You're not interested."

He wasn't sure if he still felt that way, but better that Sadie believe it. One thing remained: he didn't want or need a serious relationship at this stage of life. Not with so much to still figure out about his future.

They were both quiet for a moment, but her thoughts were so loud he could almost hear them.

"I'm worried about you sleeping on the porch," she finally said.

"Why? I'm a big guy. If a coyote comes around, I can take care of myself."

"I know, but…someone is going to see you."

"Like Eve?"

"She won't care. But maybe one of our renters. They're going to think I have a boyfriend that I kicked out of the house because…because maybe he was too drunk."

He nodded. "I've slept under the stars before instead of driving home tanked."

"Do you *want* people to think you're passed out drunk on my porch?"

"They might think we fought over something else." He leaned back and stretched his legs. "Maybe I caught you flirtin' with some other dude."

"Exactly! And they're going to think I'm a floozy."

"No one thinks you're a floozy. Whatever that is."

She pointed. "I don't *cheat*, Lincoln Carver. And I don't want people to think that I do."

He didn't know how he'd found himself in this weird conversation about imaginary events. But he didn't mind.

He crossed his arms behind his neck. "What's your solution to this quagmire?"

"Beau might see you, too. I don't know when he'll be home." She fiddled with a pillow and wouldn't look at him. "I think you should sleep on my couch."

Beau would prefer to see him on the porch, Lincoln guessed, though he might prefer not to see him anywhere near his sister's house at all. That would be Beau's problem, because by now he'd likely grown accustomed to the attention his little sister received.

"Deal."

She perked up. "Great."

"Now, what should we do for the next few hours? You need to stay awake."

. . .

SADIE WOULD NOT likely fall asleep, concussed or not, with Lincoln in her cabin all night. She had plenty of ideas of how to stay awake for hours, but Lincoln's thoughts didn't seem to follow hers. Oh, she'd noticed him lower his gaze to her legs, a moment she'd thoroughly enjoyed. He hadn't seemed thrilled to see her get-well gifts, but not because he was jealous. Because he felt so *responsible* for what happened. And instead of flowers or candy, he'd brought her an ice pack and gum. So very practical of him.

Not waiting for her to answer how they should spend their time, he stood, grabbed an ice pack from the freezer, squatted in front of her, and placed it on her head.

"You have a bump forming. Means you haven't been icing it enough."

She held it in place and her fingers brushed against his before he lowered his hand. This time, he caught her staring and a tense moment passed between them.

There were so many questions she wanted to ask him, such as why he'd never dated anyone for long. Why, when even Jackson had been engaged, Lincoln never had been. Not even once, and he was thirty-two. Naturally, there were rumors. Some women called Lincoln a player who would never settle down. But if he did, you better believe it would be with an out-of-towner. He toured so much with the rodeo, he'd meet someone sooner or later, if not already, and bring her home to Stone Ridge. On the other hand, who knew? Maybe he had a girl in every state.

As long as he was clear and above board to women about his intentions, Sadie wouldn't judge him. She'd been pursued but was still single. Maybe there was something wrong with her, or her standards were too high.

Her mother wondered all of this out loud. Frequently.

"Can I ask you a personal question?" Lincoln said.

The hair on her arms stood on end. Could he hear her thoughts? "S-sure."

"Why haven't you settled down with any of your many admirers?" He slid a gaze to all the flowers.

She lowered the ice pack. "I don't know."

"Maybe you just *like* being chased." One corner of his mouth tipped in a half-smile.

"Or maybe I've just never been chased by the right man."

He appeared to be considering this. Then, as if maybe she'd hit her head too hard, she remembered.

"I forgot something."

"What's wrong?"

"I promised Jimmy Ray's mother I'd stop by today for a chat. She needs moral support. Jimmy Ray is really acting out."

Jimmy Ray was so much trouble that Sadie finally phoned his mother, Pamela Ann. Sadie was on a fishing expedition, true enough, wondering if something was going on at home. Never dreaming she'd guessed right.

She glanced at the digital clock on her oven. "School let out a couple of hours ago, and she'll be expecting me."

"Jimmy Ray will tell her you got hurt. She'll understand."

"But I'm fine and perfectly capable of dropping in on her. She's lonely and having such a hard time. She kicked Derek out about a month ago."

Lincoln pinched the bridge of his nose as if he realized he wouldn't win. "I'll drive you."

She quickly changed back into a dress and her best boots, then, almost as an afterthought, grabbed the pie.

"I hate to come visit anyone empty-handed."

She again accepted Lincoln's hand to climb into his huge truck. She gave him directions, though he seemed to know the way. Then again, Derek would be about Lincoln's age, so they'd know each other. Derek and Pamela Ann married young, just out of high school, and they now lived in a trailer on a parcel of land belonging to Pastor June. One night, Sadie listened to a broken-hearted Pamela Ann spill her guts. She'd suspected Derek had cheated on her with a woman from out of town. He'd been drinking since he lost his job. It all came to a head when Pamela Ann issued an ultimatum. Stop drinking, and get your shit together, or get out.

He got out.

Sadie swallowed as Lincoln pulled up to a trailer on the outskirts of town on a large and empty field. She'd expected more of a mobile home, but this looked like a Winnebago you could just hook up to a truck and move.

"Pastor June lets them stay here on her land," Sadie said. "Derek can't seem to hold down a job."

The afternoon was clear and bright, a wonderful September day, but Sadie made a mental note to make sure Pamela Ann would have enough heat this winter. The ladies of SORROW would help. The society had been founded during World War II when there were actually less men in Stone Ridge for a short amount of time. The women wanted to do something to help the war effort and they'd started by knitting baby blankets for expectant mothers.

The problem began when all the babies born that first year were boys. Pink blankets went unused. After the war, some of the more fortunate men returned, and nine months later there were more boys. And then later even more boys, with a lucky one or two girls born to amazed and grateful mothers. Encouraged and searching for another way to help, the founding members decided that they'd put together a primer: The Men of Stone Ridge. They were determined for word to get out about how lucky the women of Stone Ridge were, with such handsome and plentiful men to choose from. And somehow with false promises of handsome cowboys and romance, lure more women back to town.

A little peculiar, sure. But the ladies were also the first to organize fundraisers and gather supporters for those in need.

Pamela Ann opened the screen before they'd even reached the door. "I didn't expect you. I heard about what happened. Oh, hello, Lincoln."

"Hey, Pamela Ann." He nodded.

"I brought you a pie." Sadie stepped inside, Lincoln following close behind her. "Lincoln is just a little worried about me so he's drivin' me around for today."

"Good idea. The way Jimmy Ray describes it, you were knocked out cold. But then, he exaggerates."

"Not this time," Lincoln said.

"Where is he?" Sadie asked.

Pamela Ann pointed to a little partition toward the back that divided the trailer. "He's playing video games."

She carried the pie and led them to a small table in the kitchen area. The windows were decorated with red and white gingham curtains and their surroundings were spotless and clean. Small but tidy. Sadie sat on one side of the booth and Pamela Ann on the other. Lincoln stood by for a few moments, but as they chatted, he eventually wandered over to Jimmy Ray.

"How are you?" Sadie asked.

"I think I should be asking you that question."

"I'm fine, just a little bump on the head. I tripped. After Lincoln...lassoed me."

"Jimmy Ray said the whole thing was his idea. I hoped he was kidding."

"Don't blame him. The grown-ups were in charge."

Pamela Ann laughed. "Well, it sounds like the kids loved it."

Sadie reached for Pamela Ann's hand. "Have you thought about any way I can help you through this rough patch?"

"Just someone to listen helps. I have a job picking peaches

this season. Thanks to you and the new school, Jimmy Ray can be in school while I work."

"You homeschooled him until now, right?"

She nodded. "He likes math but struggles with reading."

"Good to know. I can work with that. I'm testing the kids to see where they fall. Jimmy Ray seems very bright. He just has impulse control issues."

"Always has, but they got worse after Derek left us."

"The more I know about what's going on at home, the more I can help. We just need to stay in touch and back each other up. When we work together, Jimmy Ray benefits."

While she talked with Pamela Ann, Sadie stole glances in Lincoln's direction. For the first few minutes, he stood hand in his pockets, quietly observing whatever Jimmy Ray was doing. But a few minutes into her talk with Pamela Ann, she glanced, and didn't see him anymore.

CHAPTER 5

Jimmy Ray wasn't playing Warcraft or any game which included explosives and blowing up imaginary enemies. He was playing Mario Brothers and looked up briefly to catch Lincoln watching him.

"You know this game?" Jimmy Ray asked.

"Mario Brothers."

"I'm surprised you know the franchise."

Lincoln blinked and almost laughed. For a moment, Jimmy Ray sounded a lot older.

"The *franchise*? I grew up playin' this game."

A few minutes later, Sadie still spoke in hushed tones with Pamela Ann, and Lincoln had an ear worm from the annoying song.

"Wanna play?" Jimmy Ray offered him the controller.

"Why not?"

The women were talking quietly, and he had nothing to contribute to that conversation. Nothing they'd want to hear, anyway. In his mind, Pamela Ann should be grateful to be rid of Derek. In high school, he'd been a punk who knocked Pamela Ann up and then bragged about it.

He squatted in front of the small space with a monitor and started jumping rows. He managed to stay alive three seconds. "Let me try again."

Losing to anything fueled his competitive spirit.

"My dad is really good at this game. He's better than me, and I'm a lot better than you."

"You are."

"Maybe you just need to practice more."

"That's probably true." Lincoln pushed buttons. "I don't get much time to practice on the ranch."

"Jimmy Ray, it's time to put the game away and get washed up for dinner."

Lincoln looked behind him to find both women smiling. Jimmy Ray took the controller from Lincoln and shut off the console. He'd been sitting here all this time, losing to a kid. *Derek's* kid.

"Thank Mr. Lincoln for his time today," Pamela Ann continued. "He's a busy man and took time out of his schedule to come see your classroom."

"Thank you for coming today, sir," Jimmy Ray said and looked at all three adults earnestly. "It was *my* idea that he lasso Miss Sadie."

"Not sure you should be proud of that," Pamela Ann said, ruffling his hair, but smiling.

"None of this was your fault. I'm going to be fine. See?" She touched her head and smiled.

Jimmy Ray nodded. A few more niceties, Pamela Ann once again thanking her for the pie, and they were finally out the door.

"Is this something you do often?" Lincoln asked as he got them back on the road. "Seems above and beyond."

"I don't think of it that way. Look, I believe teaching is a calling. I know it isn't for every teacher, but it is for me. It's more than a solid career. I've always wanted to make a difference in a child's life."

Ranching could also be a calling. There were no holidays, or paid vacations. No 401k. If you didn't love the lifestyle, you could be assured to lead a horrible life.

He'd never thought of teaching as a calling, but Lincoln fondly remembered his fifth-grade teacher the same year that his mother left them. Mrs. Flynn was his refuge in a storm. From time to time, she'd remind Lincoln that as a kid himself, he shouldn't feel so responsible for his younger brother and sister. He'd been half in love with her.

He could picture Sadie being that teacher for a kid someday. Maybe even Jimmy Ray. "How about an early dinner? Where do you want to go?"

"The Shady Grind?"

"Nah, I can do better than that. Why don't I take you out of town to eat?"

"That's *really* not necessary."

"My pleasure."

While waiting for her and playing mindless video games with Jimmy Ray, Lincoln hatched his plan. Like it or not, Sadie would get checked out at the hospital. First, he'd get a meal in her. Then, when they were a few miles away from the closest hospital, he'd drive her there. Any objections would be squashed by her gratitude for a nice dinner. He could dream, anyway.

Forty minutes later, he pulled into a steakhouse in Kerrville. He guided her into the restaurant, hand on the small of her back. When they were seated, he pulled Sadie's chair out for her. Mostly because it would be unthinkable not to offer this basic function to a woman. Heck, he did the same for his sister and grandmother. It didn't mean anything special.

They were *not* on a date.

"This isn't a date." He added after the waitress took drink orders.

"No, of *course* not," Sadie said, perusing the menu.

"It's just two friends going out for a meal together."

She met his gaze. "*Are* we friends?"

"What do you mean? Of course we are. We practically all grew up together. You're Eve's best friend, who was engaged to Jackson."

"Yeah, and when Eve ditched him at the altar, you hated Eve, and me by association. Y'all didn't talk to me for a year."

He snorted. "I doubt it was a year."

"It was," she said, going back to the menu. "I counted."

"Okay, that was a rough time for all of us. We took sides. The whole town did." He glanced up from his menu. "And *you* could have stopped her."

There. He'd said it. They'd never talked about this. For years, he'd wanted to take Sadie aside and question her. Why hadn't she *told* anyone that Eve changed her mind? When did she know? In other words, what did she know and when did she know it?

"I couldn't stop her. I tried."

"By drivin' her away from the church where everybody was waitin' for her?"

Her lower lip quivered, and guilt spiked through him. "I tried to talk some sense into her. I did. You weren't there. You don't *know*. She was so...so upset."

"Upset?" Lincoln tamped down the hot streak of anger that pulsed through him. "You should have seen my *brother*. She might as well have ripped his heart clear out of his chest. It would have been kinder."

"I'm so sorry, Lincoln." She glanced up at him briefly, then lowered her gaze.

Before those eyes that shimmered with tears spilled over, he pulled back. "I know you are. And it wasn't *your* fault."

"Thank you," she said, seeming to acknowledge his generosity in forgiving her.

"Eve came back to town, Mima forgave all, Jackson is doing great, and now we're all friends again."

While that oversimplified things, he didn't see any point in continuing to peel back layers of skin just to look at the blood and tissue. There was no reason he and Sadie couldn't be friends now.

"I guess so." She shrugged. "Except friends see each other sometimes. They talk. Have fun together."

"What do you call this?" He waved to their surroundings.

"I call it you feel guilty. Oh, and don't forget 'responsible.'" She held up air quotes.

"You got me. I did say that. But I'm having fun, and we're talkin'."

She went all wide-eyed. "You're having fun?"

"Aren't you?"

"Well, yeah, but..." Her cheeks flushed a little then. "Never mind."

"It isn't that I don't like you. You're beautiful and sweet. Maybe...just a little too sweet for me."

She made a face. "You know, I hate being called sweet probably as much as you like being called *nice*."

"You can't fight who you are."

"I'm not doin' that. It's just that I'm a *little* more complicated that everyone thinks. Give me some credit, yeah?"

"Okay. But you love kids, you're taking a pittance of a salary to be the town's first teacher, you visit the struggling parents of your students. You bring them pies and listen to them complain. You ask your friends to do career day for the kids. You tell the children you love them all. And you don't want to *bother* anyone who might want to take you to the hospital to get checked out."

"That's *not* why I don't want to go." She met his eyes. "Now, you answer a personal question."

He swallowed, not knowing what to expect. "Go ahead."

"Why don't *you* date any women from Stone Ridge?"

He relaxed at the question. An easy one. "Look, I compete on the rodeo circuit. Not interested in competing for a woman's heart, too. That's just supposed to...happen."

"Aha, so you do believe it *could* happen."

"I mean, sure, it's possible. Just not likely. Look at Jackson and Eve. Epic disaster. They were way too young to get married and look what happened. Then he marries a country singer and it lasts three whole months. My parents didn't work, either. Same for Eve's parents. And now there's Derek and Pamela Ann, just the latest in a hit parade of breakups."

"Those couples were all young."

"Yeah, I guess."

She quirked a brow. "Lincoln, we're not that young anymore."

"Doesn't change facts. Not for me."

"Well, I'm sad for you." She straightened and closed her menu. "I'm gettin' married someday and probably soon, too. I want three children. I'm going to be a teacher and have summers off to be with my children. My husband and I can both work."

"Sounds like you have it all worked out."

He wanted to dislike her for planning her future husband's life before he knew what hit him. But he found her way too adorable and sexy to be mad. Plus, he'd smiled more in the past few hours than in recent memory.

"I know what I want, now I just have to find the right man."

"You're definitely in the right town. Plenty to choose

from. But I have to believe that your future husband will not be too happy to find out the way men chased after you."

"Oh, no. Once I'm taken, I'm taken. Everyone will know it."

He changed the subject. "Funny you should mention that teaching is your calling. I guess the rodeo is mine."

"I thought you would say ranching."

"Ranching, in my case, is more of a legacy than a calling."

"Is it hard to juggle both?"

He'd never been asked that question. Normally he'd spit out an answer to that question in two seconds. The rodeo was the only thing he could truly call his own. He hadn't been born into it, unlike ranching. But lately the circuit drained him, and not just his wallet. Even if successful, he couldn't win every single time. Losing hurt. No cowboy liked to lose but Lincoln hated it more than most.

"It's not hard," he lied.

"I bet the kids on the circuit love you. The children here like you. Especially Jimmy Ray."

"If I'm good with children, it's because I pretty much raised Jackson and Daisy after our mother left. Hank wasn't much help and Mima and Pop were aging. Pop was already sick with a weak heart, and so I chipped in more as the oldest. Once I got my driver's license, I drove us all to school and back every day. Helped them with homework. Sometimes cooked dinner."

"It's like you've already raised a family."

He nodded. "I know what makes kids happy. They want to be the center of attention at all times."

"That's not true, but if it is, that's not what they *need*. Kids need to learn that they can't be the center of everything."

"Tell that to a little girl who's crying for her mother every night." Lincoln shut his menu and signaled for the waitress. "I'm having the T-bone."

. . .

SADIE SWALLOWED hard at the turn of their conversation. She pictured poor little Daisy crying all night for her mother. And she wondered if, after he'd gone to bed and no one could see him, Lincoln also cried for his mother.

What kind of a woman would abandon her family? Her young *children*?

No one talked about Maggie Carver anymore. Once, Sadie asked her mother about Maggie, only to hear Mom say, "If I can't say anything nice, I don't say anything at all."

Silence followed, long and deep.

Sadie didn't know Lincoln carried such a responsibility for his family, but now that she'd heard it from him, it made sense. It might be why he appeared so serious most of the time. Not just a rancher but a stand-in father. It would also be why he felt so responsible for what happened today. And the reason he'd taken her to dinner.

She sighed, rapidly losing all hope that he might be interested in more than her concussion. At one time, she and Eve planned their lives with the Carver men. Eve and Jackson were high school sweethearts, and Sadie put herself front and center with Lincoln frequently. But he'd never seemed to notice her, other than as an appendage to Eve.

Still, she'd foolishly daydreamed that someday she and Eve would actually be not just best friends but sisters-in-law. Family. Side by side, they'd raise more Carver cowboys. A few girls thrown in for good measure, if they were lucky.

But she lived in the real world now.

Her heart already broken once, Sadie understood life wasn't all unicorns and rainbows. After dinner, they rode quietly for a few minutes and then Lincoln made a turn that would take them farther south.

"Where are we going?"

He took his time answering, adjusting his mirror first. "To the hospital."

"What?" she turned in her seat. "Are you *serious*? You tricked me. Take me to dinner, and then the hospital? Was this your plan all along?"

"No. I only came up with it when we were at Pamela Ann's."

"Great, Lincoln. Nothing like running it by me first."

"You would have said no."

"You know what? Technically, I think this is called kidnapping. You're taking me somewhere I don't want to go."

"I'm taking you someplace you *need* to go. Why are you being so damned stubborn about this?"

"Because I'm fine. And…they'll want to do a CAT scan."

The unwelcome tug of fear crept in slowly, ready to pounce. She'd had a CAT scan once, in college, when a thorough doctor wanted to rule out anything more serious contributing to her occasional migraines. Her college boyfriend, Martin, dropped her off, not even coming inside with her. And she'd discovered a huge weakness. Tight, enclosed spaces. After her complete meltdown, the doctor informed her that next time, she could consider a mild sedative.

Conversation stopped as Sadie gave Lincoln the silent treatment. When he pulled into the parking lot of the hospital, he turned to her. His eyes tipped down at the sides, giving him a constantly worried look.

He squeezed her hand. "Please, sweetheart, do this for me."

She went absolutely liquid at the sound of his deep and sultry voice. Those blue eyes. Please. Sweetheart.

Yeah, she was a goner.

"Um…I…see the thing is, I'm kind of afraid of tight…spaces."

"Aw, okay. Not a big deal. I don't like them, either. All you have to do is picture your happy place. Just close your eyes and have a little dream."

Close your eyes and have a little dream.

What did Lincoln dream about? Winning the championship? Hooking up with that year's rodeo queen?

She shook her head to clear *that* image. Well, it could be different this time. It had been a few years since her last CAT scan. This time would be easier, with Lincoln here, waiting in the lobby. Holding her hand if she got lucky. He led her into the emergency room, hand low on her back, completely unaware of how she tingled at the weight of his hand. Such a good man. So strong.

And don't forget annoying.

"Hi, I'm...I fell earlier today?" she explained to the triage nurse. "No big deal."

"Knocked out cold," Lincoln said from behind her.

She glared at him. "He's exaggerating."

"Nope, he's not." He actually winked at Sadie.

After she'd filled out paperwork and had an admittance bracelet taped to her wrist, they both walked to the waiting room. Lincoln stretched his legs out and sat on a plastic chair in the sterile room. The sounds of the ER in a larger city enveloped them. A doctor rushed through the "personnel only" double doors. A child cried. The occasional squawk of the public address system rang out.

"Code Blue, room ten. Code Blue."

Someone crashing. The entire crash team would be on their way to room ten.

"It could be a while, you know. Hope you don't mind spending your Friday night in the Emergency Room," she grumbled.

"That's okay." He crossed his arms and tipped his Stetson

to partially cover his eyes. "I'll wait for you here and nap. Unless you want me with you."

"No," she said too quickly. "I think only family is allowed, anyway."

"Right. I'll be right here."

She sure didn't want Lincoln to see her have another meltdown. He would feel responsible, all over again. And he'd been responsible for enough people in his life. She hardly wanted to add herself to the mix. This was, after all, her only weakness.

Two long hours later, in which she sat beside Lincoln deliberately not talking to him, the nurse finally came for her. That meant they'd finally arrived at the non-emergency patients. She didn't want to break it to Lincoln, but someone who walked in with a possible head injury, able to formulate complete sentences, would not be seen first. That's what triage nurses were for.

Another hour of waiting by herself, and the nurse finally took Sadie to the machine and asked her to lie down. She pictured her happy place, at the moment, the lush forest of Humboldt County. Her favorite romance series was set there, with a handsome bartender played by Lincoln, and a pretty nurse midwife played by herself. Naturally.

But no matter how hard she tried to imagine fly fishing on the river and the quirky people of the small town, she could not forget that she was trapped. In a tight and dark space, where it became a bit harder to breathe with every passing moment she slid farther from the opening. What happened if the machine broke down? Power outage? What about an earthquake? Would everyone run out of here and forget about her? Would she then die of oxygen deprivation?

Could she crawl out of here on her hands and knees? Was there even enough room to turn over? Once she could no longer catch her breath, she realized she was hyperventilating. Or possibly having a heart attack. Her hands were numb and her chest tight. She was suffocating.

Lord, she was going to *die*.

And all this without telling Lincoln that she might love him a little bit. Too bad if he didn't like it. Damn the stupid cowboy. She didn't want to be attracted to him. Not with this wretched one-sided infatuation that had lasted over a *decade*.

"Are you okay in there?" the technician asked.

"No," she whined quietly. "I…I think I'm dying."

"We're almost done, honey."

"Please…please get me out of here."

To her horror, a single tear slid down her cheek. Shortly after, another. And then more where those came from. Sloshing down her cheeks and wetting her lips. But she stayed, because God *forbid* she neglected to follow doctor's orders. Lincoln was right. She followed the rules, and here, doctors were the authority. Because Sadie was always an excellent student, a great girlfriend, a good daughter, and sister. Always. Because she followed expectations and did as told. Not like Beau, or even Eve, who did what she wanted, damn the torpedoes. Or something.

Finally, thank you Lord, they slid her back out of the giant tube. Her legs trembled and shook.

"Honey, why didn't you tell us you're claustrophobic?" the technician said, offering his hand.

"I only had one other CAT scan and I thought maybe…I don't know…" She sobbed.

The technician's face went white. "Oh, hey, hey, there. Wait right here. I'll get your husband."

"H-he's not…my husband."

"Okay, I'll get the man who brought you in here."

"No. I'm fine." She wiped tears away. "I just need to get outside. Fresh air, lots of room, and I'll be fine."

"All right, then." He eyed her dubiously and handed her a

tissue. "I'll get these films to my attending, and we should know something shortly."

"Sure," Sadie said. "I'm sorry. And thank you."

With that, she ran out of the room like the hounds of hell were on her heels. She wanted oxygen.

Room. Wide open spaces.

CHAPTER 6

*L*incoln paced the white linoleum floors of the emergency room. Nap? Ha! He'd been deluding himself. Sadie had been behind those double doors for a long while. Yeah, sure, he knew that these things took time. Maybe they were waiting for the doctor to read the results. No point in bringing her all the way here if they weren't going to have an answer tonight.

He just wanted her to be okay.

Needed her to be okay.

Lincoln pulled out the phone he rarely used. He required a distraction. Even with cell reception spotty in parts of Stone Ridge, he carried the phone around anyway. He couldn't discount the fact that at some point he might actually need the thing and be able to *use* it. This might be one of those times.

He stepped outside into the now cold dark night. His brother Jackson answered on the fourth ring.

"Hey, bud! What's up?"

Should Lincoln tell him about Sadie? Nah, he wanted a distraction from all these intense emotions she'd brought up in him. Best not to mention her name. Jackson acted squirrely about the mention of something or someone even remotely having to do with Eve. Not visiting home for years, he didn't quite understand that life moved on and people in a small and tight-knit community couldn't stay angry at each other forever.

"Just waitin' for a friend. I'm in Kerrville."

At the hospital waiting for Sadie to get a scan since she got knocked out cold when I lassoed her. He didn't say any of this out loud because he hadn't phoned to give Jackson a laugh.

"How's the Nashville scene?"

Maybe if he heard about all the beautiful women, both starlets and groupies, he'd forget about Sadie.

Because there were far more beautiful women in the world than Sadie Stephens. Some rodeo queens, for instance. He'd slept with a couple and found them empty-headed. He feared the emptiness might rub off on him. With Sadie, there seemed to be an internal light that gleamed from somewhere deep inside and lit her up. Her bright eyes were always brimming with intelligence. She also seemed to notice the smallest of details. And she had the most incredible smile. Not classically beautiful, but nevertheless a knockout.

And a first-class klutz.

He'd call that her only fault, but he couldn't forget the fact that she'd planned out her future husband's life without telling him. But she wanted a family, and she should have one. She loved children and they loved her.

"...Anyway, I think this new recording contract might be the one that takes me to the next level. I like the producer. Got some great songs," Jackson was saying.

"What about the women?"

"The *women*? What, you want to come tomcat around with me?" Jackson chuckled.

"Maybe." If he got away from Stone Ridge, at least for a little while, he'd stop thinking about Sadie Stephens.

"You know you can come out to see me anytime you want." Jackson changed the subject. "Any more buckles to add to your collection?"

"Yup. And more are comin'. The circuit starts up again in a few months. You know I'll be there."

Another thing he wouldn't lay on Jackson? The disillusionment he'd started to feel about the rodeo. Having kept the dream for so long made it difficult for him to admit the rodeo didn't live up to expectations. But if he didn't have the rodeo, nor the buckles to cement his self-worth, then maybe he had nothing.

"Daisy and Mima okay?"

"Ornery as ever."

"Good. And how's the old man?"

Generous of Jackson to ask after Hank. If Lincoln and Hank had a tense relationship, Jackson's relationship with their father could be compared to the grating sound of fingernails on an old-fashioned chalkboard.

"Still drinkin'. Still callin' it a backache."

Jackson snorted. "Runs in the family. Seems like the women in our life push us into the bottle and it's our job to climb out."

"And how are *you* doin' with all that? Still got it under control?"

"Yep. Nothin' like your own band threatenin' to kick you out to straighten up." He paused. "And the ranch? Y'all are still hanging in there, right?"

Lincoln could almost hear the guilt laced through those words. But he wouldn't let his brother know that he sometimes resented being the only Carver left to run the ranch. That there were some months they struggled to turn a profit. Jackson had every right to pursue his dream. Lincoln considered himself lucky that his own dreams fell in line with ranching.

After a few more updates, Lincoln hung up with Jackson, and went back inside the hospital to pace. Two hours after she'd been taken back, Lincoln thought he would lose his mind. He finally asked the nurse, who was not helpful. A few minutes later, when he thought he'd worn a new pattern on the squeaky waxed floor, Sadie rushed out from behind the double doors. She didn't even stop on the way out, if she noticed him at all, but just ran outside.

For a moment, shock kept him rooted to the floor. A nurse followed on Sadie's heels and stopped in front of Lincoln.

"You brought her in, didn't you?"

He nodded, robbed of words for the moment. It couldn't be bad news. They wouldn't have let her go.

Unless she refused medical treatment...again.

"She didn't tell us she was claustrophobic."

"What?"

"Claustrophobia. A phobia of tight and small spaces?"

"I know what claustrophobia is," he said with irritation.

His gaze followed Sadie. She stood outside, her back to him, her body framed by the ambient light of a streetlamp. Arms crossed and head bent.

"We'll have results shortly. Just hang in there."

"We'll be outside."

He stopped a step behind her. Her shoulders were slumped and damn...shaking. Her entire body trembling. Her hands shook as she held a tissue to her nose.

"Sadie."

"I-I'm okay. I just needed to be outside...to get some fresh air."

Lord, he was an idiot. He couldn't seem to stop being one around Sadie. Maybe he should have considered that she

83

wasn't *trying* to be difficult, but that she had a reason to avoid a CAT scan. She'd told him in the truck, but he didn't take her seriously. No one liked tight spaces. Not everyone was *mortally terrified* of them.

He took that last step and closed the distance between them. One arm around her waist, he tugged her to him, her back to his chest. He lowered his head to her shoulder.

The delicious scent was in her hair. "Sweetheart, I didn't know it would be this bad."

"Me, either. I'm s-sorry. I hoped I'd be over this. That this time I wouldn't be...out of control." She leaned into him, and tiny sobs wrenched through her body.

And damn it, straight to his heart.

"I can't stop hurting you. First, I give you a concussion. Next, an anxiety attack. Maybe you should just stay away from me."

For several minutes, she didn't speak. As her sobs ebbed and her breathing slowed, she stopped shivering. Then his heart finally stopped convulsing in his chest but still he didn't let her go. He simply wrapped another arm around her. He should let her loose now, he understood, because he didn't want to mislead her. Sadie was vulnerable, especially now. But his arms, as if independent of his brain, continued to hold her close.

"You meant well. I should have been checked out," she said quietly. "He said I'll have results in just a while longer."

Right. The results. "It's going to be okay."

She turned in his arms to face him. "I think so."

"You can say, 'I told you so' then." He briefly tapped the tip of her nose.

Her eyes smiled even though her lips didn't. They were just pursed slightly as if considering it. Her nose a little pink. All her eye-makeup had wiped away, leaving her long and dark lashes damp. This made her hazel eyes pop and take over her whole face with their intensity. When did she...oh, hell, yeah, she was *far* more than pretty.

His heart rate kicked up, and before he could talk himself out of it, he palmed the nape of her neck, and drew her close. His mouth came crashing down on hers and he expected one of two things: he'd be slapped, or the kiss would be sweet and tender, as expected. Then he'd move on from this fantasy that had consumed him since the day she drove out to the ranch in that short dress.

But he didn't get slapped.

And the kiss wasn't at all sweet but just a little bit...wild.

Sadie met him with passion, opening for him, and holy shit, this was good. So good. Amazing. And perfect. From the slide of her hands up his arms to his hair, to the lowering of his hand to her behind. He pulled her even closer. She made a tiny whimpering sound in the back of her throat which made him deepen the kiss, somehow seeking the end of this moment. In a minute this would all stop. It would come to a grinding halt. He felt sure of this. She'd pull away from too much, too soon. Or *he* would, but honestly, he didn't see *that* happening.

The sweet and nice girl next door, the teacher, the volunteer, and everyone's friend...she'd become his fantasy lover. Finally, he broke the kiss. He managed to do this with the same force of will of waking at four in the morning even when he'd gone to bed at midnight. Willpower. You didn't get to be a cattle rancher or a rodeo champ without strength and fierce determination.

Still not ready to lose all contact, his fingers traced the curve of her jawline. "We should go back inside."

He took her hand, threaded her fingers through his, and led her gently back into the waiting room. They sat next to each other on the uncomfortable plastic chairs, with nothing less than everything having changed between them. Fortunately, not much longer, a doctor met them in the waiting room.

Looks great, no brain bleed, no swelling.

You were wise to come in.

Can't ever be too careful. I'll send these images to your primary care physician.

Follow up if you get any headaches, nausea, or dizziness.

Lincoln heard it all but didn't fully register the news. His thoughts were on that mind-blowing kiss. On Sadie's mournful sobs. He didn't know how to react to what he'd instinctively recognized in her.

She'd been embarrassed to have a weakness.

He could relate because he detested weakness. But now *she'd* become his weakness.

"Concussion duty, tonight?" the doctor asked Lincoln, which made him snap to attention.

"Uh, yeah. Yeah."

"It's better to be safe. Good man." The doctor slapped his back. "Take care of your girl, now."

*She's not my…*Lincoln almost said out loud but didn't bother correcting the man this time. Anyone who'd witnessed them outside a moment ago would have every reason to believe they were together. And why bother correcting the doctor when she felt very much like his girl. At least tonight. The first time in his life he'd felt responsible for someone but didn't quite mind.

He drove quietly back to her cabin with every intention of staying.

"You heard the doctor. Concussion duty."

"Since it's already midnight, I don't think we'll get anyone else at this point."

They'd already had this conversation, but she was probably drained. Emotionally spent. Maybe that's why she'd allowed the kiss from a man who'd just told her that he wouldn't have a long-term relationship with anyone. They'd both had a long day, and he'd guess like him, she was an early riser. He wanted to get her home and into bed so she could sleep off this day from hell. Tomorrow would be better. He mentally prepared his "rah-rah" talk in case Sadie would need it. He'd had plenty of experience as a cheerleader.

Of course, you can be a Nashville superstar, little brother, you have got what it takes!

Daisy, any guy who doesn't see you're beautiful just the way you are, is an idiot.

Yes, Wade, you're right. You were robbed. You probably should be the reigning rodeo champ of the world. No one else should even try. Heh, heh.

Good morning, Beau. I slept on the couch.

Okay, that last one was for him.

When they arrived, there were several bouquets of flowers lined up and blocking her front door. He was beginning to feel like a total screwup for bringing ice packs and gum.

"Oh, good grief," Sadie said.

"Must be nice to have so many admirers."

"You realize this is just because I got hurt. This doesn't happen all the time."

"It would be okay with me if it does."

He helped pick up the flowers and carry them inside. Obviously, this town was filled with men who didn't need their eyesight checked anytime soon. And as one of the few eligible ladies, Sadie would have no trouble finding that husband and three point five children.

Once she'd placed the flowers in water, Sadie bent under her bed and came up with some blankets. She brought them to the couch and handed them over to him. Briefly, she met his eyes, but broke her gaze away quickly. She was back to being shy with him after their powerhouse kiss. A minute later, she threw him an extra soft pillow from her bed. He caught it midair. It smelled like her, a fruity, coconut, soft, sweet scent.

Jesus, sweetheart. Now you're killing me.

She no longer argued with him about staying, even after she'd gotten the all-clear from the scan. Maybe too spent, also, to say, *That kiss was a bad idea. What were you thinking? I told you I'm getting married and having three children. What, you suddenly want children? Uh-huh. That's what I thought. I'm no buckle bunny, mister.*

"I'm going to bed," Sadie announced.

She disappeared into the bathroom. When she came out, she wore a long-sleeved tee which fell to her thighs and black leggings. She'd pulled her hair into a high ponytail. She climbed in bed and shut off the light. In the dark, he kicked off his boots. He took off his shirt but kept the jeans on, removing his belt. Attempting to stretch out on the couch, he found it too small. Or maybe he was just too tall. He curled his legs and knew that if he slept this way he would wind up with a kink in his back.

"Are we just not going to talk about the kiss? Ever?" Sadie suddenly said into the thick quiet.

He winced. "What do you want to talk about?"

"Why did you kiss me? Was it because I cried, and you felt bad about dragging me there?"

"Hell, no. Sadie, don't even think that for a minute."

"I thought for a minute you'd given me a pity kiss."

"Jesus! No."

For a moment, she went silent again. "Then, why?"

"Because…you're beautiful."

And I wanted to check something out. Do you taste as sweet as you look?

"I guess I lost my head for a minute and forgot that you'd

just shared with me you want all the things that I *don't*. So, forgive me."

"I forgive you." More silence, and just when he'd hoped she'd fallen asleep, "It was an amazing kiss. Right?"

"Oh, yeah."

A few minutes later, quiet enveloped the room. Lincoln set an alarm on his watch so he could get up and check on Sadie. He pulled the covers up and tried to find sleep. But two hours went by quickly, filling them as he did with thoughts of Sadie. Naked. Riding him like a bronco. When his alarm went off, he rose and took the few steps to her bed to nudge her. Simply rolling over would be enough. He didn't need to fully wake her.

She rolled over with a little sigh and left a huge and empty space on her bed.

He looked at the short sofa.

Her bed.

The sofa.

And because his Mima didn't raise no fool, he grabbed his blankets and climbed into the empty space beside Sadie.

CHAPTER 7

Sadie woke to the sound of a dog howling. Or a *coyote.* She sat up ramrod straight and saw a man in her bed. A man! In. Her. Bed. Sleep tugged at her with such heaviness that she automatically recoiled. Until she remembered. This was *Lincoln Carver* in her bed. Lincoln, who kissed her so long, hard, and deep that she'd nearly lost sensation in her limbs. He'd kept kissing her, as if shocked and happily surprised to find the chemistry between them.

Assured that she wasn't sleeping with a stranger, Sadie settled back on her pillow and studied Lincoln. In the ambient moonlight filtering through the window, his beautiful thick brown hair seemed a shade lighter. And oh boy he didn't have his shirt on. The blankets rested just beneath his chest. She resisted the urge to pull them down to his waist and check out those washboard abs.

Instead, because he seemed solidly enough asleep, she tentatively reached for his hair. Softer tendrils than she could have imagined curled through her fingers. Lincoln was so strong, tall, and solidly built that she assumed he'd even have tough hair. But no, instead, silky strands slipped through her fingers. He smelled like soap, and leather, and some kind of delicious cologne.

She'd been such a mess earlier tonight, but he'd comforted her in a way that she didn't know anyone possibly could. She'd wanted to be nowhere other than in those strong arms, pulling her against him. But her thoughts and feelings were plain stupid. She would get hurt falling for him. He would make her cry. Falling in love with this man? Not smart. She'd already been with a man she couldn't trust. Martin took her trust and wrecked her.

Loyalty, trust, and *faithfulness* were everything.

Lincoln moved and she quickly drew back her hand. Eyes still closed, he rolled to his right, taking her with him. She almost squeaked in surprise. Oh, dear Lord. Spooning. She was literally *spooning* with Lincoln. His rock-hard forearms around her waist, he held her close. She didn't move, choosing to die in this bed, in this position, if it came to that. She prayed he wouldn't say another woman's name in his sleep. Did he have another woman that he slept with on a regular basis? Maybe someone that understood what he wanted and accepted it.

Please, please, please. Don't say anything and ruin this fantasy for me.

Just for now, in this slice of a moment's time, she could pretend. They were lovers, Lincoln her partner and best friend. They slept together every night just like this.

But in the light of day, the fantasy wouldn't last. Not for her. Maybe Lincoln liked women a little too much. She'd already been there, done that. She should stay away from him. She'd find another man in her town filled with eligible men who would do. Someone who could kiss her until her bones dissolved, but also give her security, a family, and the future she wanted.

Sadie didn't go back to sleep and saw the first rays of

sunlight as dawn broke. She felt Lincoln move next to her and closed her eyes. She didn't want him to realize what he'd done, quite by accident, and then regret it when he realized that she might make more out of this moment. She wouldn't. She'd try not to, anyway. She would let him get back to the sofa and pretend he'd slept there all night so she wouldn't be the wiser. In her heart, she'd know. She'd always know that she'd been in Lincoln's arms for a few blissful hours.

But she didn't sense him get off the bed. She didn't feel the spring of the mattress move with his weight. Instead, she felt fingers thread through her mess of bed hair and tried not to sigh.

Then lips replaced fingers and she heard a softly whispered, "Sadie."

She didn't move. A few seconds later, his hand skimmed down her back. "Sadie?"

Oh, yeah. He was trying to wake her. She then performed her best imitation of someone waking up.

"Um…huh?" She stretched, rubbed her eyes, and turned to find herself face to face with Lincoln.

He made no move to hide the fact that he'd been lying in her bed. Was still *in* her bed. Shirtless. Perhaps he wanted an award for being a gentleman. Or he was so excruciatingly honest that he wouldn't try to hide the truth.

"I tried, but that sofa is too short for my legs. And then you rolled over and I realized that this is a pretty big bed."

Excruciatingly honest it is. However, big bed or not, that had not stopped him from curling up to her.

"Yes, it's a king-size. California king, I think they call it."

That's right, Sadie, blather on about the size of your bed. Tell him how you bought the bed so that it would be large enough for two. Especially for a man with long legs.

"Anyway," he said, rising and quickly finding his shirt,

"hope you don't mind. A rancher doesn't need any early back problems."

"I don't mind." She sat up, legs hanging off the side, and scrubbed a hand down her face. "I slept well. There's plenty of room on my bed. I should have suggested it in the first place. Didn't even realize you were there."

His shirt clung to his shoulders, still unbuttoned as he tugged his boots on. And how on earth did he look even better than he did with it off? Maybe because all that tanned taut skin played peek-a-boo. When he moved one way, she got a glance of his abs. Another way, she got to see one side of his chest. He began buttoning the shirt and she may have sighed.

"Thank you for concussion duty," she said. "You're a prince."

He slid her an easy smile. "Not exactly a hardship."

"Let me make you some coffee. I at least owe you that."

"Nah, that's all right. I'm already gettin' a late start." He tugged on his belt, grabbed his hat, and shoved it on.

"Um. Okay. Thanks for career day. The kids loved it."

He winked. "Until their favorite teacher got hurt."

"Oh, I bet they knew I'd be fine. I'm made of tough stuff."

He gave her a little once-over, as though he didn't quite believe that, and broke out in a slow smile. "Yeah, but you're pretty soft, too."

Gulp. She didn't know quite what to say to that, so she blinked twice, hoping that wasn't Morse code for "I love you."

She walked him to the front door.

"Had a good time hanging out with you," Lincoln said, squeezing her hand.

"Even in the ER?" She gaped.

"Yeah, even there." And then he spun her right into his arms and kissed her.

She seriously did not know what to *do* with him. Except kiss him back. Her hands fisted his shirt, pulling him close. He deepened the kiss, which seemed to last forever. When he broke the kiss, she traced her bruised lips, missing him already.

"Okay. I'll see you later." And then he shut the door behind him.

She stared at the shut door. That's *it*? He'd kissed her, set them both on fire, and then given her the complete brush off.

See you later?

See you *later*?

She wanted to stomp and scream and yell obscenities out her front door, but this was *her* fault. She'd laid out her life plans to him. Should she be so surprised that she'd scared him off?

Damn it, damn it, damn it!

Sadie finished brushing her teeth and heard a knock on her door. She prayed there would be no more flowers. Chocolate she would take in a heartbeat.

Eve brushed by Sadie and went straight to the coffeemaker. "Tell me everything!"

"Lincoln just left."

"I know, I saw him. I waited until he'd left." Quite comfortable in Sadie's kitchen, Eve reached for the coffee grinder and scooped beans inside.

"I don't know what's going on. I'm so confused." She sat with a plop on one of her two kitchen stools. "Lincoln kissed me."

The whir of the coffee grinder going, Eve suddenly stopped the noise and turned to stare. "I'm sorry, I thought you said he *kissed* you?"

Sadie nodded. She should be happier than this. But she didn't know what it meant when a guy kissed you and left with no plans to see you again.

"He didn't just kiss me, he *kissed* me."

"Not on the cheek?" Eve cocked her head.

Sadie quirked a brow. "With tongue."

Eve gaped. "Well, butter my biscuit!"

"But when we were at dinner—"

"Wait. He took you to dinner?" She held up a palm in the universal stop sign.

"Right before he kidnapped me and drove me to the hospital!"

"Good grief, a lot has gone on!" Eve covered her mouth. "Oh, no. Did you have a CAT scan? Was it okay?"

"No," Sadie said miserably. "The same thing happened. I panicked. And the worst thing? That made Lincoln feel guiltier. It wasn't bad enough that he felt responsible for my concussion, he got to see me have a meltdown, too. That's the first time he kissed me."

"The...the *first* time?" Eve forgot all about the coffee, simply holding the filter in her hands, not moving.

Sadie rose to take the filter from her and take care of coffee-making duties. "The second time? Right there. Over by the front door. Out of the blue he just grabbed me and kissed the stuffing out of me. I thought I would dissolve."

"Oh, my."

"And then he said, do you want to know what he said? Sure, you do. He said, 'See you later.'" Sadie held up air quotes. "Then he *left*."

"That's it?"

"Okay, so it's not just me! I'm not overreacting. No, 'hey, I'll call you later today.' Or, 'how about we go out sometime?' Not even, 'hey, I sure liked kissing you. How about we try that again sometime?' Nothing!" Sadie shoved the filter into the coffeemaker with force.

"Yeah, that's weird."

"But the thing is, I keep thinking that it might be because

during dinner, well, I mentioned how I wanted to have three children. That I wanted to get married, and probably soon."

"That's...wow...not something you want to say to Lincoln. Or probably, you know, any man. At least not the first time you're out on a date together."

"But isn't honesty good? That's what I want, after all, and he said it isn't what he wants. So, there it is. At least we know."

"Um, okay."

"I'm an idiot, right?"

"Well..."

Sadie went hands up. "I don't know what I was thinking!"

"It's just...how can I say this? I mean, if y'all just give yourself a chance, you know, he *could* change his mind. Who knows what could change if he falls in love? There's a thing called compromise. How's he going to know if he doesn't ever give you two a shot?"

"Right."

"*But* if you're asking him straight out the gate to be ready for babies, car seats, and spit-up, I don't think that's going to work too well for you."

"Did you and Jackson talk about babies before y'all got engaged?"

Sadie already knew the likely answer to that question. They were teenagers when they started to date and twenty-somethings when they were planning a wedding, so they'd had plenty of time ahead of them for that sort of thing.

"Not at all, but we probably should have. Even when we were engaged, we never talked about any of those things. We were our entire world. We never gave much thought to anything or anyone else." Eve's expression grew soft and weary at the same time and Sadie regretted bringing Jackson up.

"Well, I feel like I'm running out of time," Sadie said, changing the subject.

"You're twenty-eight!"

"My mother had *two* children by twenty-eight, as she so often reminds me."

Eve waved that away. "You have a career. And a calling, I might add. What you do is important."

"Thank you, Eve."

Maybe Sadie should just throw herself into her career and give up on the quest for true love.

It wasn't going well anyway.

Later that Saturday, Sadie drove out to the General Store for the weekly delivery of her mother's homemade jam. Since her parents were out of town on a rare vacation, Sadie offered to take on this chore. After her children were grown, Wanda Stephens wound up with too much free time on her hands, so she kicked the fruit canning into overdrive. That led to jams and jellies, and when she took them to her book club and everyone raved, she started to sell them to her friends. Wanda's Jam was born. The General Store offered to stock them and just like that Sadie's mother became a businesswoman. Her bestseller? Peach jam from her own trees. Sometimes Sadie wished she could bathe in the stuff.

She pulled her truck up to the back-alley entrance of the General Store and opened her tailgate.

"Hey there, sugar," said Lloyd Hayes, Beulah's long-suffering husband. "Got your mama's jam for me?"

"Two cases."

"Well, that ought to last us a week if we're lucky." He carried a case inside through the back door, and Sadie brought up the rear with the second one. "Got to say, I didn't expect to see you walkin' around like nothing happened. Lenny said you looked like you'd gone on to glory and then he saw you breathing. We're going to be offering some prayers of thanks tomorrow."

"Aw, thank you, but it wasn't that bad. They gave me a CAT scan and I'm absolutely fine."

"Well, helps to have a hard head, I guess." He set a case behind the register and reached for a box cutter. "Heh, heh, heh. That was a joke, sugar."

"You're funny, Mr. Hayes." Sadie laughed and shook a finger at him.

The bell over the store entrance jingled and Ada Armstrong walked in. "Sadie Stephens, sweetheart! Let me look at you! Oh, good Lord, you look like you've been through hell without a passport. Leave it to that *awful* Carver cowboy to lasso you for career day. Whoever put that fool idea in his head?" She waved behind her, barely taking a breath between sentences. "I want you to meet someone."

Sadie usually couldn't get a word in around Ada, today being no exception. She'd started to explain that the whole lassoing thing had been her idea, or rather a student's idea she'd foolishly agreed to, when a handsome man entered the store behind her.

Ada waved him over. "Get on over here, honey. Sadie, I want you to meet my nephew, Judson Grant. He's a doctor!"

She said this with the same enthusiasm one might say, "We have a cure for cancer!"

This would be the nephew Ada mentioned. He was surprisingly good-looking.

"Oh, well, isn't that...nice. Congratulations on being a doctor."

Judson offered Sadie his hand with a wince. "Sorry about that. She's just a little bit proud."

"Isn't she beautiful, Judson? Didn't I tell you?" She elbowed him. "I tried to tell you, but sometimes you just have to see for yourself."

"Aw, you're so sweet, Miss Ada."

"She's right," Judson said. "And she wasn't exaggerating. You are quite beautiful."

Judson wasn't so bad himself. Jet black hair, eyes the shade of a strong espresso, and he wore glasses, giving him a real doctor vibe. But he did look a little out of place wearing chinos and shoes with tassels on them.

"Judson is thinking of moving here, maybe opening up a clinic. I'll let you two get acquainted." Ada bustled over to the vegetable aisle.

"My aunt is getting ahead of herself. I'm here for a visit just to see if it might be a good fit for me and if it's possible to set up shop." He smiled. "Just looking at you, I'm already encouraged."

"That's sweet. Where are you staying?"

"With my aunt's family for now. Keeping my eyes open for a place."

"You should look into the cabins by Lupine Lake. My daddy rents them out. I think we might have one coming up next month or so. I'd have to ask him."

"Great. I don't know if I can last an entire month with my aunt, though." He winked. "What do you do, Sadie?"

"I'm a teacher."

"That's amazing. And you like it?"

"I do. Very much."

"Teachers are the lifeblood of a community, aren't they?" He tipped back on his heels.

Judson didn't have any trouble making conversation, and he seemed interested in Sadie's profession. How refreshing.

"I like to think so. It's a calling."

"That's the same way I think of medicine."

Sadie thought it should be, but she also knew plenty of doctors who went into medicine to become wealthy. There wasn't anything wrong with that. On the other hand, she'd accepted the fact that she'd never be rich, or even close to it, as a teacher.

"Would you like to go out sometime, Sadie?"

"There isn't much to do around here."

"We could drive into Kerrville, or San Antonio. I have my car. Whatever you'd like."

Sadie rubbed her arm. Strangely, she almost felt like she'd be cheating to accept a date with Judson. She and Lincoln had kissed, twice, and maybe they'd started something. Maybe he would call her in a few days. Maybe she should just stay open for that possibility for a little longer. Because maybe "see you around" meant he would eventually call her.

Or maybe not.

"Well, um, I just…"

"I'm sorry to be so forward," he said. "I didn't even ask if you're seeing someone."

"No, I'm not really."

"Well, then, would you think about it?"

He had a nice smile. Honest and trustworthy.

She could almost hear her mother's voice: *if Lincoln isn't interested, keep your options open, young lady! Those eggs aren't getting any younger.*

"Of course, I will."

And she gave him her phone number.

CHAPTER 8

*T*he afternoon sun beat down on Lincoln's back as he drove the last nail into the broken-down fence. Nearby, Hank complained every two seconds. Loudly.

"This took too long. We're lucky we didn't lose more cattle."

When Lincoln didn't reply but kept working, Hank kept talking. "I'm thinking of hiring another hand or two."

"Couldn't hurt. You hire help every time I'm gone."

"Wouldn't have to hire anyone at all if your brother would get his sorry ass back home now and then."

Lincoln plucked another nail from between his teeth. Said nothing.

"Sure must be nice to make a living prancing around on stage like you got good sense."

Lincoln talked to Jackson regularly, so he knew show business wasn't all fun and games. But he kept his mouth shut. This diatribe ran on auto-repeat every time Hank got frustrated with anything on the ranch. Jackson wanted to play guitar and make an easy living on a stage instead of helping run his family ranch. And if Jackson were still here, according to Hank, he'd be married to Eve, because on the day of their wedding she'd just had a bad case of the jitters. Life would then, of course, somehow be wonderful.

"If he'd get his butt back home, you and I wouldn't have to work so hard."

Or maybe if Hank didn't have so many bad days they'd get back on a schedule and not always be behind.

"If you really want Jackson to come home, you're going to have to respect his choices," Lincoln finally said. "He's a grown man, not someone you can boss around."

"If he wants my respect, he's going to have to give it first." Hank viciously hammered away at a nail.

"Jackson loves his family. That's a given. Maybe if you went to just one of his concerts. Just one."

"Hell, I don't have time for that."

Almost every member of the family went at least once to see Jackson and his band. They regularly toured through parts of Texas. They'd all attended at least one concert with the exception of Hank. Somehow, he believed he'd made a bold statement with that choice. Instead, old and painful beliefs were reinforced. Jackson was their mother's favorite. She'd kept him close, and protected him, which infuriated Hank. Unable to see how much damage their mother's eventual abandonment did to Jackson in particular, Hank continued to resent their mother's "favorite."

He reminded him too much of Maggie.

Daisy was a toddler when their mother left the family. An ugly rumor occasionally floated through town that Hank might not even be Daisy's real father. That she could be the result of Maggie's tryst with a rodeo cowboy when Hank had been away at an auction. But Lincoln refused to believe that the beautiful mother he remembered would leave behind a daughter that wasn't actually her husband's biological child.

Hank continue to complain about Jackson, as if he were

to suddenly materialize out of thin air all their problems would be solved. Whether the old man would admit it or not, he missed his youngest son like he might miss his right arm. Lincoln sympathized because he also missed his brother, but hell, he was having a bad day.

Hank didn't care two hoots and a holler about that.

Now, Lincoln couldn't see himself going with his original plan to cut loose some weekend and find himself an eager buckle bunny. Not when he'd have Sadie on his mind. Not when he'd compare anyone else to that full sensual mouth that knew how to kiss a man. When he'd compare someone to the way they'd fit together in bed. He'd slept with her all night, the operating word being *slept*, when he'd never done that with a woman. But he'd eyed the bed, and the comfort of the bed, and not at all considered whom he'd be lying next to. Because he certainly hadn't intended on waking up with her in his arms. He couldn't have expected for the whole experience to be so enticing that he didn't want to move for several minutes after waking up.

He didn't want to leave, either, even as he went through the motions of getting the hell out of dodge before she got any ideas. But instead of doing just that, he'd gone ahead and helped himself to another kiss which by all rights he should not have done. She'd responded with a passion which wrecked him. Now he faced a real situation. He wanted to hook up with sweet Sadie. The town's first teacher, his friend's sister, Eve's best friend, *everyone's* friend, and practically the girl next door.

This was *not* a good idea and he should stay away. Maybe in a few days this attraction would pass. He would stop thinking about her and find some other feminine distraction. Because Sadie Stephens scared the stuffing right out of him. She was the kind of woman who tied a man down. Permanently.

But two days later, not much had changed. Lincoln drove to the Shady Grind for a cold beer every night and seen hide nor hair of Sadie. Jolette Marie showed up every night, but he still didn't want to leave the bar with her. Fortunately, Jolette Marie always bounced back and accepted every one of his lame excuses.

By the end of the week, Lincoln decided he'd bring Sadie some flowers that he clearly *owed* her for giving her a concussion. It seemed like the right thing to do and he'd failed to do this the first time. Her injury had been his responsibility and all. Wouldn't have happened without him. He picked up a bouquet of yellow daisies from the General Store, endured Mr. Hayes's teasing, ("better late than never, son. Heh, heh, heh.") and got himself over to Sadie's home late enough in the afternoon that he knew she'd be home from school.

"Lincoln," she said, opening the door. "What are you doin' here?"

"I owed you flowers." He stuck them out like delivering the morning paper.

She took the flowers from him but made no move to invite him inside. "That's nice, but you didn't really have to."

"I know."

"Thank you, I guess." She gave him a tentative smile.

"Can I come in?"

"Um, okay. Sure." She moved aside and walked to the kitchen to set the flowers down. He felt gratified to see there were no others left. "I'm fine, which you would know if you'd *called*."

"Thought it would be better to drop by and see for myself."

She held her arms out to the sides. "See for yourself."

Lord above, he did see. She wore another short dress paired with her ever-present cowgirl boots. These were red.

She must have them in every color because many times they matched her dress. He'd never seen a woman look *quite* that sexy in boots. Usually that sort of leg porn took heels. Her blond hair fell to her shoulders in soft waves he wanted to feel running through his fingers again.

"You look good, Sadie."

She blinked and smoothed the skirt of her dress. "That's because I—"

"C'mere." But he didn't wait for her to come to him. Instead he hauled her into his arms, and slowly lowered his head to meet her lips.

She didn't offer any resistance, her hands immediately wrapping around his neck. Her fingers threaded through his hair and he might have groaned. She felt so right flushed tight against him, all soft and enticing curves. He moved his mouth over her lips, taking possession, wishing he could take her to bed right here and now.

She broke the kiss. "Wait."

He waited, holding her tightly, but she didn't say another word. Two seconds later, she kissed *him*. Jesus, she was good at this. Her lips were smooth and soft and her tongue... damn. Warm and perfect. His hand lowered to just above the curve of her sweet behind and all rational thought left him in an almost audible sound. Nothing remained but a buzzing in his head.

Minutes later when they came up for air, he realized they were still standing in the middle of the room. Tugging on her hand, he gently led her to the couch. That movement seemed to jar Sadie and when she sat, she braced her hands on his chest, holding him back.

"I didn't expect you," she said. "You didn't call."

"I know. And I'm sorry."

"Okay. But...but why didn't you call?"

"Sadie, please. Can't we just make out and forget all the talking?"

"No, we *can't*."

"I was afraid of that."

"And…I have a date tonight."

She might as well have thrown ice cold water on him. Why would she kiss him like this on her way to a date?

"A *date*?"

"Yes, you know that thing that two single people do when they want to get to know each other?"

"I know what a *date* is. With who?"

"You don't know him. He's new in town." She cleared her throat. "But if I knew you were coming over, well, maybe I wouldn't have accepted the date."

This felt like a trap. If he simply professed his undying devotion to her, this imaginary date would disappear. He'd been through this game before. Playing the jealousy card? Not unfamiliar territory, but it surprised him coming from Sadie. She was one of the most grounded women he'd ever known.

"So, if I'd called first…"

"If you'd called after you kissed me, then said 'see ya later.' I had no idea what that meant."

"It meant see ya *later*."

"Right. How much later? Two days? Two weeks? Two years?"

"Not two years." He scoffed. "But you *know* that I'm busy."

"Take it easy, Lincoln. I'm not asking you to do anything you don't want to do."

"Thank you."

"But what you seem to want to do is kiss me. A lot."

"To be fair, I just recently discovered that I like kissing you. It was an accident."

Her neck made a jerky movement. "Kissing me was an accident?"

Mentally, he face-palmed. He seemed to be digging himself a grave with a spoon. "No. I meant that I didn't expect it to be so good."

"I'm a good kisser?"

"Yeah, and if we stop talking, maybe we could do some more of that." He took her hand, brought it to his lips, and brushed a kiss across her knuckles.

"But I have my date." She glanced at the clock and stood. "He'll be here soon. You should probably go."

"You seriously have a date?"

"Of course. Why? You thought I would lie to you?"

"All right. I'll go." He stood, confused beyond belief.

He'd never been kicked out. He'd always been out the door before that even became an issue. Never one to outstay his welcome. But things were different in Stone Ridge. He didn't like to get involved with women in his town. Too many other men. He liked to call the shots, not the other way around.

"You...maybe you could come back," she said from behind him. "Later."

He turned to face her. "What? You don't expect the date to go well?"

"It's a first date. I don't really know him, or I'm not sure..." She trailed off.

"Sadie, look, it's cool. You and I don't have anything real going on. Just a few kisses that distracted us both. If you want to get married, well, maybe this dude could be the one. Your shot."

"Yes." She twisted her hands together. "Maybe."

The doorbell rang and damn, Lincoln realized he would meet this guy. Shit fire.

"Want me to go out the back?" He winked.

107

"Don't be ridiculous. We have nothing to be ashamed of."

She opened the door to a man wearing Dockers, loafers, and a blazer. He reminded Lincoln of a sports commentator on TV. Every hair in place. Trendy glasses which gave him the appearance of intellectual superiority. He disliked him immediately.

"Hi there, Judson. You're right on time," Sadie said.

"I always try to be."

Yeah, and he probably called ahead, too. Didn't just get a sudden feeling that he wanted to see a girl he couldn't get out of his head. Even if he did, well, he'd certainly *call* first.

Lincoln stuck his hand out. "How are you doin'? I'm Lincoln Carver."

"Dr. Judson Grant," he said.

That made sense. His hands didn't appear to have seen a single day's worth of fence work. But on the other hand, Lincoln would bet his ranch that this guy would give Sadie the children, security, and family she wanted. Probably without breaking a sweat.

"Lincoln stopped by and he's on his way out," Sadie said.

"That's right. You two have a good night, then."

With that, Lincoln stepped outside and ignored the uncomfortable slash of envy that snapped through him. He had no right to be jealous What's more, he didn't quite understand why he did. That sucker was going on a date with a woman who'd already mapped his life out for him. He'd likely have no say in the matter. She'd hook him and reel him in like today's catch.

Lincoln drove himself to the Shady Grind for a cold beer, but he wasn't looking forward to it.

A KNOT the size of Texas formed in Sadie's stomach. She should have waited for Lincoln a few more days. If she hadn't accepted this date with Judson, something might have changed between her and Lincoln. Granted, he was about as romantic as a turnip, but with *such* potential. She could feel it in the way he kissed her, making her feel both precious and breakable, but hotly desired at the same time.

But as Judson blabbed on about the strange weather in Texas (winter in the morning, summer in the afternoon), and the horsepower of his BMW, Sadie tried to talk herself into having fun on this date. She'd agreed to it, after all. It wouldn't be fair to Judson not to be all in. At least for tonight. Then she'd see.

"Where did you go to medical school?" she asked between breaks of his lecture on BMW versus Mercedes Benz. BMW was a superior machine according to him.

"University of Maryland. Residency at Stanford. I briefly considered going into general surgery, but that meant more school. I wanted to get started on my family. I'm a general practitioner, something you don't hear about anymore. We're a dying breed. That's why my aunt thought I should be a country doctor." He cleared his throat. "Sadie, if you don't mind my asking. Who was that guy? Lincoln? I mean, you said you're not seeing anyone."

"I'm not. Lincoln is...he's just a friend. I've known him for a long time."

"Great," he said, taking her hand. "Because I don't like having any competition."

Boy. He was certainly new in town. She wondered if he'd heard about their town's strange demographics. She kept quiet, unwilling to assure him he had no competition. He had a jumbo-size competition in the form of one clueless rancher.

They arrived at a French restaurant, a place so upscale that Sadie felt out of place in her best boots. But at least she didn't have to worry about what to order because Judson did that for her. Good thing, since she didn't know what on earth to order.

"It was a little hard to find a French eatery, but this place has five-star reviews," Judson said. "Do you like French food?"

"I don't think I've ever tried French food."

"You're in for a treat," he said, and then took her hand again. "So, Sadie, how many children do you want?"

"Um...possibly three?"

"Perfect! I want three as well. Some people say two, so the children don't outnumber the parents. Some say four so they each have a playmate. But I think three is reasonable in today's day and age. We do have to consider overpopulation, carbon footprint, that kind of thing."

While that made a lot of sense, Sadie couldn't remember why she'd settled on three children. She'd hatched those dreams long ago.

"I didn't plan for my wife working outside of the home, but a teacher is the perfect job, isn't it? You'll have summers off to be with our children."

Did he say our children? Sadie sucked in a breath. Judson was coming on so strong. She removed her hand from his.

"I-I didn't get into teaching just to have summers off."

"I'm sure you didn't. It's a noble profession."

"Um...are you planning on getting married soon?" She half expected him to drop to one knee and propose right now in which case she would have to run out of here screaming.

"Well, we're not getting any younger, are we? And you don't want aging eggs. That could mean complications, such as learning disabilities, if not worse."

"I'm twenty-eight," she said, as a gentle reminder.

She'd like to believe her eggs might still be young enough to be wearing orthodontia, thank you very much.

"And I'm thirty-five. I'm finally in a great fiscal position to make all my dreams come true. A beautiful home, wife, and children. I've already started college funds for the children."

"Wow." Sadie's elbow started to itch. "You're very responsible."

"I hope that's an attractive quality."

She nodded because who in their right mind would disagree with that.

Her elbow began to itch in earnest. Their food came, and grateful for the distraction from the talk of college funds and fertile eggs, she took a generous bite. Then another. Judson went on and on about private school versus public school, and when he began to name their future children, Sadie thought she might rub her elbow raw.

"Are you okay?" Judson asked, suddenly aware of something other than his future family and large suburban home with a cabin in the mountains for annual ski vacations.

"I'm not sure. I'm suddenly very itchy."

"Let me take a look." He held her arm, turning to view the elbow. "Maybe you're allergic to something here?"

"I think so."

And she believed that something could be Judson Grant.

What was *wrong* with her? He was good looking, sweet, and almost perfect. He'd said all the right things, even if she favored public schools versus his desire for private school. Also, she refused to name a child *Ace*. Sure, he moved fast but she admired his honesty. Far better than someone stringing you along for years, lying the entire time.

Been there, done that.

But Lord, did she sound like *this* to Lincoln? She wondered why he'd even wanted to see her again. But he'd come back to her cabin when he didn't have any reason to feel responsible for her anymore. And kissed her.

"Maybe I should just go home. Call it a night."

A few minutes later, he drove her home, a little sulky.

"I'm just going to soak in some Epson Salt and go to bed."

"That's what I would prescribe."

She couldn't stop him from walking her to the door, grateful when he didn't attempt a kiss. Once inside her cozy cabin, Sadie finally let her shoulders unkink and the itching eventually stopped. Until that moment, she didn't realize how badly she wanted to get away from Judson. He'd made her nervous. Antsy. She wanted to be alone tonight. Alone with a book and a glass of wine.

When she'd gone away to study at Baylor University, none of her new girlfriends could imagine being young and single in a town in which men chased women. They'd called her "blessed" and compared Stone Ridge to Alaska. Even though life was different at Baylor, Sadie still waited for a man to ask her out first. And then she'd met Martin and thought her life would soon be complete. He'd loved her from day one, or so he said, from the moment he'd first laid eyes on her. There'd been no one else for him but her, he'd said. No one.

Martin called her darling, which no one had before (or since) then. She'd been madly in love with him, too, with his sweet Australian accent and gorgeous boyish smile. Martin was her first lover. He'd loved that, too, proudly taking her virginity and calling himself her "one and only." The relationship lasted all four years, and Sadie expected a marriage proposal at the end of it. Martin wanted her to visit his Mum in Australia after graduation. They'd made plans.

But instead, just before graduation day, one of her friends asked for Sadie's forgiveness. They might never see each other again and she couldn't keep this on her conscience. She confessed that she'd slept with Martin numerous times and deeply regretted the betrayal. And she wasn't the only one. Turned out he'd also slept with some of her other friends.

Once, with her roommate. Because sweet Martin loved women…a little *too* much. And that Australian accent, in the middle of Texas? A walking aphrodisiac to women.

When she'd confronted him, he'd almost expected her forgiveness. They could still make this relationship work. He loved her and wanted to get married. He hoped that she would overlook four *years* of cheating. Because, somehow, Sadie gave him the mistaken idea that she loved him so much he could do no wrong. That she was so *sweet*, so kind, she would naturally *forgive* him.

Martin, like so many others before and since, mistook her kindness for weakness. Worse, friends hid the ugly truth from her. Heart shattered, Sadie broke up with Martin. Though they'd always been beyond careful, she had herself checked, and discovered he'd never given her anything physically permanent, except a guarded heart.

In Stone Ridge, she felt precious and wanted. The men of Stone Ridge did not cheat on their women. It only took a rumor of a man cheating, and another would be lined up ready to take his place.

Love remained such a mystery to Sadie. How it happened, and what caused that attraction to simmer.

From the age of sixteen, she'd thought Lincoln Carver the most incredible boy she'd ever seen in her life. Abandoned by his mother, he took care of his family, and worked hard. He was kind to everyone, with a genuine smile, and honest eyes. But until the concussion fiasco, she'd never actually been alone with Lincoln.

But now it seemed that Lincoln Carver wasn't at all interested in chasing any women. Some even chased him. Except for Sadie.

She might if she could. But she didn't know how.

Remembering her students' homework, Sadie spent a night alone on her couch grading papers.

CHAPTER 9

$\mathcal{I}$t took one day for Sadie to figure out that Judson reminded her of someone very dear and special in her life.

Her mother.

All that over the top organization to detail and planning. It made Wanda Stephens a terrific businesswoman, but as a wife and mother, she'd been slightly...neurotic. It wasn't until Sadie came face to face with someone with strict and definitive plans for the rest of their life that she realized what she must have sounded like to the men she'd dated post-Martin.

It wasn't just the fear of being tricked again by another smooth talker, but the pressure she occasionally felt from her mother. Even with a working plan for her life, while away at college, Sadie learned to believe in flexibility. To accept that "the plan" could occasionally be adapted. She hadn't planned to still be single at twenty-eight, but so what? No big deal. It didn't mean she'd die alone. Eve was single, too, and not worried about it.

The most important thing in any plan was to move

forward, continually improving, shifting where needed, and finding new interests and ways of accomplishing goals. She'd decided not to date anyone seriously since graduating from college. But returning home meant back-sliding into her mother's pre-conceived notions. Sadie should be married now, or well on the way. It sometimes seemed as if Mom took this as a personal affront. As if this meant Sadie rejected everything she'd been taught to believe.

The Friday after her parents returned from their cruise, they invited Sadie and Beau over for dinner. Years ago, her father built the family's ranch-style home on five acres. Though they didn't have a working farm, he'd planted a small micro vineyard he wanted to work full time after retirement. For now, it remained his hobby. He often wore a pair of old-fashioned blue coveralls covered in grape stains and occasionally could be found wandering the rows of grapes, muttering to himself. Sadie found this adorable.

"How was the cruise?" Sadie asked at the door, giving her mother a quick hug.

"So much food! I probably gained ten pounds. All there is to do on a cruise is eat."

"Is that all?"

"And drink, of course. Your father was quite happy." Wanda made a face. "He is, of course, the authority on wine wherever we go. I don't know enough to argue with him."

"What about live entertainment?"

"Some of that. A magician. A bunch of chorus girls. A saltwater pool I *refused* to go in." She waved a hand dismissively.

"Well, as long as you had fun."

"How did the deliveries go?"

Sadie gave a thumbs up. "Nothing I couldn't handle."

Wanda controlled her business to the point that it was a

wonder she'd trusted Sadie with a simple delivery to the General Store.

Beau breezed into the kitchen a few minutes later, hugging Sadie and Wanda. "I can't stay long. Got a hot date. Let's get this show on the road."

"Beau Stephens, you are not going to eat and run again!" Wanda shook a spoon at him. "Who's your date?"

Beau winked. "Don't worry about it."

"I am your mother. I demand to know."

"I'm your sister. It would be nice to know," Sadie said.

"Where's dad? I'm outnumbered for once!" He leaned in and hooked his arm around Sadie's neck. "Should I tell y'all? I don't know, will you blab?"

"You know I won't," Sadie said sincerely.

"Mom?" Beau asked. "What about you?"

"Honey, I don't believe in *gossip*."

Both Sadie and Beau barely contained a snort as their eyes met.

"She's a woman I met while on a job in Austin. Her name is…um, Sherry."

"Oh, she sounds wonderful!" Wanda said, not as discriminating when it came to her son. "Maybe you can talk her into moving to Stone Ridge."

"That might be a stretch."

"What does she do for a living?" Sadie asked.

"She's a dancer." Beau's eyes were filled with mischief as he silently commiserated with Sadie.

She knew *exactly* what kind of dancer because her brother had a definite type. Long legs, tight behinds, big breasts.

"She must be very graceful," Wanda, completely oblivious, said.

"Yes." Beau gave a huge smile. "Oh, yes."

Her father finally appeared, still wearing his farmer

clothes, fingers red and stained from the grapes. "Hello, my children."

Sadie hugged her father. "Hi, Daddy."

"Pops." Beau fist bumped with their father.

"Beau can't stay long," Wanda announced. "He's got a *date*."

"Good, good," he said, completely oblivious to the clip in his wife's voice as he washed his hands over the sink.

"Why don't *you* have a date, Sadie?" Wanda asked, quirking a brow.

"Wanda…" her father warned.

Her father, bless him, always told Sadie that she should hold out for the perfect man. And she'd tried to do this, but until recently that perfect man showed no interest in her at all. Now, she knew he liked to kiss her. Not much more than that so far, but a step in the right direction.

"I actually went on two dates while y'all were gone. I just don't have one tonight."

"That's great, sugar," Wanda said. "Which date did you like best?"

"Well, Lincoln took me to dinner because he felt bad about the concussion thing. That was nice."

No one said a word, probably because they considered Lincoln to be a friend of the family. Long ago, everyone kindly stopped making fun of her crush on him. And since she would leave out all of the kissing and spending the night together, they'd be none the wiser.

"*And?*" Wanda pressed. "Who else?"

"Um, Ada Armstrong's nephew. Judson Grant."

At this, her mother froze mid-stir at the stove. "The *doctor*?"

"Yes, he's a doctor," Sadie said, squirming.

Wanda practically jumped in the air and did a little pirouette. Next she'd probably do a soft shoe.

"Holy hell, Sadie, you hit the jackpot." Beau rolled his eyes.

"What happened?" her father turned from the sink, looking at his wife, probably wondering what made her happy enough to dance across the kitchen tile like a gazelle.

"Keep up, Dad," Beau said. "Your daughter has nabbed herself a doctor."

"No, she hasn't!" Sadie protested.

"Now, Sadie, *please*," Wanda said, hands clasped, prayer-like. "Give him a chance, at least. What have you got against a young and handsome doctor?"

"Wanda…" her dad warned again.

"How do you know he's handsome? And I have nothing against him," Sadie protested. "I just don't know if I'll see him again."

"Maybe they're not a 'love match.'" Beau held up air quotes, in danger of rolling an eye right out of his socket.

"Nonsense! Teacher and doctor, what could be better?" Wanda said.

"Doctor and nurse?" Beau offered, a sly grin on his face.

"Teacher and professor?" Her father said, drying his hands. "Or how about teacher and farmer?"

Teacher and rancher.

"I wouldn't mind that." Sadie gave her father a wide smile.

She'd always wanted a man like her father, someone who put his family first, and loved his wife even when she acted a little kooky. Even when he didn't always want the same things she did. She'd always been a daddy's girl, and to her, her father was a little god. Tall and thin, and so handsome with his full head of strawberry blond hair. Daddy had rough, callused hands but they were gentle when he'd stroked her cheek and carried her to bed as a child.

A strong man could also be so gentle at times.

After dinner, seeing Beau off to his date with an obvious

stripper, and helping Mom with the dishes, Sadie joined her father on the deck. Here, they had a perfect view of his vineyard. He sat nursing a glass of Pinot Noir from California. The traitor.

The twilight sky flashed before her, a beautiful orange mixed with tinges of dark blue. She loved this time of the day when the waning daylight flirted with the evening. The sweet smell of grapes wafted through the air and would forever remind her of Daddy.

She scooted her chair closer to her dad's. "I told Judson that you might have a cabin comin' up for rent. He's lookin' for something short-term."

"Those cabins aren't fancy enough for a *doctor*."

"Yes, they are."

He patted her knee. "Well, you tell *me* if I should rent him a cabin. I'd charge him top dollar. But maybe that would put him in too close proximity to you. Unless that's what you want, but sure didn't seem that way."

"No." She sighed. "I am sorry about that. Why is it so hard to fall in love? I don't understand."

"It's not hard at all, Sweet Pea. All you have to do is risk your heart. Open up a vein and bleed."

Sadie swiveled her neck. "Oh, is *that* all?"

"No, but it's the toughest part."

And ever since her college boyfriend, she'd guarded her heart. No man would ever fool her again. Whenever she'd been asked out, she made her expectations clear. And most of the time, there was no second date. She'd scared every one of them off. Good riddance.

"I have this image in my mind that the right man is just going to walk right up to me and say 'Hello, where have you been all my life?' And then I'll *know*. But every single man who chases me is not the right one."

"Just you wait. It won't be that way forever. Don't settle,

baby. Never, ever, settle." He patted her hand while he sipped his wine.

Her mother would just tell her to get on with it, that no man would ever be perfect. They were *men*, weren't they? Hence the lack of perfection, sort of built-in. But Sadie didn't need perfect. She just wanted someone perfect for her...the *one*. Mom would laugh at that, too. There is no "one." With plenty of great men in Stone Ridge she should simply be grateful for all of the choices.

But when there was just one man a woman wanted it didn't really matter how many others there were.

Lincoln was simply always around her, in one way or another. She'd never been alone with him until recently, and now, she didn't quite know what to do. But letting him know about her date with another man? Not smart. He might not even come over again, much less call.

Later, Sadie drove back to her cabin where more student papers waited to be graded. Instead of going inside, she walked over and knocked on the door to Eve's cabin. She opened it with a smile, holding her latest rescue, a little orange tabby.

"How do I chase a man?" Sadie blurted out.

"Well, hello to you, too." She turned and Sadie followed her inside.

She plopped on the worn-in couch Eve had purchased at a garage sale. Eve didn't have much after veterinary school loan payments, and Sadie's father gave Eve the same good deal on the cabin that he gave his own daughter. Her Daddy always helped a neighbor in need. And everyone helped Eve whenever and wherever they could. She'd been through a tough time.

"I've never gone after a man. Never made the first move. You know, they always do that sort of thing for us here. I did the same thing in college. I waited until Martin asked me out," Sadie said. "Force of habit."

"That doesn't mean we can't chase after who *we* want. I mean, look at Jolette Marie. She doesn't seem to have any problems."

"I don't know what to do. I want to chase Lincoln."

"Yes, well, that's probably what you would have to do to get Lincoln. He's always been his own man."

"He came over before my date with Judson. And he kissed me. Again."

"Wow. Okay." She set the kitten down on Sadie's lap. "So maybe he *is* chasing you?"

"Well, he brought me flowers, and…" Sadie stopped petting the kitten mid rub. "Oh, boy. Maybe that's true, but he has terrible timing. Plus, he left *encouraging* me to go on a date with Judson if I wanted a relationship."

"You two already have a relationship, anyway. A kind of relationship, at least. Just go with that."

The kitten meowed, as if in agreement.

"You're right. I'm overcomplicating things because—"

"It's what you do." Eve finished Sadie's sentence. "I'm the same way. That's why we're best friends."

"It still hasn't solved the problem of how to chase him."

"How about you just study what the men do, and do that, but in reverse?"

"In reverse?"

Eve smirked. "You'll be the one wearing the dress."

"So, I just walk in, tip my imaginary Stetson, say 'c'mere,' and wait for him to walk right into my open arms?"

"Um…" Eve seemed to be biting back a laugh. "I think you'll figure it out."

Sadie stood and handed Eve the kitten. "That's it! I'm sick of this. Tired of waiting and wondering 'what if?' I'm goin' down to the Shady Grind for a cold beer."

"What? Why? I have cold beer in the fridge."

"Oh, Eve, you're so clueless. A beer at the Shady Grind means something *else*." She pointed from herself to Eve. "It means 'I'm going to be there, and if you're there, little lady, maybe something will happen.' It's the way men *talk*."

"I see."

She walked with purpose to the door. "Are you comin'?"

"I'm sorry, hon, I can't. Not tonight. I'd have to get Anna-beth to cat-sit. This is my first week with this little kitty and he hates being left alone. Can you do this on your own?"

"I'll have to." She saluted in the doorway. "Wish me luck."

And with that, Sadie shut the door, and sprinted back to her own cabin. Inside, she fixed her hair, leaving it down, and curling it at the ends. She wore mascara and dared to smooth on red lipstick like a floozy. If she wanted to be happy with the man she thought could be the right one for her, she would need to take a risk. But this time Sadie would take a calculated risk.

Time to open up a vein and bleed all over the damn place.

CHAPTER 10

*L*incoln was having another shitty night after a back-breaking day. He'd come to the Shady Grind for a beer because here was the weekend, and he still couldn't get a certain woman off his mind. He kept picturing Sadie kissing that doctor the way she'd kissed him. Some people would call that cheating. Okay, not him, but still. He didn't like the idea at all.

On the big screen in the background, the Astros were striking out. This night moved from bad to worse. Plus, the bar was peppered by cowboys, and very few women, not adding to the ambience. Even Jolette Marie was MIA tonight. Didn't much matter anyway when he couldn't get his mind off Sadie. No one else would do. Wonder if a lobotomy would help? He should ask Jackson what to do about this problem, since he'd been hit by the love stick early in life and somehow managed to survive. Barely.

He pulled his phone out to call Jackson when the door to the bar swung open and in walked Sadie Stephens. Not surprisingly, every man turned his head to check her out. She looked better than fine tonight, wearing her hair down, blue suede boots, and a short blue dress. *Red* lipstick. He nearly swallowed his tongue.

She came right up to him, sat up on the stool next to where he stood, and ordered a draft.

"Hey, there," she said, turning, as if she'd just noticed him.

"Where's the *dentist?*" He took a pull of his beer and immediately hated himself for sounding like a jealous boyfriend.

"He's a general practitioner, and I don't know where he is tonight."

"Here you go, sweets," Priscilla said, setting Sadie's beer mug down. "That's twice now in one month. Good to see you come out tonight."

"Thanks, 'Cilla. I got bored at home all alone." She tipped her mug and eyed him.

No date. Interesting. He turned to face the room, leaning his back against the bar, legs crossed, holding his bottle.

"This isn't the right place if you're lookin' for fun and entertainment. The Astros are on their last leg. It's all over," Lincoln said, shaking his head.

"I don't care."

"Ha. That's almost un-American."

"What if I don't care about that, either?"

He snorted. "What's wrong? Bad day?"

"Not at all."

"What is it? You want to get stinkin' drunk?"

"I could do that at home, Lincoln. Eve has cold beer at *her* place."

He should probably read something into this, but swimming in an oasis of confusion, he simply scowled.

"Oh, forget it! I can't do this." She tossed her hands up, climbed off the stool, and stomped outside.

"What'd you say to her?" one of the Henderson brothers

asked. There were three of them, each more annoying that the last.

"Not a thing." Lincoln shrugged.

"Maybe that's the problem." Sean, the youngest brother, snickered. "Go after her, man, or I will."

"Don't even think about it." Lincoln set his bottle down and followed her outside.

She stood at the entrance to the bar, still on the top step of the short staircase. Not moving, she held the bannister, and faced the street.

"All right, what did I say?" He held his arms out in his "lay it on me" gesture.

"Nothing." She turned around. "This isn't your fault."

"First time for everything."

"Okay, listen." She threw her palms up. "Here's the truth. I *like* you."

He smiled, feeling the night take a delicious turn, even with a sudden memory of junior high school. "Thought I'd been tossed aside by the dentist."

"Well, you weren't! We had one date. I didn't even kiss him goodnight. Okay?" She swore under her breath and covered her face. "Oh geez. I don't know how to do this."

"Do what?"

She lowered her hands. "Chase a man. Make the first move."

He chuckled at that. "You're doin' fine. And I kissed you first. Remember?"

But the realization that Sadie Stephens was after *him* didn't make him want to cut and run. Her expectations were clear. She seemed to be in a big hurry for marriage and babies. He should go back inside the bar. Drink another cold beer. Try to forget about her even if that didn't seem to be working. But instead he walked toward her just to be closer.

He didn't quite know why but his boots had a mind of their own tonight.

"Hey." He stepped into her space and tipped her chin to meet his eyes. "I'm not good at this, either."

"Liar. Women just flock to you."

"Not always. I chased after girls when I was younger. And stupid." He cleared his throat. "But I don't want to disappoint you, of all people. You're like this bright light and I'm…"

"What?"

"Practically a curmudgeon." He tried a smile as his thumb traced the silky curve of her jaw. "At thirty-two. Maybe I'm jaded."

He'd witnessed his parents' marriage implode under accusations of infidelity. Saw Jackson shatter after Eve abandoned him. And now here he stood, going after the one woman in town probably most *like* Eve. As if he, too, wanted a shot at the agony his brother had endured.

But then her hands wrapped around the back of his neck and warmth spread straight to the soles of his boots. He pulled her in tight against his body.

"Can we forget everything I said to you on the night you took me to dinner? I think I should get a do-over. Concussion and all. Not in my right mind. I *don't* have any ready-made plans for this. For us. I'm wide open. I just like you so much and I want to be with you. I want…more kissing." She looked up shyly. "Is that alright with you?"

"Sign me up."

He covered her mouth and felt the intoxication flood him again. She tasted like the sweetest drug. Like his own addiction. He shouldn't want her, but he couldn't get enough of her. Taking them away from prying eyes, he moved her to the side of the bar and pressed her against the wall. When they came up for air, her lips were bruised from his kisses, and her hazel eyes shimmered in the soft ambient moonlight.

"Sadie." He pressed his forehead to hers. "What are you doin' to me, girl?"

Her hands slid up and down his forearms and he felt every tender touch press through his flannel shirt and jean jacket.

"I'm not going to sleep with you," she breathed. "Not yet."

He fixed on the "not yet" like a dog with a bone.

"You've already slept with me," he teased, nibbling at her ear, knowing exactly what she meant, and not eager to hear it confirmed.

She smiled into his eyes. "I don't know, can you handle that?"

"Girl, I'm a cowboy. I've been kicked by an angry bull and thrown from my horse a few times. Fixed fences until my hands bled. I think I can handle *this*."

"I think you can, too."

"Doesn't mean I'm going to enjoy waiting."

"Me, either."

He would ask why they were both waiting when neither of them wanted to but thought better of it. Sadie was in his arms. She might just be worth waiting for. *When* they hooked up, not if, it would be explosive. And it would be soon, too. He would bet his life on it.

"You have to promise me something," Sadie said. "I want one hundred percent honesty between us. If you want someone else, just *tell* me first. And don't think I'm so fragile and *sweet* that I can't handle the truth. Apparently, everyone seems to think I need to be sheltered. And I don't."

"Honesty. You got it." He kissed the column of her neck. "What's next?"

"Some of that making out you were talkin' about."

"Oh, yeah."

. . .

SADIE NEARLY FLOATED HOME LATER that night. After walking her to her truck, Lincoln sent her on her way home with one of the most heartfelt kisses she'd ever experienced in her life. He put his entire body in a kiss. Not a simple meeting of lips and tongue. He held on tight when he kissed. They were hip to hip, one of his hands on her butt, the other one around the nape of her neck, him keeping her close.

This time, there was no "see ya later." He'd said, "See you tomorrow."

Sadie couldn't sleep for hours, so she went next door and updated Eve on everything.

Lincoln would never string her along. He'd never make false promises and lie to keep the peace. He'd proven just how painfully honest he could be, and she'd let him know in no uncertain terms she wanted the truth. So yeah, this could be good. She could do this. Just one day at a time.

The next morning, she was in such a great mood that she woke excited to grade papers. In other news, Jimmy Ray made her laugh with his answers even though they were one hundred percent incorrect. Even when he paid little attention, he might be the most creative genius eight-year-old she'd ever met. She'd done a short lesson with the third graders on earth science and on one of the questions she'd wanted an explanation for their answer so she could check reasoning skills.

Under "How do you know?" Jimmy wrote:

I read the book.

Not quite what she'd asked but he'd been very literal. Earlier that week, when she'd asked the children how they earned money at home doing chores, Jimmy Ray wrote:

I don't. I'm a freeloader.

That answer made her chuckle, as she silently wondered where he might have heard *that* phrase before. Pamela Ann was still picking peaches, probably not making much doing it, and Derek nowhere to be found. Sadie wished she could help more than she already did, but she'd let the ladies of SORROW know. Beulah organized a canned drive to help with food. Sadie kept a barrel in the classroom which already brimmed with soups, canned beans, and vegetables.

One of Beulah's biggest planned fundraisers would happen today, and the entire town would turn out. One of their famous town barbeques would take place in the center of town. The meat was donated by several local cattle ranching families, including the Carvers, and the Hendersons. Sadie's father would bring wine, a shock to no one. Priscilla would provide beer, soda, and chips. Others were bringing baked goods and raffle items which included a lot of hastily knit hats from a recent knit-a-thon. They expected all residents to pay generously for the food, drinks, and cake, in support of funds to repair the old church building.

Sadie opened her door to Eve. She carried a small box filled with aluminum foil–covered items. "Are you ridin' with me or on your own?"

"I guess we should ride together."

"Right." Eve winked. "You never know, you might just come home with someone else. I have no idea who. I'm just putting that out there."

"He'll be there."

Eve put the box down. "Honestly? Can I tell you how happy I am for you? Let me hug you."

For the first time, Sadie almost felt guilty at being this giddy. Maybe she should have contained her joy, somehow, at least for the sake of Eve.

"I'm still sorry it didn't work out for you and Jackson," Sadie said through the hug.

"That's okay, honey. Now it's your turn to go grab some happy." She pulled back and met her gaze. "Please do better than I did."

"I'll try."

Eve squeezed Sadie's shoulders. "You'll do better than try. You're going to rock his world."

Sadie didn't know about that, but she would have to trust herself again. Overall, she believed she made good judgements about people, and her old college boyfriend was simply an aberration. She'd been away from home. Lonely, she'd gone for the first bright and shiny attraction who'd chosen her.

The party had started when Sadie and Eve arrived. The grills were on, many of the older men gathered around them, including, not surprisingly, Hank Carver. He rarely came off his hill unless it involved a fundraiser. To Sadie, Hank was always just a bit scary. Tall and imposing with a full head of white hair, you'd be as likely to get a smile or a scowl out of him, depending on his mood. He didn't seem like the kind of father to give his daughter heartfelt advice about falling in love. Poor Daisy.

"Hello there, Sadie."

Sadie whipped around to find the source of the male voice, not too surprised to see Judson behind her. "Oh, um. Hi."

Instead of the Wranglers and boots most men wore today, Judson wore a pair of khaki shorts and a white polo shirt with a designer emblem. "I thought you'd be here."

"Hi, I'm Eve Iglesias." Eve offered her hand. "I don't think we've met."

"I'm Dr. Judson Grant, a friend of Sadie's. Ada Armstrong is my aunt."

"Judson is here to consider possibly opening up a clinic," Sadie said. "And Eve owns the only clinic in town."

"I'm a veterinarian."

"Ah," Judson said with a smile. "We're both doctors."

Eve nodded. "We do need a health clinic. Everyone either

drives to Kerrville or just patches themselves up and gets right back on their horse."

Judson quirked a brow. "Where do pregnant women go when they're in labor? Do you have a midwife?"

Sadie and Eve exchanged a glance. Their midwife left town a few years ago practically under the cover of darkness. No idea why.

"No," Sadie said. "Women either make it to the hospital in Kerrville or they give birth wherever they are."

"Right," Eve said. "Lenora tried to cross her legs, but she didn't make it to the hospital and gave birth to Ellie in the back of her husband's Land Rover."

"Oh, dear," Judson said. "I'm beginning to think my services here would be greatly appreciated."

"Eve!" Annabeth rushed up to them, carrying a box. "Here you go. My contribution today."

Sadie peeked inside the box when Eve took it. "What's that?"

"I made a bunch of knit caps. My first try at knitting and I think I'm pretty darn good." Annabeth turned to Judson. "Oh, hello. You *really* shouldn't have worn white today."

Eve pulled out a knit hat and Sadie noted that it seemed to have a large hole on one side. "Well, okay. I'll walk these over to Lillian. She's selling them."

Annabeth followed Eve as she headed to the table where Lillian Carver sat.

"Are you busy later, after this?" Judson asked.

"Yes, I'm sorry. Busy, busy."

Sadie didn't know what else to say. She would have thought that her feelings about their one date should be perfectly clear to Judson. But she didn't want to hurt his feelings, either. It wasn't his fault that he'd become her mirror and what she'd witnessed terrified her.

"How about another day?" Judson asked.

"I, um, well…" Sadie glanced up and saw her mother and father arriving. "Oops. Gotta go, I see that my parents have arrived."

She rushed to meet her father, joining him at the tailgate where he removed a case filled with bottles of wine. "Hey, Sweet Pea. Why don't you help your mother with the jam? I've got this."

Sadie went to her mother's side, where she was counting jars. "I've brought forty of my latest stock. I hope that's enough. If we sell at $10 a jar, and Lord knows it's worth that, we could raise $400."

"Thanks for the donations. Everyone loves your jam."

"I do want my daughter to eventually teach in an actual building, of course, not one of her father's portables."

"There's nothing wrong with that portable," her father grumbled.

"May I help you?" A male voice came from behind Sadie.

Judson, who Sadie couldn't seem to lose today. "We're fine."

"I'm Dr. Judson Grant. Nice to meet you." He offered his hand to Sadie's mother.

Sadie didn't miss how he always introduced himself with "doctor" as if this was his name at birth. Eve never introduced herself as "Dr. Eve Iglesias" and Sadie knew plenty of Ph.D. candidates in education who didn't, either. Wonder if Judson would refer to Sadie as "doctor" if she decided someday to go for her doctorate in education.

"Oh, my goodness! So nice to meet you. I heard you're dating my daughter. Welcome to the family!" Wanda gushed.

"Mom, no. We went on one date. We're not *dating*."

"I'm seeing if I can remedy that, though," Judson said.

"Well, son, you have my blessing."

Seriously? Sadie slid her mother an incredulous look.

Smiling, Judson picked up a single box of jam, leaving the rest for Sadie and Wanda.

For the next few minutes, Sadie visited with her students, most of whom were here with their families. Jimmy Ray arrived with Pamela Ann and shyly said hello. Mother and son needed a fundraiser themselves, but Pamela Ann came anyway, ready to help where she could. She'd brought some items for the bake sale and an old quilt for the auction.

"This is beautiful," Sadie said of the quit. It looked familiar. "But isn't this…"

This could be her wedding quilt from the ladies of SORROW. They sewed one for each bride and all carried a distinctive look. But all the cross stitching where Pamela and Derek's names and their marriage date were had been removed. In its place were simply the words:

Stone Ridge Elementary
Established 2021.

Pamela Ann nodded. "Don't worry, it's been dry cleaned. Some of the ladies' best work. Back before Beulah had arthritis."

Sadie couldn't imagine the sacrifice needed to give something this meaningful up for the sake of a school. "This is *yours*."

"It's not being used, and I wanted to give it a new life. Besides, the memory is fading fast."

"Still no word from Derek?"

Pamela Ann gave a slight shake of her head. "I wanted him to clean up his act, not disappear from his son's life."

"I'm sorry," Sadie said. "Jimmy Ray must be having a tough time, though he's been a lot better in class."

"That's because he has a raging crush on his pretty teacher. I think he'd do anything you asked of him. Would you move in with me?" She grinned.

"Hey." That voice could only come from one male, a deep

scraping sound that made her special places wake up and do the Macarena.

"Hi."

Vaguely aware that Pamela Ann left, saying something about her son, Sadie simply stared at Lincoln, just drinking him all in. He wore clean Wranglers and a blue button down that matched his eyes. His sleeves were already pushed up his forearms as the day began to warm.

"You okay?" He grinned, tucking a lock of hair behind her ear.

"I was just looking for you and wondering when you'd get here."

"Had to wait for Daisy. Want to put me to work, every little boy's crush?"

She might have blushed. "You heard that?"

"Yep," Lincoln said, tipping back on his heels. "He'll have to get in line. But I say, play to your strengths, sweetheart. You've got him where you want him."

"I feel terrible for him. Derek still hasn't shown up."

"If I know him, he's sleeping off a bender somewhere."

"He needs to come home, if for no other reason than Jimmy Ray."

"Lincoln!" Jolette Marie walked up, all tall, thin, and gorgeous.

"We could use your help at the grill," she said. "I think Hank wants a break from the smoke."

"Sure," Lincoln said and giving Sadie a wink, tucked hands in his pockets and headed that way with Jolette Marie.

Sadie watched as Jolette Marie slipped an arm around Lincoln's waist, tilting her head to give him her full attention.

And a little spike of fear and dread clutched her.

She couldn't compete with Jolette Marie, former beauty and rodeo queen. But rather than feed her insecurity, Sadie got busy and spoke with every person who'd come out today to support the school. She talked with the parents about her plans for the year and how they could help now and in the near future. Judson was never far, and she wound up introducing him a great deal. He did eventually strike up a conversation with Beulah, who seemed just as enthralled with him as Sadie's mother.

Lincoln never moved far from the grill, hanging out with his friends Wade, Beau, and Riggs Henderson, occasionally sliding Sadie a wink when he caught her looking. Hank seemed glued to Eve's side, her mother Brenda never far from either of them. Lillian sold out of all her knitting and was trying to give Annabeth a quick knitting lesson. Apparently every one of Annabeth's hats had a large hole in them. But Eve took one, threaded her ponytail through it, and walked around advertising a new kind of hat.

Many families with young children began to leave after lunch. But when the sun started to slip down the horizon Sadie noticed Pamela Ann wandering around the town square. Alone.

She ran up to Sadie when their gazes met. "I can't find Jimmy Ray anywhere."

CHAPTER 11

*L*incoln half listened to Hank discuss current cattle prices with Riggs Henderson when out of the corner of his eye he caught Sadie running toward him. The wild look in her eyes spun a rush of fear straight through him.

He jogged over to meet her halfway, heart already pounding.

"Jimmy Ray is missing, and Pamela Ann can't find him anywhere."

"How long has he been missing?" Lincoln asked Pamela Ann.

"I don't know...I just...he was playing right over there with his friends," she pointed toward the shaded tree area in the center of town where games were set up for the children. "I don't know how long it's been."

"Did you ask any of his friends?" Lincoln asked.

"Yes, and they don't seem to know a thing," Pamela Ann said.

"Any idea where he could have gone?" Lincoln pressed. "Maybe he has a favorite place around here?"

"I've looked everywhere." Biting her lower lip, Pamela Ann seemed on the verge of panic.

Lincoln looked over his shoulder to meet Wade's eyes. The men surrounded him in seconds. Hank, Riggs, Wade, and Beau.

"How can we help?" Wade asked.

Within minutes they'd devised a plan to comb every inch of the surrounding areas. Some would go on foot, others drive a short distance, and then go on foot. They'd meet in the middle. Except for the strip of downtown, this area led to thick brush and streams a few feet away in some areas. The idea of a kid near the water unsupervised made everyone move quickly. Lloyd handed out walkie-talkies from the General Store to those who needed them.

The women sat Pamela Ann in a circle surrounded by Beulah, Mima, Brenda, and Wanda. They were all holding hands, heads bent in prayer.

Lincoln grabbed a walkie-talkie and a flashlight to add to the one in his glove compartment. He shut his driver's side door and turned to find Sadie when Jolette Marie came up behind him.

"I'll go with you," she said.

Sadie stood right behind her. Without a word to Jolette Marie, he reached for Sadie's hand. "C'mon, sweetheart."

For a minute, Jolette Marie looked like someone had sprayed her with a firehose but then quickly saved face. "Oh, right. You should go, you're his teacher."

As he drove them to his assigned area, he reminded himself that he'd need to have a talk with Jolette Marie at some point. To inform her their temporary and occasional "arrangement" was over. Even if they hadn't been together in months, she'd expect something from him at some point. An explanation. A word or two.

"I'm so scared," Sadie said. "What if someone grabbed him

and he's miles away by now? What if Derek did this? Maybe he was just waiting for the right opportunity to snatch him from Pamela Ann."

He took her hand and squeezed it. "Try not to imagine the worst. This could all have a logical explanation."

"I'm trying to believe that. But all I can think of right now is this little boy who's so confused and scared because his daddy is suddenly gone. He must think it's his fault."

Lincoln's thoughts went to Daisy, who at three, just couldn't understand her mother was gone.

"Where's she? When she back?"

These questions were often directed to Lincoln, but also to Jackson, Hank, and really anyone who would listen. She'd looked for their mother everywhere. In every bedroom. The kitchen. Barn. Pastures.

"She'll be back, baby, soon," Mima said, rocking Daisy to sleep every night.

He pictured that little face now, dried tears streaked down her pink cheeks. The unbridled resentment Lincoln felt for his mother rose to the surface. Even some animals did not abandon their young. At that time, he'd simply been angry because she'd left so suddenly and without explanation. He figured when she came back, he'd let her have it. He'd unleash all the pent-up anger, maybe he'd call her an ugly name or two, and get sent to bed without dinner. Totally worth it. He'd tell her what she'd done to her baby girl. How she'd cried every night. He'd remind her to *never* leave like that again.

But he didn't imagine she'd never be back.

He hoped that for the sake of Jimmy Ray, if nothing else, Derek would show his ugly mug in town again.

"Could he really have walked this far?" Sadie said now, as Lincoln pulled off the road.

He'd clocked half a mile, and yeah, it was unlikely, but

possible. Why he would have walked this far was the real mystery. Maybe he'd thought he could walk home. But again, why, exactly? Some classmate might have made fun of him. Maybe he was upset with his mother. It could be anything.

"We've got to look everywhere. And this is how we start. We have a plan."

"It's almost like you guys have done this before."

Not true, but yet many of them were in the military at one time, such as Riggs, Wade, and Lincoln. They understood how to fall in line, how to execute a plan, pull together, and both take and give orders.

"We've all had a horse or cow get loose in these hills at one time or another. We'll find him."

"If he walked this far, he'd probably feel lost. This road seems to go on forever and there are no more landmarks for miles."

Lincoln grabbed his jacket, as the temperatures were falling, and took his extra flashlight from the glove compartment.

Sadie accepted it. "This one's for me?"

"Yes. But I need *you* to stay here by the truck."

"What? Why did I come if I'm not going to help you look?"

One hand on the nape of her neck, he pulled her close. "Because I spent all day by the grill feeding folks and didn't get to see you. And also, you'll help me *when* I find him."

"I like the way you said when not if."

"Oh, I'll *find* him if he's out there but I'm not good with crying kids."

"You think I am?"

"Hopin' like hell you're better than I am."

Lincoln gave Sadie a quick chaste kiss and climbed out of the truck. No one reported back on the walkie-talkies, meaning no success in finding the kid yet. With a flashlight, bottle of water, handset, and the gun he didn't tell Sadie about tucked under his jacket, he set off into the tree line. There were coyotes in the brushy areas that sometimes roamed farther into town, especially after nightfall, hunting for food. On the ranch he used his rifle but kept a handgun in his truck. He'd never used it, hoped to God he never would, but it was there just the same.

He turned back one last time. Sadie stood outside the truck, her flashlight pointed toward him and the trees.

"Jimmy Ray!" she called. "Jimmy Ray!"

He joined her and did the same, calling the kid's name out as he went. An owl hooted nearby, and the crickets rang out into the now cold night. Pretty soon the dropping temperatures could make this a dicey situation. It wasn't that a kid couldn't survive out here overnight, but conditions weren't optimal. He'd be dehydrated before long. And Lincoln hoped for no worse than that.

"Anything?" A voice came through the handset, sounding like Riggs.

"Just got here, heading out."

The sound of Sadie's calls grew distant as he walked farther into the tree line, making a pattern. He marked each tree as he passed it, further insuring he'd cover new ground. Twigs snapped under his boots and leaves crunched. His flashlight caught nothing but dead vegetation and plenty of critters who ran for cover when the light caught them. Before long, he'd walked the acreage assigned to him and still no sign of the kid. He'd have to head back now and check in.

"I'm headed back," Lincoln said into the handset. "Nothing here."

"Nothing here, either," Riggs said gruffly.

Ah hell, a few more feet couldn't hurt.

"Jimmy Ray!" he called out after a few minutes of walking, frustration bubbling. "Damn kid, where the hell are ya?"

Crunch. Snap. And then the lone howl of a coyote.

"Shit fire." Lincoln touched the handle of his gun and shouted into the dark night. "Jimmy Ray! If you're out here, son, now's a great time to say something. Game over."

"Game over?" came a little voice straight ahead.

Shining the bright light in the direction of the sound, Lincoln found Jimmy Ray at the base of a knotted tree. He appeared to have just woken from a nap.

Lincoln jogged over to him and squatted in front of him, handing him the bottle of water.

"Your mother is lookin' for you. What do you think you're doin' out here?"

He rubbed his eyes. "I got lost."

"No kiddin'." Lincoln held his hand out and pulled Jimmy Ray up. "Where were you headed?"

"I was *goin'* to find my dad."

The kid's voice took on a challenging tone, that of a little boy trying to call up some false bravado for his misguided plan. Lincoln found it far too familiar, but he also didn't miss the dried tears on the boy's cheeks.

"I beat his score on Mario Brothers. I need to find him and tell him."

Of all the reasons Lincoln might have suspected, this would be dead last. "Did you think of letting your mom know you were off on this journey?"

"She would just say no. I can't see my dad."

"Listen to your mother." Lincoln talked into the handset. "Got the kid."

"Seriously?" Riggs's voice crackled. "I'll be damned."

"Who's that?" Jimmy Ray asked.

"Just one of the men that are out lookin' for you. You set off a search party."

"I did?"

"Yeah, well, we don't like to see a cryin' mama."

"My mama's cryin'?"

"What do you think?" Hearing the howl of the coyote again, this time decidedly closer, Lincoln turned the kid in the direction he'd come. "We need to head back now."

"Is that a c-coyote?"

"Yeah, but don't worry. I'm right behind you. He'll get to me before he ever gets you."

"But I don't want him to get you," Jimmy Ray whined.

"He won't." Lincoln laid a hand on the kid's shoulder and shone the flashlight to light a path and lead him. "Just keep walking toward the light."

After a few minutes of silence, Jimmy Ray piped up. "My mama cries all the time now anyway."

Lincoln winced. Kids noticed everything with zero filter. "Yeah, but you don't need to give her another reason. Do ya?"

Halfway back, Lincoln realized the boy might actually be tired. He'd walked all the way here in the first place. He should be exhausted.

"Stop," Lincoln said, placing a hand on Jimmy Ray's shoulder.

Once the flashlight confirmed no coyote in their vicinity, Lincoln bent and hauled the kid up to his shoulders. "Hang on tight, buddy."

He hiked the rest of the way back and soon enough he heard Sadie's calls coming closer.

"Jimmy Ray!" She sounded a bit hoarse now.

Hell, he sounded that way, too.

"That's Miss Sadie," Jimmy Ray said. "What's she doin' here?"

"You didn't think your teacher would want to find you?"

"Did *she* cry, too?"

"Not really," Lincoln lied, thinking that Sadie came close.

But it was one thing to make your mama cry, another to be the reason for your first crush's tears.

"Put me down," Jimmy Ray said. "I can walk now."

Lincoln lowered him to the ground, and Jimmy Ray did everything but smooth his hair back. Lincoln smiled because he understood. Sadie did the same sort of thing to him. Made him want to straighten up, tuck his shirt in, check his hair, and simply be a better man.

Sadie's flashlight shined on them and she ran to meet them.

"Jimmy Ray!" She went to her knees and grabbed him in a bear hug. "You're okay. Thank God!"

"I'm okay, Miss Sadie," Jimmy Ray said. "I just got a little lost."

"Your mama sure is worried about you."

"I'm sorry."

"You found him." Sadie met Lincoln's gaze, making him feel every bit the superhero he wasn't. "You said you would."

"I got lucky."

They settled Jimmy Ray into the back seat, buckled him, and were on their way back within seconds. Pamela Ann met his truck before he even pulled into the parking lot, running up to it. She yanked on the rear-passenger door before Lincoln came to a full stop.

"My baby!" Pamela Ann climbed in the back seat with him. "Let me look at you. Are you okay?"

"He's okay." Sadie turned in her seat to watch the emotional display. "Just a little dirty."

Lincoln flashed a smile in Sadie's direction and caught her hand in his, threading his fingers through hers. He didn't know why this moment made him want to touch Sadie, but any moment that he touched Sadie was a good one. Behind Pamela Ann came a group of residents who'd stayed. Others probably left the minute they heard the boy was found. He didn't blame them. It was one long day for him and would be an early morning as usual.

Jolette Marie was in the group of those who'd stayed, and she slid him a confused look, quirking a brow meaningfully. He'd have that talk with her sooner rather than later. They'd never had anything close to a commitment. But their relationship, while of a temporary nature, had probably lasted on and off a bit too long. It was a two-way street from the get-go, but guilt coursed through him because recently, he hadn't been honest with her. He should have told her the night he'd run into her at the Shady Grind that whatever they'd had was over, *not* that he'd take a "rain check." Because it would never rain that hard again.

No surprise, the doctor stayed behind, and when Pamela Ann took Jimmy Ray out of the truck, he knelt to examine him. Well, at least he was good for something. While the crowd dispersed and Sadie talked with Pamela Ann, Lincoln put his gun away and cleaned up the bed of his truck.

"We need to talk," Jolette Marie said, at his elbow.

"Yeah. We will. Just not now." He shut the tailgate.

"Why *not* now?"

"Because it's late, I'm tired, and I'm takin' Sadie home."

She went hand on hip. "Are you *serious*?"

"I am." He met her gaze, hoping she'd see the firm resolution in his eyes.

"Yeah. I guess we *will* talk later, or maybe not at all." She stomped off.

If only it could be that easy. But nothing ever was for Lincoln when it came to women. His "lucky" nickname sure didn't follow him into his love life. Every time he thought he'd been close to something real the feeling slipped away. Maybe falling in love just wouldn't happen for him, but Sadie made him want to try again.

He found Sadie and stood next to her for a few minutes while she said goodnight to everybody in the world.

Or this town. Either way.

"Ready?" he asked.

"Yes." She walked hand in hand with him to his truck.

He opened the passenger door and held out a hand. "I thought maybe you'd missed saying goodnight to someone. Couldn't have that."

"No." She grinned. "Couldn't have that."

He hauled her against him and bent low to kiss her. He didn't care who saw them, but he hoped that the doctor did. He'd been on Lincoln's last nerve today, following Sadie around all day like a puppy dog.

Lincoln drove to Lupine Lake, but of course, Sadie had questions. He'd expected that. Where he'd found Jimmy Ray, what did he say when he found Jimmy Ray, was Jimmy Ray crying? He answered the volley of questions he eventually expected to answer for Pamela Ann, too.

"When you found him, did he tell you where he'd been headed?"

He cleared his throat. "To find his daddy."

"Oh." Sadie's hand went to her chest, as if it physically hurt to hear those words. "Poor kid."

"Yeah, apparently he reached a new level in the Mario Brothers game and just wanted to let him know."

Sadie bit her lower lip. "I should tell Pamela Ann just in case he doesn't."

"Might be a good idea."

"What are they going to do if Derek never shows up again?"

"Won't be easy, but they'll survive. Maybe even be better off. We'll all be there for Jimmy Ray. Help him grow up to be a good man."

She went silent for such a long moment that he took his eyes off the road to glance at her. And found her studying him.

She squeezed his forearm. "I'm sorry. I forgot about your mother. Tonight made me think of that."

"It's okay."

"It must have hurt so much to feel abandoned."

"We didn't just *feel* abandoned. We were." He pulled up to her cabin and turned off the truck. "Anyway, it was a long time ago."

"How could any parent...I don't understand." She shook her head.

"That's because you're Sadie Stephens. You wouldn't abandon a difficult *student*, much less your own child."

She unbuckled, drew closer, and cupped his jaw. Then he was kissing her again, because she was his truest addiction. Other people needed beer, gin, and weed. He wanted Sadie's kisses. She tasted like sweet tea and honey and he couldn't drink in enough of her.

When he broke the kiss, they were both a little breathless.

"Come inside," she said, hand on his chest.

He couldn't say yes fast enough.

CHAPTER 12

*S*adie's hands trembled as she unlocked the front door. The last time Lincoln was in her cabin, she'd left on a date with another man. And the time before that, they'd spent the night together, and he'd kissed her for the second time without much explanation. She felt even closer to him after tonight, but there was still so much he didn't know about her. There were still things she felt compelled to share with him, right or wrong.

Because when she gave her body to a man, when she let him have that sacred part of herself, she wanted to know his heart. And even if she'd known Lincoln for half her life, she didn't know the most intimate details about him. He'd already shared some of his pain, and now it was her turn.

Open up a vein and bleed.

Her stomach burned and she gnawed at her lower lip. "You want a beer?"

"Sure." He followed her to the kitchen. "If you're having one with me."

She untwisted the cap of her beer and they clinked bottles together. "To reunions."

"Reunions," Lincoln said and took a pull of beer. "That was a little dicey tonight. I'm glad we found him before he wound up spending the night out there alone."

"I can't even imagine."

"Did you hear the coyote?"

"I'm kind of embarrassed to say I jumped back in the truck for a few minutes."

"Don't be." Lincoln chuckled. "Smart girl. Knew I didn't have to worry about you."

"All this happening tonight made me wonder. Do you think...would you ever want to see your mother again? Like if she showed up in town someday."

Lincoln didn't even hesitate. "I would. Certainly loved her enough. And, I'm not angry anymore. Enough time has passed that I think I'd be able to listen now. Not that it would make much difference."

"That's generous of you."

"We all make mistakes. Hers was pretty epic but I figure I'm no one to judge her."

"If anyone has the right to judge, it's you. She left you to feel...responsible."

He shrugged. "Maybe that's not such a bad thing."

The man before her was strong but compassionate and everything he'd been through formed him. Sadie set her beer down and went into his arms, which opened wide for her. Strong hands slid down to her waist, holding her close. He gave the best hugs on earth.

"It took me a long time to get to this place. I was angry and bitter for a long time. I'm no angel."

She buried her face in his neck and breathed in his warm scent. "That's okay. I'm not as sweet as everyone thinks that I am."

"People who don't know any better. I've known you're a

force to be reckoned with since the moment you stood up for Eve." He chuckled. "I still remember you standing outside the General Store, holding a paper bag, wagging a finger, telling everyone who would listen that they could stop hatin' on Eve because they didn't have the whole story."

"I'm a loyal friend."

"Even though I was mighty pissed at Eve, I never managed to be as angry with you. We were both in the same position, hurting for the people we loved."

"But you need to know, I tried to stop her. Please know that. You have to understand, I was terrified, too. A whole church full of people were waitin' for her. But Eve didn't see it that way. You know how proud she's always been and when she gets an idea in her head no one can stop her. I know she loved Jackson, probably still does. She was just scared they were too young. That Jackson should go to Nashville or he'd wind up hatin' her. When I drove her home, I thought Jackson would come after her, and there would be a wedding after they talked."

"But he never did."

"It's not that I blame him...I just thought—"

"They'd work it out somehow." He scrubbed a hand down his face. "We all did. C'mon, they were *Eve and Jackson*. Together forever."

"Together forever." She couldn't meet his eyes. "I can see why that would make you jaded."

He took her hand, raised it to his lips. "But not you. You're the farthest from a jaded person that I've ever met. No one's like you, Sadie."

"And for me, there's never been anyone like you."

She kissed him, and this time the kiss wasn't quite as sweet as the intensity of it grew and blossomed. Their tongues tangled as their mouths slanted against each other, seeking more. Breathless, she broke the kiss and took his hand, tugged him toward her bed. In case there were any questions, she kicked off her boots and pulled her dress off, leaving her in a black push-up bra and matching panty thongs.

Gratified at the very male sound that came out of Lincoln, she absorbed the knowledge that he didn't look at all disappointed. In fact, he appeared stunned as his gaze raked over her body, from her breasts to her legs.

"God, Sadie. You're beautiful. So beautiful."

His callused fingers gently traced a path from her bra strap to the cup, tugging it down. Then he bent low to take her nipple in his mouth, licking, teasing, and tugging until she moaned.

He met her gaze intently, his blue eyes the darkest she'd ever seen them. "Are you sure?"

"You wouldn't be here if I wasn't."

"That's all I need to hear." He unbuttoned his shirt, letting her help, and quickly divested himself of his boots and pants.

She stood for a moment just admiring his body. Anyone could tell that Lincoln didn't spend a lot of time behind a desk. He worked physically hard every day of his life and it showed. His shoulders were wide and muscular, his stomach flat, tapering down to strong muscular thighs.

He gently laid her on the bed and covered her with his warm body. He kissed her, hot and deep, plundering her mouth. When he had her breathless, his tongue took a leisurely tour of her body, from the column of her neck, down to her belly button, leaving tendrils of heat in its wake.

"I want to take my time, but I don't know if I can," Lincoln said. "I want you so much and you're driving me out of my ever lovin' mind."

"You don't need to go slow or be careful with me. This

time," Sadie said. "Right now, I want you hard and fast. And, like, yesterday."

He blinked. "Damn, girl, you are constantly surprising me."

"I hope so."

Desire pulsed through her body and she bucked under him, then her hands were on his ass, lowering his boxer briefs. She sucked in a breath at the sight of him completely naked now because he was um, large there, too. She probably shouldn't be surprised.

He caught her staring and grinned. "Are you okay?"

"Y-yes."

"But not so sure about hard and fast anymore? Don't worry. I'll make this good for you."

"I know you will." Sweet emotion spiked through her and she bit her lower lip to keep from crying. "I can't believe this is happening."

"Oh, it's happening."

"You have no idea how long I've wanted this."

"Yeah?" he grinned. "Show me."

LINCOLN WAS ABOUT to go out of his mind with lust. He'd felt intense desire before, but this felt completely new. This? Sheer madness. It took everything in him not to ravage her the minute she'd brought him to her bed. Because damn, she was unbelievable. So gorgeous, with soft peachy skin and dear Lord, the underwear…Sadie wore of the sexiest panties he'd ever laid eyes on. He wanted to tear them off with his teeth, but it looked like she'd paid a lot for them.

Then she'd bucked underneath him and told him what she wanted. He went almost still with surprise. He'd fanta-sized about this moment, but though their kisses were hot, he didn't expect a wild woman in bed. Slow would be better, if he could manage. She certainly didn't make this easy.

"Condom," he said and reached for his pants, pulling the shiny package out, and ripping it open.

He put it on and lowered himself to her, kissing all over her body, feeling her writhe under him and open up, spreading her legs wider. His fingers probed inside her and she wasn't just damp, she was sopping wet. That final check was all he needed. Slowly, he slid into her and gave her a moment to adjust to his size.

"Okay?" he asked, nibbling at her neck, and tried not to move inside her, which required a herculean effort.

"Oh God, yes, please. Lincoln. I need to move."

Then she bucked beneath him, and he was a goner. All control slipped and he just pounded into her, riding her like she'd asked, hard and fast. She clutched at his shoulders, her hips meeting him with every powerful and deep stroke. She was incredible, taking every last inch of him. It wasn't long before she moaned, calling out his name, and he felt the first waves of her pulsing and clenching around him like a vise. It milked an orgasm out of him faster than he could have ever believed possible. Better and more intense than any in his life.

He groaned and emptied himself into her. But after, even with all her enthusiasm, he still worried he'd hurt her. He rolled with her and tucked her to his side.

"Damn, girl. You didn't have to take me all at once like that." His hand glided up and down her spine, soothing her, feeling gratified at having left her breathless.

"Once you were inside of me, there was no other way."

"Are you sore, baby?"

"I don't think so, but I also can't feel anything right now. I'm not even sure I have a body. It feels like it dissolved and floated up to heaven."

He chuckled and pressed a kiss to her temple. "You're amazing."

She played with the hairs on his chest and glanced up at him, a playful smile on her lips. "Not nice and *sweet*?"

"Well, you certainly *taste* sweet. How about that?"

"I'll take it."

"You will," he said and rolled to brace himself above her. "And then you'll take some more."

"Oh, yes."

And with that, he lowered his head between her legs and proceeded to rock her world.

It was still dark when Lincoln forced himself to disentangle from Sadie and get dressed. They'd been at it all night long, which meant that whether she wanted to admit it or not, Sadie was sore. He'd been gentle the next time, taking his time, slow and easy, but still she'd come harder than he'd ever seen a woman do.

But it was time to go. Playtime was over. Their ranch hands were always given Sunday off for family and church, which meant a longer day for him, seeing as they were already shorthanded. Usually he'd manage to find some time for himself on Sundays, though, if nothing else because Mima insisted he, Daisy, and Hank join her for dinner. Tonight, he would move heaven and earth (or more like a couple of cows) to see Sadie again.

He bent over her naked and sleepy form to kiss a bare shoulder, as it peeked out from under the covers. "Don't get up."

"Don't go," she said lazily, reaching to pull him close. "I wanted to serve you breakfast in bed."

"Cook me dinner instead. Or I'll cook you dinner. Either way, I'll be back."

"Yeah?"

"You don't think you're getting rid of me now, do you?"

He stroked her butt one last time through the sheet and then went out the door, locking it behind him. A random ray of moonlight illuminated beautiful Lupine Lake. Dawn broke over the horizon as he drove up the hill to his cabin for a shower and change. Within a few minutes he was fully caffeinated and mucking horse stalls. He hated Sundays because of this one chore that he didn't usually have to do. Eve often took this job for extra cash, but Mima insisted she have Sundays off.

Next he saddled his gelding and rode out to the north pasture to check on the fence line.

That's when he saw Jolette Marie riding in the distance. Her family's horse ranch abutted the Carver ranch, but they rarely ran into each other. Both families owned plenty of land, with the ability to avoid each other if needed. The Trueharts never required any help from their neighbors. Wealthy and influential, Mr. Truehart had been married five times, each time to a younger woman. He employed a full staff, including a maid and a cook who lived on the property.

Lincoln could go on avoiding Jolette Marie but that wouldn't work for him. This was a small town. Much as he hated it, this conversation would happen. This was his fault, for taking advantage of the easy situation that Jolette Marie offered. Now he had to get out of this quickly, with the least amount of damage to a woman he thought of as a friend.

He rode to the fence line and dismounted, a clear signal that he wanted to talk. Jolette Marie joined him almost immediately, smiling widely as she hopped off her horse.

"I knew you'd be back. We've got a new horse coming in for training, but I can meet you tonight."

"That's not going to work for me."

"What are you thinkin', then? Tomorrow?"

He shook his head, realizing he'd misled her just by

meeting her here. "This thing between us is going to have to be over."

"Are you kidding me? Is this about Sadie?"

"Okay, listen. You and I were never serious. Nothing permanent. That's the way we both wanted it."

"That's the way *you* wanted it and I went along."

"It wasn't just me. We've been together maybe twice in all the time we've known each other. If you wanted more, you would have said so. You have lots of other men in your life and I never cared. We never promised each other anything."

"Because you didn't want to settle down. With anyone. If that's true, why are you dropping me?"

Because I feel like someone hit me over the head with a baseball bat.

Stunned. Seeing stars.

Because I'm thirty-two years old and I've never felt this way about a woman. I didn't even know that I could.

He wouldn't say any of those things to Jolette Marie and risk making her feel second rate.

"I haven't been fair to you. You deserve better."

Jolette Marie climbed back on her horse and took the reins. "What if I don't mind?"

"Doesn't matter. I do."

She scoffed. "This *is* about Sadie. I knew it. You're *such* a fool. She's sweet and nice but she's *not* going to keep a man like you happy and satisfied."

At one time, Lincoln would have bet the same. Now he knew far better. God, how much better. They were going to get along just fine. What's more, they had a connection that he'd never had with anyone else.

"You'd be surprised. But that's my business."

"You're *going* to get bored. When you get bored enough, let me know and I *might* consider taking you back."

Sadie would *never* bore him. "Please don't."

"You're an ass," she said and turned her horse in the direction she'd come.

"I'm sorry."

She galloped off but not before giving him the one-finger salute.

He turned to the gelding. "Well, that went well."

The gelding snorted.

CHAPTER 13

The morning after the school fundraiser, Lillian rose later than normal, made herself a quick breakfast, and without even bothering to write to Albert, set off for town. There were times when she didn't need any advice from the old man. Those were the times when a mother and grandmother knew what to do and didn't want anyone to stop her.

There would be some clean-up downtown today, considering that they'd all been otherwise occupied searching for Pamela Ann and Derek's boy. Poor child. Lillian would bake some cookies and her homemade fudge for the boy soon, as well as figure out how to get ahold of his no-account father. There simply seemed to be no end to her chores. The list just kept getting longer, not shorter.

Today, she would need to have a talk with this new doctor in town. Judson Grant, Ada's nephew. He seemed to be under the mistaken impression that Sadie was the woman for him. Ha! Lillian would set *him* straight. Lincoln had finally noticed Sadie, thank you Jesus. Yesterday, Lillian's gaze followed Lincoln throughout the day, and *his* gaze followed Sadie's every move.

She truly did not understand *why* men continued to move to their town. Most of them grew up here, but every now and then a young whippersnapper came along like he had good sense. With their shortage of women, it was Lillian's duty to make sure her grandson got a good one. Not that her Lincoln needed any help in that department, as he did seem to be particularly gifted at attracting women, but she would prefer him to marry one of their women, and not someone he met on the rodeo circuit. And it couldn't hurt to cut away all distractions from his and Sadie's path straight to the church altar.

Speaking of Trinity Church, she did of course make her appearance at morning services. Lillian considered it her duty to show up not only for Hank and his children, who couldn't be bothered, but for all the other heathens who refused to darken the doorway of a church. Bless their hearts.

She didn't see Sadie this morning, and she was a regular. Lillian otherwise saw all of the usual suspects. Beulah and Lloyd Hayes, Brenda Iglesias, Eve. Wanda and Merle Stephens, Ada, and her nephew. While Ada schmoozed with the Pastor, trying to advance her one-way first-class ticket into heaven, Lillian offered to buy the wonderful Dr. Grant a coffee over at the General Store.

Kill them with kindness, her blessed mother used to say. Or was that her father? Well, either way.

"Of course, Mrs. Carver." Judson (whom she refused to call "doctor" as he looked twelve) crossed the street with her. "I would love to have coffee."

"Order whatever you want, young man," she said once they were inside. "I don't mind paying five dollars for a cup of coffee. It's the way of the world these days."

"Now Mrs. Carver, I can't have you buy my coffee. This is my treat."

He made points with Lillian for being a gentleman. Any man of Stone Ridge would happily be impaled in the town square before he let an old woman pay for anything. Impressed, she sat and waited for him to be back with her order. They didn't make coffee here any better than Lillian did at home, but she enjoyed occasionally being out and about and off the ranch. One couldn't lead a full life with only cowboys, cattle, and horses for company. People needed each other and community.

"I understand that you're thinking of opening up a clinic here," Lillian said, because that rumor had already wound its way through town twice.

Lillian loved the idea, though she'd prefer a woman start one. Still, one couldn't be picky.

"I certainly believe that I'm needed and would do well opening up a practice here, but it's expensive to start a clinic. All the equipment, a location, hiring a staff."

"We'd love to have you, but you do understand the peculiarities of our small town?"

"The shortage of women? Yes. It's a bit…disturbing."

"Uh-huh. That's right."

"I admit I have plans to be married soon."

"Oh, you're *engaged*?" This would be easier than Lillian thought.

He shook his head. "What I meant is, I have a plan. I need to find a wife and preferably soon. That could be difficult here. And unfortunately, the young woman I have my eyes on has a terrible skin condition."

"Really."

"Sadie Stephens. We went on one date, plenty of fun, but it ended early because she broke out in a rash. Something she ate, I'm sure. She's a beautiful girl. So sweet and kind."

"She is. And very much taken."

He quirked a brow. "*Taken?* We went on a date."

"Oh, dear. Here's what you need to know about our Sadie. She's far too sweet to say no to a friend. And she wanted to welcome you to town I'm sure."

"I'm confused. Who is she "taken" by?" He held up air quotes.

"My grandson, of course, Lincoln Carver."

He blinked. "I thought they were just friends. I met him on the night of our date."

"Understandable mistake."

"Well, this explains a great deal. She did put me off for another date and she wouldn't give me the time of day at the fundraiser."

"It's not like Sadie to be rude, but she might have been trying to spare your feelings any further. No point in wasting your time."

"I appreciate that since I've got no time at all to waste."

Pamela Ann and Jimmy Ray walked inside the store and headed straight to their table. "Dr. Grant, thank you again for looking Jimmy Ray over last night."

He stood. "My pleasure. Well, not my pleasure, I mean… obviously it's not a *pleasure* to have your child missing for hours."

"I knew what you meant," Pamela Ann said shyly, holding Jimmy Ray's hand. "He's not gettin' far from me for a while. Jimmy Ray swears he'll never do that again. Right?"

"Yes, ma'am." Jimmy Ray nodded.

Lillian kept her mouth shut because she had nothing good to say. Jimmy Ray was the image of his father. But despite the overabundance of genes he'd received from Derek, hopefully he'd grow to be a fine man of Stone Ridge anyway. One could hope.

"I've got some cookies and fudge coming your way, young

man." Lillian wagged a finger. "I'll send them to school with Miss Sadie."

The boy's eyes lit up. Lillian made award-winning fudge, after all.

"What do you say?" Pamela Ann tugged on Jimmy Ray's hand.

"Thank you, ma'am."

After a few more pleasantries they were on their way. Lillian noted with some surprise the wistful look in Judson's eyes as he watched them. *Pamela Ann?* Really? Well, well. Why not, after all? A pretty girl, many believed she'd been far too good for Derek. Imagine if she were to marry a doctor! Of course, first she'd need to get divorced.

Although Lillian wasn't really in the market to match up anyone but her grandchildren, this one sort of fell in her lap. She simply needed to keep Judson in town. Pamela Ann would bring Jimmy Ray for regular check-ups and love would blossom. *After* the divorce.

She patted Judson's hand. "I would love to hear you tell me how I can help you bring a clinic to Stone Ridge."

SADIE MISSED church on Sunday morning. She'd slept in after Lincoln left. *Lincoln.* He was an amazing lover. Powerful and strong, he could be so gentle with her, worried he'd hurt her. Kissing her tenderly, making love to her slowly the second time, but still giving her orgasm after orgasm. Far from hurting her, he'd delivered the most erotic night of her life.

She'd wanted and waited for him for so long. For him. For something real. Someone she could trust again since trusting hadn't been possible for years. She would refuse to worry or feel insecure about any other women in his old life. That was the old Sadie. The Sadie who, post-Martin, would notice every time a man would so much as glance at another woman. She assumed a man couldn't be faithful to her. Pathetic. Therefore, relationships were ruined before they got started. She offered zero trust. No one had the patience to deal with her need for constant reassurance and eventually she'd faced facts: this was her problem and hers alone.

She spent the rest of the morning cleaning her cabin and made a list for the market. One of her skills was in the kitchen. Mom taught her to cook and Daddy always said Sadie was his second favorite cook in the world. The first? Julia Child. Ha! Sadie made a succulent pot roast and delicious lasagna. In the middle of making her list, the landline rang in her kitchen.

"Hey, baby."

Oh, sigh. *Lincoln.* "Hi. Good morning. Hi."

He chuckled. "I forgot something. I know you said you'd cook me dinner, but Sunday is the one family dinner that Mima insists we all have together. You'll have to cook me dinner another time."

"Oh. That's okay."

Sadie could understand why she wouldn't be invited to a family dinner yet. They were new. No pressure or promises. She refused to be a female Judson Grant. It didn't mean anything not to be invited.

"What time should I pick you up?"

"What *time?*"

"Yeah, unless you want to drive out here. We have dinner around six."

Sadie couldn't breathe. She was completely…speechless.

"Baby? You there?"

"I'm…invited?" she finally squeaked out. "Tonight?"

"Yeah, well, I'm selfish. I want to see you and was looking forward to dinner…and after dinner."

"Me, too."

"You know what? I'll pick you up. I'll be there at 5."

A sweet ache of pleasure buzzed through her body. Dinner with the family. Sadie spent the next few hours deciding what to wear. Nothing she owned seemed adequate.

She finally phoned Eve in desperation. "Please come over. I have an emergency. Stat!"

Eve came over within two seconds with her First Aid kit. "What happened? Did you fall?"

Oh, fine, fall a couple of times and everyone thinks you're a walking emergency.

Sadie went hands on hips. "This is a *fashion* emergency."

"Oh, whew!" Eve plopped down on the sofa. "Where were you this morning, missy? I saw Lincoln's truck here late last night."

"I overslept. Believe me, he wore me out." She held up two dresses on their hangers. "This or that?"

"Where is he taking you?"

"Wait for it: dinner with the family."

"Then why are you dressin' up? The first time I ate dinner with them I wore my Wranglers and a T-shirt."

"Eve, you were *sixteen*." Sadie let out an exasperated breath. "I have to make a great impression."

"Mima adores you!"

"But Hank doesn't. He scares me a little. He's always so…quiet."

"Aw, Hank is a pussycat."

"Because he's always liked *you*. I don't think he likes me very much. And I want him to like me."

"Well, he doesn't really like a lot of people. But, sweetie, he won't care *what* you're wearin'."

"It's a ranch. I should probably wear Wranglers. I do have a pair. Somewhere."

"Don't be silly. If you're not wearin' a dress no one will recognize you." Eve pointed to the blue and white dress.

"Maybe you're right. I think Lincoln likes me in a dress." Sadie plopped down beside Eve.

"I'll just bet he does." Eve elbowed Sadie. "And also, out of a dress."

"Yes, he does. We're so good together. But I'm nervous I'll do something wrong tonight."

"Don't worry, there won't be any question as to which fork to use." Eve rolled her eyes.

"I *mean* do something wrong to spoil this thing with Lincoln."

"Like, date another man? Too late, he already forgave you for that," Eve quipped.

"Get jealous over another woman. Like Jolette Marie. It's pretty clear that she has a thing for Lincoln."

"Who *doesn't* Jolette Marie have a thing for? I know she's had her eye on Jackson forever. She's never forgiven me for falling in love with him. Now that he's in Nashville, I wouldn't be surprised if she online stalks him."

"What is her problem?"

Eve shrugged. "Not sure it's a problem. She just likes men. Don't forget she holds the title for runaway bride. Three times to the altar but changed her mind at the last minute."

Although Eve was technically also a runaway bride, Sadie of all people knew it hadn't been that simple for Eve. She'd loved Jackson enough to let him go.

"I think she's spoiled rotten."

Eve snickered. "The only daughter with three brothers and a father who's wealthy? She did dressage for years and owned her first prized horse at *five*."

A sore subject for Eve, whose mother still worked as a maid and cook for the Trueharts. She and Eve lived together in one of the cabins on Truehart land after Eve's father abandoned the family. Eve knew Jolette Marie better than most people. At one time they'd even been close friends, but then Jackson noticed Eve, and the rest was history.

"I don't like the way she looks at Lincoln," Sadie confessed. "Like she'd like to eat him up."

"You should care about the way he looks at *her*. From what I've seen, with little interest at all. Don't let her do this to you. Jolette Marie smells insecurity. She'll take that and run with it. And jealousy can destroy relationships."

"So can cheating," Sadie felt compelled to add. Once, in truly dramatic style, Sadie said to Eve, "As God is my witness, I will never be cheated on again!"

"Honestly, there's more to Jolette Marie than any of us realize. Remember, she's never been loved by anyone. Not even her own father."

"You're right." Sadie remembered how all of the men she'd been engaged to marry were her father's business acquaintances. Very old-school of him. "I should be more understanding."

Eve nodded. "You've got to know what you have with Lincoln and trust him. Otherwise this won't work."

"I know Lincoln is a good man, but it's hard to remember that sometimes. Men cheat."

Eve quirked a brow. "Not *all* men. Remember that."

CHAPTER 14

*L*incoln came by promptly at five o'clock to pick Sadie up. She'd been ready since three. No sooner did she open the door than he nearly tackled her, picking her up in his arms and carrying her inside. Large warm hands wandered under the skirt of her dress giving her a full body tingle.

"I missed you, too."

"There's more than one reason I love you in a dress," Lincoln said with an easy smile. "But do you mind wearing jeans tonight?"

"I almost did. But why?"

"Because I want to take you somewhere after dinner and a dress would make that difficult."

"Where?"

"It's a surprise."

After she'd changed into Wranglers and a T-shirt (perhaps hoping for Eve's fortune and blessing at the Carver table), he drove them to the ranch on the outskirts of Stone Ridge.

Lincoln reached for her hand. "Don't be surprised if my father talks bull sperm at dinner. Mima has *tried t*o stop him."

"Bull *sperm*?"

"Just one of the many fascinating conversations you're bound to hear at a cattle rancher's table." He rubbed his chin. "Hank is trying to find a champion stud."

"What a coincidence, so am I." At his quirked brow she laughed. "Kidding! What do they usually ask your dates?"

"Well." He went quiet for a moment. "I wouldn't know. You're the first woman I've brought home since I was a teenager, I guess."

"*Really?*" She was far more pleased by this than she probably should be.

He shrugged. "Yep. I guess Carla Lynn Marshall, now that I think about it. She insisted. Said if I was taking her to the prom, she wanted to meet my family."

"Seems logical."

Sadie remembered Carla Lynn. Four years older than Sadie, she'd moved away from Stone Ridge a few years ago and wound up marrying a man from Dallas.

"I don't know how logical it was but as a pretty horny teenager I would have done anything at that time."

"So, what you're saying is that you haven't changed much?"

He snorted. "Guess I never wanted to bring anyone home."

She allowed that knowledge to settle, warm and sweet. "Hank scares me, you ought to know."

"He scares a lot of people." He brought her hand to his lips and brushed a kiss across her knuckles. "I've got you. And you'll do fine."

Sadie had been to the Double C Ranch many times with Eve, but not for a while. She loved this part of Hill Country, where large family ranches dotted the land for miles. The Carver cattle ranch happened to be one of the most successful in the county. A family business from the get-go, passed down from one generation to another. More like a legacy than a business. When Albert Carver died, the entire town came out for his funeral. The Carver family was among the founding families of Stone Ridge.

Mima greeted them at the door. "Sadie Stephens! I'm so surprised. Look at me! Am I surprised or what? Do I look surprised? Of *course* not!"

"Maybe because I told you?" Lincoln said with a smirk.

"That, too, but this beautiful girl is finally here at the family table."

"Mother, don't marry them off just yet," Hank said.

Lillian cackled. "Alright, I won't!"

They walked to the large open room adjacent to the kitchen with the large ranch table that seemed to seat twelve or more. Lincoln held her hand, so wonderful since she wanted the support. She'd never had trouble making friends, even while at college, but nothing mattered quite like sitting for the first time at the Carver family table. Making a good impression on Hank. Gratified that Mima seemed happy for her to be here, that didn't negate the fact that her nerves were getting the better of her.

She realized that she hadn't said a word yet besides hello. "I'm so happy to be here."

"Great," Hank said. "I hope you like chicken and dumplings. If it's Sunday, you know it will be chicken and dumplings."

"That's what Lincoln told me," Sadie said. "I love chicken and dumplings."

"Are you complaining, Hank? I don't appreciate your tone. Please tell me you're not complaining about a home cooked meal." Mima shook a finger at him.

"You know I prefer beef. I'm a cattle rancher for the love of Pete."

Lincoln let go of her hand, which he'd been holding the entire time. "I'm gonna get us a couple of beers."

He walked past Daisy as she arrived, and they fist bumped.

"Hey, everyone." She took a seat near Hank and noticed Sadie. "Hi. I didn't know we could bring a date."

"*You* can't bring a date, pumpkin," Hank said. "Lincoln just sprung this on us."

Sadie's smile froze. Sprung *this* on us? She was *this*? "I'm sorry to intrude."

"You're *not* intruding, sugar," Mima said. "Lincoln told me he didn't want to break your plans. Hank just has the manners of a bull."

"Excuse me," Hank grunted. "Maybe I hang around cattle too much."

"What's happening?" Lincoln asked firmly when he walked back in the dining room. He sat, handing an uncorked beer to Sadie.

She took a pull of it. "Nothing."

Lincoln took her hand again under the table and squeezed it.

"Can I do something to help?" Sadie asked Lillian.

"No, sweetie, but thanks so much for askin'."

Before long the food was served. Hank, though, kept getting up to fill a shot glass, and then returned to eat a bite or two.

"Y'all will never believe who I saw at church today," Mima said. "That lovely doctor. Ada's nephew. Judson is his name."

Sadie hoped that she wasn't the subject of any conversations between those two. Given this had all happened so quickly between her and Lincoln, she didn't have a chance to explain. Not that she owed Judson anything. They'd had one date. One eye-opening date.

"Who's that?" Daisy asked. "Never heard of him."

"He's Ada's nephew," Lincoln said. "I met him."

"Lovely, *lovely* man. I'm trying to fix him up with Pamela Ann."

"Lord above! Not this again," Hank said. "Stop trying to fix people up. It never works."

"Not to mention that Pamela Ann is *married*," Lincoln added.

"To that awful Derek," Mima said. "And I'll wait for the divorce, *son*, I'm not a heathen. But I don't give it much longer."

"Considering no one knows where he is, that's probably a safe bet." Lincoln took a big bite of dumplings.

Lord, Sadie loved to watch him eat. Liked it nearly better than eating, and she *loved* food. She'd been mostly quiet and self-conscious about the subject of Judson, because she didn't want to add to that conversation. But now she felt compelled to speak for Jimmy Ray.

"I wish Derek would come back for Jimmy Ray," Sadie said. "Even if he doesn't love Pamela Ann anymore, he shouldn't abandon his son."

A dead silence hung in the room, and too late Sadie realized how that statement would sit with the Carvers. Hank's eyes narrowed as though the memory of his loss pierced him. He slammed the rest of his shot.

Beside her, Sadie felt Lincoln tense as he took her hand and squeezed it. He slid Hank a harsh look, almost like a warning.

"He's my student," Sadie said, trying to recover and move the conversation from deadbeat parents, both male and female. "He's actually very funny. Quite talented."

"If he's anything like his father, he's an idiot," Hank said harshly.

"I...I don't think he should be judged by what his father is like," Sadie said carefully. "I'm his teacher and I see nothing but possibilities."

"Which is what a teacher should see!" Mima interjected. "And why you're a *wonderful* teacher, sugar."

"That she is," Lincoln said, hand splayed on her thigh.

"I bet all the little boys have crushes on you," Daisy said.

Sadie shook her head. Just Jimmy Ray.

"Back to what I was sayin'," Mima said, passing the gravy. "I think we need a clinic in town. I know I'm tired of driving to Kerrville for my check-ups. This young doctor seems interested."

Sadie didn't like the idea of running into Judson on a regular basis, and he certainly wouldn't be *her* doctor, but she could appreciate his use for the community. For emergencies.

"I think we need to convince him to settle here," Mima said.

Everyone but Hank nodded and chewed.

After dinner, Sadie of course offered to help with the dishes. Both she and Daisy helped but after a few minutes, Lincoln entered the kitchen.

"If y'all don't mind, I'd like to grab Sadie before it gets too dark."

She turned and at the sight of Lincoln her heart skipped, but in a good way. One hundred percent cowboy stood arms braced in the doorway of the kitchen. He wore a different Stetson, one that appeared a bit more weathered. Ditto with the Wranglers, which fit him like a glove. He wore a blue and gray flannel shirt and appeared to have a tee underneath, leather gloves on his hands. The smile he slid her seemed almost dangerous and enticing.

"Go ahead, hon. We're almost done here." Mima hip checked Sadie in Lincoln's direction.

"Um, okay." She took Lincoln's outstretched hand and he led her outside to the family stables and the horse pens.

"Do you ride horses?" he asked.

"Well, of course. What do you take me for? Do you think I could be best friends with Eve and never ride a horse?"

"Guess I never actually saw you on one."

"Granted, Daddy never bought me my own horse when I desperately wanted one. We owned the land, but he said horses would be too much maintenance."

"He's right." Lincoln opened a stable door with ease. He led a beautiful tanned quarter horse out, a burst of white on her forelock. "This is Thimble. She's gentle. In tune with emotions. Eve swears she can read her rider's mind."

As if she understood his words, the horse nuzzled Lincoln. Sadie smiled but then pointed to the other stall when a dark horse that reminded her of Black Beauty stood regally. "And that one?"

"That's Taco, Jackson's gelding. He's not quite as easygoing. I'll ride him."

"We're going riding?"

"You thought I just wanted to show you the horses?" He cinched a lead on Thimble and walked with her.

"It's been so long for me. I hope I remember everything."

"It's easy with Thimble. She comes by her name honestly." He reached for a pail nearby and began to brush her. "I used to think it was just a cute name, but Mima reminded me the thimble is what keeps your thumb from getting stuck by the needle."

"Who named her?"

"Not sure." Lincoln cocked his head. "I think Eve did. It's not her horse but it might as well have been."

Sadie joined him in brushing Thimble because it seemed

172

like the thing to do and she found the task soothing. She loved just being with Lincoln, side by side this way. They didn't even need words as they quietly worked together. Finally, Lincoln saddled Thimble. Then he led Taco out of his pen, and they both went through the same process with him.

"Where's the horse you use for the rodeo?" she asked, listening to the bristle of the brush glide against Thimble's coarse hair.

"That's Lucky. I keep him up the hill with the other cow ponies. He doesn't work too hard, but I sure don't want him to get a big head. Or get too soft."

By the time Lincoln gave her a hand to climb on Thimble, the sky had turned into a beautiful gray as the sun began its long slide.

"Where are you taking me?"

"Patience. You'll see."

Sadie settled into the saddle, thinking that if it were true a person never forgot to ride a bicycle, the same could be said of a horse. All the riding she'd done as a younger woman came back to her and Thimble responded so well to the reins, Sadie began to feel like they moved together almost like the same person. They both followed Lincoln and Taco, first at a canter, then a straight-out gallop. Finally, after a few minutes, when it felt like they were surely miles away from the house, Lincoln slowed. He hopped off Taco, then came to offer Sadie his hand.

She wisely jumped right into his arms, knowing he could take her weight. He did, easily, then held her in the circle of his arms.

I love you, I love you, I love you.

The words were stuck, weighed down with the worry she was moving too fast. Feeling too much. He needed time to catch up with her nearly lifelong love affair from a distance.

"Sorry Hank was a grouch tonight. Something is going on with him and I intend to find out what it is."

"Don't worry, I'm fine. It's okay if he doesn't like me."

But she wasn't fine. Not okay. Somehow it still mattered too much that *everyone* like her. She needed to get over that.

He tipped her chin. "You're a *fairly* passable liar, you know."

Caught, she bent her head to plunk her hard head against his chest. "No, I'm not."

He chuckled, his hand gliding up and down her spine. "That's one of the things I like best about you, baby. Your terrible poker face."

"Are you going to tell me why we're here?"

"This is my favorite spot on the ranch. All the acres and acres of land we have, and yet this patch right here is the best one to see the stars."

A thicket of trees stood a few feet away, and in this spot no trees blocked any of the view. Just a wide, open sky, with hues of pink and red as the sun finally set.

"Aw, and you wanted me to see it." She reached to run her fingers through his hair, not an easy feat given their size difference. "You know, that's almost romantic."

"Almost?" he said, sounded disappointed. "Hey, I'm trying."

He towered over her, but she never felt intimidated. Wrapping her arms around his waist, she turned her head up to him. "And, baby, I love that you're trying."

He pulled her down on the grass and settled her between his long legs. "See why I wanted you to wear jeans?"

"Life on a cattle ranch is not compatible with wearing a dress."

"But please don't stop wearing them." He nuzzled her neck.

"Eve said if I didn't wear a dress no one would recognize me." She laughed.

"I would."

Those two words were laced with meaning and her heart swelled. They sat quietly as the sun disappeared over the horizon and they were surrounded by utter darkness and a bright spread of stars. They covered every inch of the velvet black sky.

"You're right. Beautiful. This is my new favorite spot, too."

"Where's your old one?"

"A place by the lake where a willow tree's branches hang so low, they touch the water. It's almost…spooky. But also, beautiful in the moonlight."

"I need to see that." Lincoln pulled her closer, his strong arms around her waist, and he lowered his head to her shoulder. "I come here when I want to be alone. When I'm tired of obligations. I've never shared this place with anyone else."

She leaned against him, never feeling so safe. Secure. So… loved. The words were on her lips before she could hold them back.

"I love you."

His body froze for a moment, but then he simply squeezed her tighter. "Say that again?"

A spike of fear churned in her stomach, but he honestly sounded like he hadn't heard her. Welp, she could take it back. She'd never been shy with the words "I love you," telling her family and friends often. But with Lincoln, it was different. It carried a weight and hadn't been as easy to say. Until now.

Why not just speak the truth and get it over with? It wasn't as if this feeling would ever change.

"You heard me. I love you."

He still didn't return the words, but she didn't expect him to. He didn't need to. This was her thing.

Open up a vein and bleed. Take the risk. She felt his love for her. That was enough for now.

He kissed her temple and spoke gently enough to sound like a whisper.

"Baby, I'm new to all this. I've had relationships before. There were two, both with women from Oklahoma that I met on the rodeo circuit. Long distance, but I was faithful. I'm not sure they were. Both ended because something was missing. I wouldn't leave Stone Ridge; they didn't want to move here. But a million other small things were wrong, too. And I didn't care enough to work on them. I'm not sure I ever really fell in love."

"Don't be too hard on yourself."

"I think sometimes I'm not hard *enough* on myself. I'm probably going to screw up sometime with you, and not just by bringing gum instead of flowers—"

"No, don't say—"

"And you have to understand that with me…it's one day at a time." He turned her to face him. "But if you can handle that, Sadie, I'm in."

If a heart could shimmer, hers did at that moment, and surely as bright as the stars in the sky.

I'm in.

In some ways, those words were better than simply parroting "I love you."

"What changed your mind? Am I *that* great of a kisser?"

"The moment I realized you wouldn't tell me how terrified you were of tight spaces because you didn't want *me* to feel bad for dragging you there. You were trying to take care of me even then. That's a first for me. The way you care for Jimmy Ray, who's a little punk unless he's around you. Everyone loves you. You're amazing in the way you care about *everyone*." He chuckled. "And then…the kissing. The way you wreck me. Yeah."

He'd always been in charge, caring for his family at a young age. She wanted more than anything to change that for him. To give him a soft place to fall.

"That's all I want." She leaned her head back, pressing against his shoulder. "I want to take care of you."

"You already do."

They did some more of the explosive kissing that changed their relationship in one single night. The pull between them felt almost flammable with intensity, but gratification pulsed through her to know it went deeper than physical. For her, it was deeper long ago. And then she'd locked the door on that dream and told herself that since she couldn't have him, she'd need to find someone else.

But she'd *never* found anyone like Lincoln. No one ever cared like this. She kissed him and kissed him until she felt salty tears roll down her cheeks.

He wiped one away with his thumb. "Is this good crying?"

She nodded. "This is what I've wanted for so long. I've been so lonely."

"Even with all these men chasing you?"

"No one right for me."

He nuzzled her jawline. "I hope you know I'm not perfect. Not even close."

"Well, you know *I'm* not. I tried to plan my future husband's life. Remember?"

He gave her that slow easy smile that made her womb contract. "And what changed your mind about all your detailed plans?"

"I heard what I must have sounded like." She brushed away a tear. "That date with Judson? He was the male version of me, but on steroids. And he terrified me. He had such plans and came on so strong. He practically started naming our future children."

Lincoln scowled. "Hope you've told him about us."

"I didn't have a chance. I avoided him at the fundraiser, but...I think he knows."

"You tell him, or I will."

"And what about Jolette Marie?"

"What about her?"

"Lincoln, she has a thing for you. It's obvious. Are you going to tell her about us?"

"Way ahead of you. Already did. And she's fine."

Lincoln stood and held out his hand to pull her up. Once more he drew her into his tight embrace. "We better get going. It's getting cold out here and we need to ride back before you freeze your cute ass off."

CHAPTER 15

Sadie found Lincoln's cabin to be nicer than hers. He lived not far from the house on the hill where Hank resided, and ranching operations took place.

"This is roomy."

A one room cabin, but definitely larger than hers.

"Used to be the house where all the cowboys lived years ago, before Hank, and later Jackson and I, were old enough to help."

All one room, with what appeared to be a bathroom toward the back.

"No kitchen?"

"Nah, I'm not much of a cook. And the place didn't have one because the cowboys were always fed at the main house, or the food brought to them outside. Thought about putting one in, but instead I'm probably just going to break ground on a house in a couple of years. Got a few acres not far from here. At least, that's what Hank and Mima want."

"Do *you* want that?"

"Sure." He shrugged. "Someday, it will be good for a family. A long way from now, of course."

"Of course."

She took in the cabin, not surprised by the shades of brown. Leather couch and chairs. The cabin screamed cowboy, with horseshoes on the walls, and many framed photos of rodeos and baseball. But she found a shelf filled with books, too. Quite a few dog-eared John Grisham legal thrillers, which made her smile. She also loved a legal thriller. In between all the books, stood a framed photo of Lincoln, Jackson, and Daisy. All three were much younger, Lincoln probably a teenager. Tall, but rangy, before he'd filled out. Jackson and Daisy were flanked on either side of him in a protective embrace.

She picked up the photo and he came up behind her, arms wrapping around her waist.

"I'd do anything for those two," he said softly.

"I know you would." She set the photo down and turned in the circle of his arms. "And they'd do anything for you."

"Jackson probably would. Not so sure about Daisy some days," he chuckled. "She thinks I'm standing between her and a great love affair with Wade."

"*Wade?* For real?"

"She has a crush on him."

"I had no idea."

"Yeah, well, rodeo cowboys have a way of turning a young woman's head."

"I guess I wouldn't know." She reached to tousle his hair. "I have a thing for a rancher."

"A rancher who's a part-time rodeo cowboy."

"Either way."

He bent to kiss her, one hand on the back of her head, pulling her as close as two people could be. "God, baby. What you do to me."

"What do I do to you?" she whispered.

He gave her an easy smile and tugged on a lock of her

hair. "It ought to be criminal. I can't stop thinking about you, thinking about being inside you again. Trying to figure out new ways I can get my work done faster."

"That doesn't sound too bad."

"Not bad. Kind of addictive." And with that, he swept her up in his arms and carried her to his bed.

Clothes were quickly removed. Boots kicked off. Shirts unbuttoned. Pants discarded and bra and panties removed. But under the sheets, he slowed down and reached for her. His warm palm caressed from her stomach down her thigh in a gentle glide. There had never been a more intimate moment than in those seconds when Lincoln wouldn't break eye contact as one hand continued to roam freely down her body. When he touched her core, she moaned, and his eyes darkened with smoldering heat.

"I could hold you like this for a million years," Sadie said on a sigh.

"And I could hold you for a million and one."

Threading his fingers with hers, he held their joined hands above, while he moved over her. He kissed her, his tongue deep, and plundering. She took every last sweet ounce of him, seeking more. More of the delicious and fiery taste that was all male. All him. He lowered his mouth to her nipple and sucked first one breast then the other until she was one raw nerve of lust. In a frenzy, she stroked him until he groaned.

He quickly rummaged for a condom in his nightstand and protected them both.

"God, Sadie. Baby. So good," he groaned as he pumped into her hard and fast.

Like the first time, the pressure inside her built quickly. Wickedly. Helplessly, she arched against him, delicious pleasure rising like a tidal wave she couldn't hold back. Her breaths came hard and fast and still she wanted more. He'd made her greedy.

"Lincoln, please. Faster. Harder."

She clung to his shoulders, thinking she'd never felt anything this...big. Their connection, the two of them joined together, made her skin too tight. Powerful aches of heady tenderness tugged at her heart. Unrelenting. Moments later, she trembled as tremors of orgasm rocked her body.

Lincoln held her close in the aftermath. "Gets better every time." He brought her hand to his lips and brushed a kiss across her knuckles. "Tell me."

She didn't have to ask what he meant. "I love you."

He got very quiet then, studying Sadie's eyes, tracing the curve of her jaw. "Yeah."

And then he kissed her, so sweet and tender, she heard the words he didn't say.

AFTER DROPPING SADIE OFF, Lincoln headed straight to Hank's to have a word with him. He found him in the kitchen with another drink, staring at his laptop, which he quickly shut when Lincoln walked in. Porn? No way. Didn't sound like Hank, who was rather old-fashioned.

He turned to Lincoln. "What's up?"

"I don't like the way you talked to Sadie tonight."

"Hm. Well, wait until Jackson hears about this. You and Sadie."

"Why should it matter?"

Jackson would have to get over it. Life goes on and all that. But the blame should stop. Maybe Eve shouldn't have walked out on him, but she'd also given Jackson what he wanted. Because Lincoln had a front seat to that show, and he remembered. Jackson was torn between marrying Eve, and an invitation to move to Nashville that was received a mere week before the wedding. He hadn't been raised to walk out on his commitments. Eve did it for him.

If they'd all eventually forgiven Eve, they should also forgive Sadie.

"We need to do whatever it takes to get him to come back home. And this won't help. How's he supposed to sit at the same dinner table with Sadie?"

Lincoln scoffed. "Same as he would with Eve."

"He won't sit at a table with Eve, either, and you know it. Sadie might as well be Eve. She drove Eve home instead of gettin' Brenda, or one of us to talk some sense into her. Just weddin' day jitters, I'm tellin' ya."

"I thought we'd moved on."

He grunted. "Forgiveness is your grandmother's department."

Except for Eve. Hank had forgiven *her*, easily, as if she had no real responsibility for her decision. His favoritism toward Eve verged on the ridiculous.

"I'm thirty-two years old and I'll date whomever I want."

"Well, now, does this mean you're *finally* goin' to settle down?" Hank crossed his arms and leaned back. "You should have been the first headed to Trinity altar."

I love you.

The words sent a spike of something he couldn't quite name. Certainly not fear. He recognized *that* feeling. At first, he'd thought he must have heard wrong. Now, he reminded himself that Sadie loved everyone. He'd heard her often calling out to Eve, "I love you." Heck, he'd even once heard her tell Jackson she loved him. But she'd never told *him* before tonight.

"Take it easy, there. I'm not getting married anytime soon. Too bad if you don't like it but I'm still not ready for all that. I'm just ready... for her."

He scowled. "I'll apologize next time I see her."

That was too damned easy. No argument. Lincoln sat across from Hank. "Think maybe you're drinkin' too much lately?"

"What's too much?"

"Somethin' is going on with you. Admit it."

"Can't a man have a drink now and then? When did you get so damned judgmental? Don't you go to the Shady Grind for a cold beer every chance you get?"

"And that's more about bein' around people than drinkin'. You drink alone, and far too much lately."

"Easy for you to say. You *have* a life. You kids were my life, and now Jackson is gone."

Lincoln scrubbed a hand down his face. "Jesus, Dad. Not this again."

"What?" He glared. "Am I supposed to just give up on him? And now, Daisy. I can't lose another one of my kids."

"What about Daisy? She's not goin' anywhere."

"You never know, she might leave."

"You're crazy. She adores you. Just because she works in Kerrville doesn't mean she's movin'."

"Yeah? And what if she's *not* my daughter? My flesh and blood? Ever think of that?"

"That's what's botherin' you? It's just a nasty rumor. People aren't even talkin' about that anymore. She's a Carver through and through. Obvious to everyone."

"She looks just like your mother."

"So? Doesn't mean she's not yours."

With that, Hank opened the laptop and shoved it toward Lincoln. There, he read an email:

If you have any doubt at all that Daisy Carver might not be your biological daughter, we could dismiss them all with a simple DNA test. Maggie Mae and I had an affair and I suspect Daisy could be my daughter. I just want to know the truth and I promise not to interfere with your lives.

Lincoln froze. Promised not to intervene in their *lives*? He already did with the first damned email. The string of email messages made it clear that Hank had been dealing with this for months. Shit fire! This was all eating away at his old man. All the drinking made sense now. All the bad days. This stranger was slowly and systematically torturing Hank. He adored Daisy, and always treated her like a princess. His only daughter. She could never do wrong where Hank was concerned.

"You should have said something to me," Lincoln said. "You shouldn't have to carry this alone."

Hank tipped his chair back. "It took me a while to believe it wasn't a joke. But I had the man checked out. He's an old rodeo cowboy from Arizona. Get a load of this: he's older than I am. Obviously passed through Texas at some point and met your mother."

"You don't know that."

"I don't know that it *isn't* true."

A punch of guilt ran through Lincoln because he'd been a part of the rodeo circuit scene for a while. And buckle bunnies. Women who got a thrill from being with a cowboy, and easily moved on. He'd never stopped to think some of these women might also be someone's *wife*. Someone's mother. The thought of his own mother, a buckle bunny. He might never get *that* image out of his head. With a home, children, and a husband who loved her, God only knew why that hadn't been enough.

"How did he even know about Daisy? *How* would he know? Seems like if he knew about her, he would have said something sooner than this."

"It's pretty clear to me. Your mother must have contacted him at some point. Maybe after she left us. To tell him he could come pick up his kid if he wanted. As for why he hasn't said anything until now, maybe he didn't want the responsibility. Maybe he'd just like to know her now as a grown woman who might someday give him a kidney. You know, spare parts," Hank said bitterly.

Lincoln's mind filled with thoughts of Daisy, suddenly finding out after being abandoned by her own mother, that the man who'd raised her might not be her real father. Simply put, it would kill her.

This man didn't have the right to randomly pop into her life and destroy it.

"I don't think you should tell her, if that's what's been bothering you."

Hank's body went from one tight and rigid coil to almost limp. If a body could sigh, Hank's did. In relief. "You think so? Is that fair to her?"

"It's protecting her, which is what we're obligated to do. It won't help her to know any of this."

"But if we do the testing, maybe that would stop the stupid rumors."

"Those already stopped. It's taking a risk. A risk we don't need to take. The results won't help Daisy either way."

And the wrong ones would crush her.

Better that Daisy never know there was even a question about her paternity.

"I don't know, son." Hank shook his head. "I can't take the easy way out, much as I want to. What's the right thing to do?"

"Dad, you let me handle this."

Daisy was Hank's huge weak spot. It would be too easy for someone to take advantage of him.

Hank closed his eyes and pinched the bridge of his nose. "What are you going to do?"

"I'll handle it."

With that, Lincoln forwarded the email to himself. If the

man wanted to deal with his family, he'd have to go through Lincoln first.

Though the men took weekends off from work on the old church, every weekday morning when Sadie arrived to the portable next door, she could see the daily progress. By the time they were done, Stone Ridge Elementary would pretty much be a brand-new building. They were currently in the process of completely replacing the roof with the funds they'd raised. Some fundraisers were ongoing, like the knit-a-thon, and her mother's jam.

This bright and crisp autumn morning, she waved to Riggs Henderson, who spent more time than most working on the building. He nodded and proceeded to carry several wooden planks over his shoulder. Lincoln would be joining Riggs for the second part of the day. When Lincoln took his day working on the building, of course, she'd sneak looks outside like a voyeur. It wasn't enough to have him in her bed or be in his more nights than not. She enjoyed finding him outside, a cowboy with a tool belt low on his hips. She hoped for days with warm temperatures when he'd strip down to a T-shirt.

They'd enjoyed one amazing week of getting to know each other, and she fell a little harder every day. She'd make dinner, or he'd bring it. They'd watch Netflix and sometimes he'd agree to re-runs of *The Bachelor*. He only groaned a little, and then enjoyed it much more once he got to poke fun. It became their guilty pleasure.

At the end of the school day, Sadie would always see each child reunited with their parent. One of the many advantages of a smaller classroom. Time for a check-in each day. Sort of a daily teacher parent conference. Most often, she checked in with Pamela Ann. Still no word on Derek. Jimmy Ray remained on his best behavior, which considerably calmed the entire class-room. Even Bobby Joe no longer constantly asked about a snack.

She'd been able to focus on individual lessons plans for the children, place them into similar groups, and monitor their progress. Ellie had already started to identify two-letter blended sounds and simple words. Sadie didn't know which one of them was happier about this.

Sadie was having a mini conference with Ellie's mother, recommending some books to read, when she noticed Judson chatting with some of the parents. She still hadn't talked to him about Lincoln.

"Hello there," Sadie said. "I'm sorry I've been avoiding you."

"Avoiding me?"

"Yes, I wanted to tell you about Lincoln. I told you we were just friends, but that's changed."

"I know," he said. "Mrs. Carver told me."

Thank God for Lillian's eagerness to pry into her grand-children's lives. Thank God, too, that she liked Sadie for Lincoln.

"That was true at the time, but then things changed. Suddenly."

"Take it easy, Sadie." He waved a hand. "You don't owe me anything. It was *one* date."

"That's what I thought, too, but Lincoln wanted me to tell you."

He blinked. "Yeah. I get it. Make sure you told him that you did."

"I will. He's right over there, working with the crew today." She nudged her chin in their direction. "That will be our new school when it's completely renovated."

He glanced over. "I love the sense of community in this town. The way you all come together."

"Yes, it's one of the best parts of Stone Ridge."

"What's the other?"

"All the great men that live here. I guess that's better for the women. Sorry." She cleared her throat. "Um, I just wondered...sorry, but have you considered that you tend to come on too strong? You know, with all your very *specific* plans for you and your future wife."

"Aha. I freaked you out. I tend to do that. It's just I have something specific in mind, and I don't believe in wasting time. Or being dishonest."

"Nothing wrong with that. I used to be a lot like you, but sometimes you have to let things play out. Don't think of it as a waste of time. Just try to enjoy the journey."

"That's...really good advice."

"Well, don't look so surprised. I can give great advice. But what are you doing here? Can I help you?"

His eyes shifty, he wouldn't meet Sadie's eyes. "I've been talking to some of the parents, getting a feel for what they think about a clinic. So far, the feedback is encouraging. But there are a few parents I can never seem to find so I thought I'd come at pickup time."

"That's a great idea. And I'll also ask them on your behalf. I meant to do that anyway." She smiled when from behind Judson she caught Lincoln's eyes and he gave her a sly wink. "Have you found a place to stay?"

"Not yet. You let me know if a cabin becomes available. I drove by and Lake Lupine is beautiful."

"I'll let you know." With everything cleared up between them, she didn't see any harm in him renting a cabin from her father.

"Jimmy Ray!" Derek came out of nowhere, it seemed, walking toward the lot, swaying a little, his arms open wide. "Daddy's here."

He was obviously intoxicated. Protectively, Sadie grabbed Judson's arm. "Maybe you should go."

Judson turned. "Who's *that?*"

"That's Jimmy Ray's father. I need to intervene. You should leave."

Judson didn't, but he took a step back.

Jimmy Ray, who had been playing kickball as he waited for his mother, ran over to his father. "Daddy! You came!"

Sadie stepped between Jimmy Ray and Derek. "Honey, you need to go home with your mother."

"He's comin' home with me," Derek said. "A mother shouldn't keep a father from his boy."

"I'm sure you two can work that out, just not...not here." She clasped a hand on each of Jimmy Ray's shoulders.

"Been tryin' to work it out but she won't talk to me." Derek stood close enough that Sadie could smell the stale whiskey on his breath.

The roiling stench made her gag. "This isn't the place, Derek. Please."

"Don't you get between me and my son."

Jimmy Ray began to whimper quietly beside Sadie.

"You're upsetting your son."

"He'd be fine if you let him go."

"I *can't* let him. Please understand. Pamela Ann didn't say you'd be comin' by to get him. He's my responsibility while at school. She's usually here by now but she must be runnin' late today."

Derek snorted. "Oh, right. Pickin' peaches must be keepin' *her* busy."

More mothers arrived but hustled their children off quickly, after they'd exchanged looks with Sadie and she gave them a quick nod. This seemed the safest course to take.

But she couldn't back down. She was the only link to safety for Jimmy Ray until Pamela Ann arrived. Her voice shook but she didn't let go of Jimmy Ray. Glancing to the roof where Lincoln was working, she didn't see him. She'd be fine. She'd take care of herself.

"Derek, you should leave b-before the men come."

Sooner rather than later, they'd be here. Across the street stood the Shady Grind and plenty of men stopped in for a beer after lunch. And Lincoln would notice this commotion. So would Riggs. She didn't want to see what might happen to Derek then. Not right in front of his son.

"Daddy, I'll see you later, like you p-promised me," Jimmy Ray said, and his tiny little boy voice sounded shaky, too.

Sadie's heart plummeted. No child should be a witness to this.

"Hey!"

The sound rang so rough, loud, and threatening that Sadie jumped. Lincoln advanced on Derek, followed closely by Riggs.

Derek turned to the sound, but seemingly unflappable, scowled. "Go away, Lincoln. This is between me and my son's teacher."

"The hell it is."

Lincoln put his body between Sadie and Derek. Riggs moved behind her. The two men boxed her and Jimmy Ray in a protective circle.

"You have a problem with the teacher, you can talk to me."

"You better go, Derek," Riggs said. "We don't want any trouble."

"I don't, either. Why is it so crazy that I want to see my son?" Derek yelled.

"Not this way," Lincoln said with a stiff jaw. He pushed Derek back ever so slightly. "I believe you've had a few."

She'd never seen Lincoln like this. His tall and imposing frame dwarfed Derek's, even though he was not a small man himself. Fists were tight at this sides. He looked ready to fight. Lord, she hoped it wouldn't come to that. Not in front of poor Jimmy Ray.

Pamela Ann pulled up just then and jumped out of her truck. "Derek! What are you doin' here?"

"I'm here to see my son, woman."

"Not until you clean up your act." Walking past Derek, she took Jimmy Ray's hand and led him away with the confidence and strength of a Mama Bear. "We'll talk then."

"You keep sayin' that!"

Riggs went with them, escorting them toward the vehicle. Walking even faster, Pamela Ann ignored Derek. But Jimmy Ray turned back once more, tears streaming down his face.

And Sadie's heart sliced in two.

Derek backed up, watching as Pamela Ann pealed out of the lot. "Damn it!"

"Time for you to go." Lincoln crossed his arms.

Derek went palms up. "Fine! You can back down. Call off the dogs, *Miss* Sadie. I'm done."

"You're not drivin' anywhere," Riggs said, in no uncertain terms.

"Great." Derek threw his keys to Riggs, outnumbered, outmanned, and outwitted.

"I'll get one of my brothers to pick me up and drive me back here," Riggs called out to Lincoln. "You got this?"

"I'll clean up." He slid an arm around Sadie's waist.

Sadie watched as they drove off, every one of her muscles releasing tension. She trembled. "What just happened here?"

"Derek just showed us that he still hasn't grown up."

"Poor Jimmy Ray."

He hauled her into his arms. "You okay?"

By all rights, she shouldn't be. "I could have taken care of that myself, you know."

He kissed her forehead. "But Riggs and I just couldn't stand by."

"I know."

She both loved and disliked that fact. But she couldn't have expected the men of Stone Ridge to stand by and watch a drunk man try to take his son. At that moment, she noticed Judson standing a few feet away from the portable, under the shade of a tree. He mopped his brow.

"I better go and talk to him. He might be a little shook up."

"Sure. Did you tell him about us yet?"

Incredible that he'd even mention this given what they'd just witnessed. She chose to take that as a compliment and smiled. "Yes, I told him, and he's fine."

"Good."

"We had *one* date, Linc."

"By your own account, he'd already named your children."

"You should be *happy* I went on a date with him. He opened up my eyes."

"That a stretch, but yeah, let's go with that." He smiled, those beautiful blue eyes flashing humor. "How about we head over to the Shady Grind for a cold beer? You look like you need one. Or two."

"I thought we'd decided to wait a while." She cleared her throat. "Beau?"

Lincoln told her that he'd be the one to tell Beau about them.

"He knows." Lincoln met her eyes and tugged on a lock of her hair. "Talked to him this morning. And he's fine with it."

Sadie breathed a sigh of relief. "I knew he'd be reasonable."

"Not exactly. He threatened to punch me into next week

if I ever hurt a single hair on your head. But I would expect nothing less."

Sadie frowned. "He can sound so violent, when I know he's just a pussycat."

"Yeah. That's your brother. A real pussycat," Lincoln said, heavy on the sarcasm.

This would be their first public outing in Stone Ridge as a couple. They weren't exactly a secret, but they also hadn't hung out at the bar since the night they'd left together. And yes, people were still talking about that night.

"Priscilla brought lunch over, and I said I'd return the favor and come by for dinner." He unbuckled his tool belt. "Just give me a little while to finish up here. I'll go home for a shower and change and meet you back here for dinner. Why don't you go by and see Eve after you talk to the doctor?"

"Okay." She gave Lincoln a quick kiss, then joined Judson under the shade of the tree. "Hey, are you okay there?"

"Does this kind of thing happen often around here?"

"Not at all," Sadie said. "You have to understand that the men around here are very protective of the women. There are so few of us, you know. "

"I get it. Your man is pretty impressive over there. It looks like he's used to this."

"He's known Derek for a long time. I don't think he would hurt him. Especially not in front of the boy." Sadie felt compelled to explain and defend Lincoln.

"I have to tell you, I'm worried about Pamela Ann," Judson said.

"So am I." A pinch of hope sprang in her. Nice to see someone else concerned about Pamela Ann. He probably had resources Pamela Ann would need. "We should both keep our eyes and ears open."

"Definitely."

"Hey, Lincoln and I are wandering over to the Shady

Grind later. You should join us for a cold beer, if you feel up to it."

He pinched the bridge of his nose. "Actually, I would appreciate a double Scotch."

"They have that, too."

"Good deal. See ya there."

Waving to Judson, Sadie went to pick up her backpack from the classroom and locked up.

So much had changed since the first day of school when she'd fallen through the floor. Not just between her and Lincoln, but between her and her students. They were making such progress, all of them, but now she couldn't help think that Jimmy Ray might backslide after this display.

Sadie walked to the clinic and found Annabeth sitting behind the receptionist desk, scrunched over her laptop.

She glanced up. "Hey. You know anything about Excel spreadsheets?"

"Oh gosh, *no*."

"Never mind, I'll figure it out." She hooked her finger toward the back. "She's in her office."

Sadie knocked on the door, then let herself in. Eve sat at her desk, staring out the window. Sometimes Sadie forgot that Eve was deaf in one ear, a result of one of the worst years of her life while away at college. She wore a hearing aide in that ear most of the time but still preferred to read lips. As Sadie approached, Eve must have seen her in her peripheral vision.

She smiled and made eye contact. "Hey, there."

"I suppose you didn't hear the commotion outside?"

"No, what happened?"

"I'm still shaking." Sadie gave Eve the details. "I feel a little overwhelmed right now."

"No wonder." Eve quirked a brow. "I'm so glad you weren't alone."

"Poor Jimmy Ray. All I can think about is how *he* must feel right now."

"It's got to be so rough being pulled between your parents like that."

"If Derek were to get help, maybe he and Pamela Ann could get somewhere. But he seems oblivious."

"I know the type." Eve frowned. "Drinking too much can certainly bring out an entirely different side of someone's character."

"You want to go over to the Shady Grind? Lincoln and I are going over for dinner."

"It's time to make it official?"

Sadie shrugged. "Everyone already knows. Even Beau."

"And your parents?"

"We're having dinner on Saturday. My mom is in a bit of denial. She doesn't think it's a big deal to have Lincoln over for dinner even though I tried to tell her why. But Daddy is happy. He loves Lincoln and always has. Unfortunately, Mom is a little disappointed I won't be marrying the doctor."

"Such is life."

"Eve." Sadie swallowed the ball of emotion in her throat. "I'm so in love with Lincoln. I can't help it."

"It's no wonder. You've loved him for years from a distance." Eve stood and coming around her desk put her arm around Sadie's shoulders. "Hey, want to go and see the dogs who are stayin' overnight?"

When Eve first joined the clinic with Annabeth, Sadie would visit often and always wanted to see the pets. She didn't have a dog or cat of her own at the cabin. Growing up, the family always owned dogs and one or two barn cats. Sadie enjoyed roaming the cages and cheering the forlorn doggies up. Separated from their families even for a night usually made their big brown eyes round with fear. This pulled at Sadie's heart and both she and Eve often sang to them, danced, petted them, anything to make them feel more comfortable as they recovered from whatever procedure Annabeth performed on them.

Tonight, the overnight room housed a small King Charles Cavalier, another small mixed dog that looked to be mostly Chihuahua, and a border collie, the most common dog for ranchers. The yips, whimpers, and barks began the moment they walked through the swinging doors.

Sadie wandered down the aisle, checking names and the procedures done. "Want to know a secret? I think Judson might have shown up today just to see Pamela Ann. I can't prove it, though. Unfortunately, he got to be a witness to it all."

"Wow. He certainly moved on fast after you."

"We had one date!" Sadie went hands on hips.

Eve chuckled. "I love to see you this happy. You know that?"

"Sometimes...it feels like a dream. Like any minute I'm going to wake up and Lincoln won't remember who I am."

"That sounds like a nightmare."

"I don't want to ruin this. I don't want to believe that *he* will. It all happened so fast for him, just boom! One night we were forced to spend together and suddenly I'm irresistible to him. What if he changes his mind about me again? That could happen."

"Lincoln doesn't easily change his mind about much, in my experience. But don't let your insecurities get ahold of you."

"What if he's just stringing me along because I lowered my commitment expectations?"

The moment she uttered the words she realized they couldn't be true. She'd told him she loved him. Were he really stringing her along, he'd have run for the hills right then.

"Did you?" Eve quirked a brow, appearing to be more therapist than veterinarian.

"I don't know."

"Yes, you *do* know."

Sadie squirmed. "Am I on trial here?"

Eve laughed. "Answer the question."

She considered the question, one she'd been marinating on for a few days.

"No. I didn't. Because Lincoln is the man I've always wanted. I still want to get married and I want children, but that will come in time. Right? No rush. Therefore, I haven't lowered my expectations. Yes! I have not. Right?"

"So glad we had this talk." Eve closed the door to the overnight room. "Hey, I could do this for a living if this veterinary thing doesn't work out."

"Oh, you're funny." Sadie cleared her throat. "Now, Dr. Iglesias, let's talk about you."

"Me?"

"Yes, you! Because you haven't dated anyone at all since you came back home. And you have your choice of men. Every eligible bachelor has their eye on you. Every Valentine's Day you get more bouquets than any of us. Why won't you go out with a single one of your admirers? The Henderson brothers sure are cute, every one of them, and I think Sean has a crush on you."

"I'm not ready for that."

"Excuse me, but weren't you the one that said I can't let my past define me or how I feel about men?"

"That's different."

Sadie immediately felt a deep pull of regret. She'd been cheated on and betrayed by a man she'd loved, but Eve lost the love of her life to the Nashville music scene. Then, she'd nearly lost her life to a man she'd dated only once.

"But there are similarities. Both of us have to get over our past to move into our future."

"I know, I know. Please don't worry about me. I'll get there. Someday. Just…not now." Eve met Sadie's eyes. "I promise. Okay?"

"All right, I can take a hint. Hey, what about tonight? You comin'?"

"Nah, I have to get home to the kitten I'm fostering. He's needy."

"Why do I think that means you're going to be eating ice cream and binging on Netflix?"

"Hey, don't knock it until you've tried it. I'm watching *Hart of Dixie* for the tenth time. I keep finding things that I missed the first nine times."

"If you want me to stop worrying about you, stop saying stuff like that."

"Can I help it if I like to escape into a southern rom-com?"

"Maybe I should try more of that."

She laughed. "Why not? You're living your own romantic comedy. Lincoln gives you a concussion, and you two wind up in love."

She could use the relaxation and escape right about now. The reminder that there were better men in the world than deadbeat dads who arrived drunk to pick up their kids from school. The hope that there could be a happily ever after even for couples who were having challenges. Even for those who would have to find it in their hearts to forgive.

"Hey."

Sadie turned to the sound of the deep voice she'd recognize anywhere. Lincoln stood braced in the doorway.

CHAPTER 16

The man certainly cleaned up well. One would never guess he'd been pounding nails a short time ago.

"Hi, Linc," Eve said with a little wave. "Y'all have fun tonight."

"Eve's not comin'," Sadie said, moving toward Lincoln.

He put his arm around Sadie's waist but looked to Eve. "Yeah?"

"I've got things to do."

"We'll catch you next time," Lincoln said.

"Love you!" Sadie called out as she said goodbye and promised to catch up with Eve later. "How much of that conversation did you overhear?"

He chuckled. "You mean the part about us living our own romantic comedy?"

"You know Eve. She's such a romantic. We were talkin' about how she's stuck on watching the same rom-com over and over again."

If that upset Lincoln, he didn't say much. He took her hand, and they both walked the few storefronts down to the

Shady Grind, where the dinner crowd was arriving. A bevy of pickup trucks, both old, dirty, and new, were parked in the empty dirt lot next to the bar.

"The thing is, Eve's still not over Jackson," Sadie added, wanting to know Lincoln's thoughts.

The subject of Eve and Jackson was off-limits for years. But they should be able to casually talk about them now.

He squeezed her hand. "Aw, damn. I was afraid of that. Jackson has moved on. She should, too."

"I know. I keep tellin' her that."

"Keep trying. I hate to see her wind up alone forever because she's waitin' for something that will never happen."

"Me, too."

Of course, Sadie thought *she'd* been ready to move on and look what happened there. But their situations were so different. Jackson never came home anymore, and Eve would never leave Stone Ridge again.

Lincoln shook hands with Riggs Henderson, who stood just outside the bar, nursing a beer. She walked inside, still holding hands with Lincoln. The jukebox played a song by Alan Jackson. The din of conversations was loud enough to match the sounds of his electric guitar. Tantalizing smells of fried chicken and burgers wafted from the kitchen.

A couple of the men frowned in their direction, especially the ones who'd brought her flowers after her fall. Another Stone Ridge woman off the market. She smiled, a little apologetically. Unfortunately, she'd always had a thing for the man who'd brought her gum and an ice pack instead of flowers. Romantic as a turnip. But she loved him anyway.

Lincoln led her through the bar heading toward a table, still holding her hand, nodding and smiling to Priscilla.

"Hey, you two!" She gave them a big grin and clasped a hand to her heart, pleased as punch, it would seem.

Sadie smiled back, when out of nowhere, a red whirlwind

came from the left. Jolette Marie flung her arms around Lincoln's neck. "Hiya, big boy."

Conversation all around them dried up to a hush. Lincoln froze in place, but he didn't hug Jolette Marie back. Didn't touch her.

"Hey."

He'd pulled Sadie flush to his side which meant suddenly she found herself extremely close to Jolette Marie. Close enough to see that her eyes were glassy, and she appeared to already be drunk.

The song ended and another one didn't seem to be queued up to take its place. More silence. Someone chuckled and someone else coughed.

"Hey there, Sadie!" Jolette Marie winked at Sadie, but her hands were still on Lincoln. They'd lowered to his chest.

"Someone put another damn song on." This was from Riggs Henderson.

A moment later, the sweet and sultry voice of Miranda Lambert sang out from someone's phone.

Crazy Ex-girlfriend.

"For the love of God," said Riggs. "You idiots."

"Excuse us," said Lincoln. "We're about to have some dinner."

"Sorry," she said, sounding not the least bit sorry. She stepped back. "Didn't mean to interrupt y'all."

Lincoln pushed through the opening, taking Sadie with him, seemingly unaffected by the exchange. But Sadie shook with anger. She wished she'd been the kind of woman who would haul off and slug someone like Jolette Marie.

"What do you want?" Lincoln perused the menu. "I'll go up to the bar and order for us."

"I want to leave," Sadie said. "Let's just go."

"No. I don't want her to ruin our night. She has to understand."

"Is that why we came here tonight? I thought you talked to her."

He met her eyes, and she found warmth in his gaze. Concern. He took her hand under the table. "I did, baby. Tell me you noticed she's drunk."

"Not too drunk to tackle you."

"What did you want me to do? Push her off me?"

But that would be unthinkable. No Stone Ridge man would put their hands on a woman to hurt her in any way. It wasn't Lincoln's fault that Jolette Marie took liberties. Even if it did make her wonder why she felt that she could get away with it. Sadie probably shouldn't say anything. Best not to make waves. She shouldn't mention that she wondered what *exactly* he'd told Jolette Marie. Better to trust.

Just excruciatingly difficult for someone with her history.

"It looks like she still wants you," Sadie blurted.

"She never *had* me to begin with," Lincoln said. "She just wants what she can't have. Why do you think she's been a runaway bride three times? Once she's got herself a fiancé, she goes all the way to the altar before she realizes she doesn't want him anymore. It's a sickness."

"I hate how familiar she is with you. I *hate* it."

"I don't like it, either."

"You're the one that wanted me to tell Judson about us, when we went on one date. How would you feel if Judson threw his arms around me like that?"

"I'd probably slug him for it." He smiled and tugged on a lock of her hair.

Sadie averted her eyes long enough to see Jolette Marie, looking no worse for the rejection, throwing her head back and laughing at something that Riggs Henderson said. Considering *he* didn't look happy, Sadie wondered what could possibly be that funny.

Or was she laughing at everything and *everyone* tonight?

Maybe laughing at Sadie, finding her too trusting and stupid? Because she didn't know that they were still carrying on behind her back? That sick feeling in the pit of her stomach made a reappearance tonight. Was she going to be the last one to know again? She'd promised herself never again to accept the delusion that people were basically good at heart. To believe that friends wouldn't keep something important from her. Friends were supposed to prevent you from looking stupid and...naïve.

Maybe she was also wrong about Lincoln loving her. After all, he'd never said the words. She could be completely delusional. Sadie gnawed at her lower lip, pushing back tears with the pads of her fingers. A small part of her still wished everyone liked her. She'd always wanted to be everyone's friend.

"Sadie, are you alright?" This came from Judson, suddenly at their side.

"She's fine," Lincoln answered for her between gritted teeth.

"I'm good but thanks for asking."

Judson waved and walked to the bar.

"What's he doing here?" Lincoln said.

"I invited him."

Lincoln quirked a brow.

"He was very frightened by what happened today with Derek!"

"Yeah."

"And he didn't exactly grab me tonight or anything."

Of course, Lincoln would likely slug him, and Judson was a smart man.

"Baby, please, let's not do this."

Lincoln hadn't done anything for her to doubt him. Then again, neither had her ex, and she'd been blind to the signs.

And how would she know if she was doing the same thing all over again?

"Okay." Lincoln took her hand across the table. "Let's go."

Intent on ignoring Jolette Marie, Sadie let Lincoln take her hand and lead her out of the bar. Without words, they quietly walked holding hands to his truck parked between the portable and old church.

"Where to now?" he asked.

"I want to go home."

"Okay." He helped her into his truck.

She wanted to be alone. Lincoln made it difficult to think straight. He made her feel, dozens of emotions like desire, lust, fear, pride, and overwhelming love. She needed to *think*. To figure out a few things because no one would ever make a fool out of her again. Ever.

When they arrived, he walked her to the door as he always did. But as she unlocked it, she turned to him. "I…I think I want to be alone."

He narrowed his eyes. "Why?"

"I have a lot to think about."

"I get it, baby, you're mad, but we have a lot to *talk* about."

"But I can't *think* when you're around."

"Then you need to start." He pressed her body against his. "Talk to me."

"No. My feelings haven't changed, it's just that I…this is about me. I need a little time."

"Okay," he said, releasing her and backing up. "Take all the time you need. I'm not goin' anywhere."

Sadie let herself inside, shutting the door gently. Back against it, she slid to the ground and let the ugly tears fall. Wet, sloppy tears that ran down her cheeks and made her breathing uneven. She obviously hadn't moved on. And though she'd been on lots of dates, most men didn't have the patience for this type of jealousy and insecurity. They'd just moved on. And if she wasn't careful, so would Lincoln.

She'd make this a self-fulfilling prophecy. Self-sabotage.

She didn't want to let "Cheater" ruin the rest of her future life, but this was about more than an unfaithful boyfriend. This was about her, too. She'd been too sweet, too trusting, too gullible. She didn't want to be that woman again. Instead, she wanted to be wise and sophisticated. A little bit more like Jolette Marie, who seemed to bounce back for the most part. She owned the kind of confidence that Sadie envied.

Right now, though, Sadie wanted that woman out of her mind. She didn't want to think about her and Lincoln together. There were two people in this relationship, not three.

If they still had a relationship after tonight.

Oh, my Lord, what had she done?

Wiping away her tears with the backs of her hands, she stood. Maybe Lincoln was still here. He might be sitting in the truck since she hadn't heard it drive away. She could explain that she'd been temporarily insane for about ten minutes. Sadie flung open the door to find him sitting on the porch, his back pushed up against a wall, his Stetson tipped so that it covered his eyes. His arms and long legs were crossed at the ankles, and he appeared to be settling in for the night. When he heard her, he re-positioned his hat to see her.

So, the "I'm not going anywhere" remark was literal. "You didn't go." Relief flooded her.

"Ready to talk already?" He winked. "I thought I'd at least get a catnap out here."

"Y-you were going to stay here all night, weren't you?" A smile tightened her cheeks almost to the point of pain.

"If that's what it takes." He stood.

"You really want to be here." The thought momentarily baffled her.

"I don't know how else I can show you. It won't be easy to get rid of me."

She barely resisted the urge to launch into his arms and forget everything, if he would be willing to do the same. "You're right, we should talk."

Outside, they were less likely to jump right into bed and resolve this problem at least for now. She took a seat on the top step of her balcony and he did the same.

He studied her. "You were crying. Baby, I never want to be the reason you cry."

She leaned into his shoulder, relishing the contact. "I meant to tell you this the first night we were together. I've already been with someone who said all the right things, who *did* all the right things. There were no signs, or if there were, I didn't see them. Too naïve to know what was happening right in front of me. Everyone else knew before I did. It's a horrible feeling to be blindsided like that. Remember when you told me you'd been angry and bitter after your mother left? I was angry, too, for a long while. For a different reason."

He went silent for a beat before he squeezed her tight. "You're going to tell me why?"

"I'm going to tell you everything."

In the next few minutes she told him about Martin. Not just *his* betrayal, bad enough, but that of so many of her so-called friends, leading her to conclude that no one had any real respect for her. She'd been the good girl, the nice girl, the friend, and apparently to them, a doormat. She ended by explaining that even though she'd always been careful, she'd been tested for diseases and received the all clear.

Lincoln quietly listened, simply holding her close. "Jesus, baby. I'm so sorry."

"That's okay. All in the past. But if he showed up here tomorrow, I'd probably...spit on him."

Lincoln chuckled. "You'd have to beat me to it."

"So, now you see why I want honesty above all else." She pulled back, searching his eyes. "And when you didn't even try to hide the fact that you snuck into my bed without permission and slept with me all night, I knew I could trust you to be honest. Even when it hurts. Oh, and also that time you said that I shouldn't read anything into you helping me, because you'd do the same for anyone you'd accidentally hurt."

He winced. "Obviously, things have changed."

"You're a good man. Maybe you're not romantic, but you're honest to a fault. I've been learning to trust myself again, and I'll get there. Maybe I backslid a little tonight, because of Jolette Marie. But I trust my instincts. I'd trust *you* with my life."

"You can. I will never hurt you." He kissed her, a sweet and tender short kiss that wrapped around her heart in a sweet ache.

"And...Jolette Marie?" Sadie asked, knowing after today, they'd had something between them. "How long did you two date?"

She'd noticed the longing looks Jolette Marie threw Lincoln's way. She'd expected to be able to go looking for Jimmy Ray with Lincoln. Sometimes Sadie didn't like to hear the raw and honest truth, but she wanted to know anyway. No one would ever make a fool out of her again.

"I wouldn't call it dating, and it's over. We didn't have a real relationship and that's the way we both wanted it. I haven't seen her in months, since before my last circuit. I've already talked to her. Whatever we had, and believe me, it was casual, it's over now. She isn't handling it well."

"I want to be the only woman you're sleeping with. I don't like to share."

"Neither do I, and even if I've never settled down, I'm a one woman at a time kind of guy."

"The man I was with said the same thing to me. And so many of my so-called friends mistook my kindness for weakness."

"And I hate that for you, but you're going to need to trust me. I'm not him. I'm not that guy who says things just because a woman wants to hear them. Hell, I almost missed out on what we have because I told you the raw and honest truth. How would I know that you'd take me any way you could? I'm damned lucky."

"I know you're different. I told you, this is my problem."

"Which makes it my problem."

"Is it too much to want to be classy, cool, and sophisticated? When I'm all of those things, then maybe weird things like what happened tonight won't bother me so much." She shimmied her shoulders. "I'll just shake it off."

He grinned at the reference to her favorite singer and ran his hands up and down her spine. "Hell, no. Don't you change. I want you to care. Don't want you to be anyone other than who you are. You're sweet, but you're my kind of sweet. You're trusting, and you've trusted the wrong people in the past. That's not on you, baby. It's on them."

"But I hate my stupid insecurities."

"Listen. I'd lay money that if we don't work out, it will because of me. Something I did or didn't do."

An icicle slid down to her heart. "Like what?"

"Bring gum instead of flowers? Spend too much time on the ranch? Make you mad because I forgot an anniversary? I can think of a lot of reasons you might dump me. You'd better believe it won't be because I *cheat*." He stood and held out his hand. "Come here."

CHAPTER 17

"*W*here are we going?"

Lincoln took Sadie's hand and led her to the lake. "I should ask you. Show me that tree you like."

"Right this way."

He let her lead, wanting a distraction, and wanting to get them past this weird night. He'd give anything to change what happened tonight. But he'd been frozen in place when Jolette Marie pounced on him. She was drunk or wouldn't have resorted to that sleazy tactic. She'd done it simply to unnerve Sadie, or maybe to piss him off.

This happened to be the one time in his life when he wanted a woman to trust him completely, and know she could.

He'd seen firsthand the way jealousy ruined relationships. He wondered if his mother would have stayed if Hank tried to appease her. As the oldest, he knew far more than he should have about his parents. He remembered late nights with yelling matches between Hank and Maggie Mae, including wild accusations from her:

You love her.

You still do.

I'm just your second choice because she wouldn't have you.

And the worst one of all:

You married me because I got pregnant.

Unfortunately, he'd never once heard Hank deny any of this. Maybe he had, behind closed doors. Lincoln wouldn't know. But if he'd calmed her fears, she wouldn't have been so insecure that she'd an affair. She might not have left them. Somehow, she'd never believed she came first with Hank, or that he loved her enough.

The whole ordeal left Lincoln with bitter memories. He'd been inclined from the first of his interest in women to keep entanglements light and shallow. Never permanent. Because his mother's brand of love was possessive and conditional. She'd tossed the word "love" around like it was a salad. Lincoln had made up his mind that when he told a woman he loved her he'd somehow have to be ready for the constant assurances that would follow. Ready for the feeling of a noose tightening around his neck daily. And he'd never reached that point.

With Sadie, it seemed different.

For one thing, he'd suddenly found himself on the other end. Wanting assurances that the doctor was out of the picture. Incredible. He'd hardly believed the words coming out of his own mouth when he'd said them.

She'd been betrayed not by just one person she trusted but by several, so no wonder Sadie doubted her own judgement. But everything he'd seen firsthand told him that there was nothing wrong with her intuition now.

Lincoln would be damned if he'd allow Jolette Marie, or the doctor, to get between him and Sadie. They'd reached a tree with knotted roots, and a canopy of branches almost touching the surface of the lake water.

"This is it." Sadie stopped.

He pulled her into his arms, hands gliding down to rest on her behind. "You're right. Kind of ghostly."

"Scary. And no match for your stars."

"Are you scared of this spooky tree? Tell me you're scared, little girl. Your big bad man will protect you."

"You're funny." She turned to him, and belly to belly, she stretched to thread her fingers through his hair.

He barely resisted groaning. Damn, those were magic fingers. "We didn't get a chance to do something I'd planned for tonight."

She quirked a brow and the expression made him laugh.

"Dance. We didn't get a chance to *dance*."

"Do you dance?"

"Not very well."

"I bet that's not true, cowboy. Something tells me you do *everything* quite well."

"Baby, you flatter me, but I assure you that's not true. I can't sing, either." With that, he lowered his head and began to slowly move with her in his arms, a Brad Paisley ballad in his head.

"With no music?" She smiled up at him. "See how talented you are?"

"It's in my head." He continued to move slowly, leading her, but were he being honest, simply enjoying the holding her part. No music required.

"Care to share?" He heard a hint of teasing in her tone.

"That's my brother's territory." Even so, he began to hum, doing his best. Hopefully he wasn't too terrible.

Once, Jackson told Lincoln that he could at least *carry* a tune. High praise indeed. But his humming must have been adequate because she stopped all the teasing, and laid her head on his chest, sighing.

"I love you, Lincoln."

He loved hearing those words. She made him feel like he was the only man in the world ever to hear them. He tipped her chin to meet his eyes, hoping she could read them and know that even though he couldn't quite get the words out yet, damn, he felt it in his heart. Something large and unyielding tugged at him.

"Tell me again."

"I love you."

She always gave the words to him again, because hers was the biggest heart of anyone he'd ever known.

"This is so much better than dancing at the Shady Grind. I have you all to myself in case I step on your foot," she said, and a few minutes later, tilted her head. "Hey. I just realized that we didn't eat any dinner."

"We could fix that."

"Yes. I'm finally going to cook you a big dinner."

"There's something I don't hear every day. As if you've been waiting for the day to cook for me." Raising her arm, he twirled her once. Look at that, she didn't fall. "You don't have to cook."

"You're going to love my cookin'. Fried chicken?" She waggled her eyebrows. "Or are you like Hank and want some beef?"

"Girl, you will never hear me say no to fried chicken."

This is where he felt most at home. Comfortable. No drama. Light, breezy, carefree. And his job to keep it that way.

ON THE FOLLOWING SATURDAY, Sadie didn't find a way to get out of helping the ladies of SORROW with the knit-a-thon they were hosting in Trinity Church's basement. Considering the results would benefit her, it felt wrong not to participate, even if her knitting pace reminded her of a snail. She'd be lucky to complete one of these knit caps in two years at her rate. The ladies could bang them out in a couple of hours.

When she arrived, Lillian sat near the wide table filled with colorful yarn. She patted the empty chair closest to her.

"Anyone heard from Eve?" Sadie asked as she took a seat.

"She was over at the ranch this mornin', but then headed out to a call. Ed's mare is calving. She'll be here when she's done," Lillian said.

"Lillian, congratulations are in order, I hear," said Beulah, passing a skein of yarn. "Sounds like another young lady has chosen herself a Carver man."

The ladies had obsessed with which man of Stone Ridge Sadie would choose to be her husband for years. It stopped while she lived away but the minute she'd come home the speculation didn't stop. Neither had the blind dates, each one more ridiculous that the last.

"We're getting to know each other."

Lillian bit her lower lip, hardly able to squash a huge grin. "Yes, well, Sadie has *great* taste."

Ada sniffed. "I thought my nephew was a wonderful choice. He would be for any young lady."

"He's a wonderful man, Ada," Sadie said, taking her skein out and placing it on the table. "Thank you for introducin' me. I think we'll be great friends."

"Great friends are *not* what I had in mind," Ada said, looking at Sadie over lowered spectacles. "I still think you should consider him."

"Well, I—" Sadie began.

"If this here thing doesn't work out with Lincoln, I'm sure she will," Beulah said, patting Ada's hand.

That seemed to pacify Ada for now, never mind that if this "thing" didn't work out with Lincoln, Sadie probably wouldn't be good to anyone. She refused to agree, not wanting to jinx anything with Lincoln. Some women loved their many choices. Sadie did not. She'd wanted to settle down since she was about twelve and first laid eyes on Lincoln Carver.

"How's your mom 'n 'em?" asked Maybelle, Beulah's sister. "Why isn't she here?"

Sadie struggled with her needles, as per the usual. She was all thumbs when it came to this sort of stuff. "She's home doing some canning. It's peach season."

"Lawd, that woman and her jam." Ada shook her head.

"It's award-winning," Lillian said. "She's already made her contribution to the cause."

Grateful for Lillian's defense, Sadie didn't add anything. Truth be told, her mother had executed a metamorphosis from the woman who'd raised her, knitting, baking, sewing, and for a short time even leading Sadie's Girl Scout troop. She might be obsessed with her business now, but Sadie didn't see any harm in that. If it made her happy and gave her life purpose, she couldn't argue.

"Anyway, I'm sure she's gettin' ready for tonight. Lincoln and I are going over for dinner."

Sadie wound the thread around her needle like she should, but when she tried the other needle, the knot slipped. She tried again. Everyone was already way ahead of her.

"See there, she has a perfect excuse. I'd be cleanin' all day to impress my future son-in-law," Lillian added and elbowed Sadie.

"Let's not get ahead of ourselves, Lillian," Maybelle said. "*My* boys are still single."

And the way things looked to Sadie, they would remain that way. All three played video games twenty-four seven from their worn-in couch.

"I'm not sure Lincoln is all that ready to get married," Sadie said, preoccupied with the knot that wouldn't keep.

She should have realized her remark would stop conversation. Self-conscious, Sadie looked up from her knitting.

Ada stared at her, appearing dumbfounded. "Then what on *earth* are you doin' with him?"

"I wouldn't say that my Lincoln isn't ready," Lillian protested.

"Sadie, hon, your eggs have *got* to be gettin' on in age," Maybelle said. "There's no time to waste."

Again with the eggs!

"I'm twenty-eight! And we're gettin' to know each other."

"Bah!" Beulah said. "You've known that boy all your life. What more do you need to find out about him?"

"Now." Lillian put up a hand. "We all realize there's a way that two young people get to know each other when they're considering married life and how they fit together."

"Lillian!" Rather than stunned silence, Beulah now gasped. "You don't mean—"

Sadie squirmed and chose silence as her best recourse. She pretended to be fascinated with her knitting, when realistically, she'd created a tangle of yarn for Eve's kitten.

"Why, getting to know each other's families better, sharin' hobbies, cookin' dinner, that kind of thing," Lillian said. "What did you *think* I meant?"

"Good Lawd," Beulah said, blushing and fanning herself. "Nobody but you can make me feel like *I've* got the dirty mind!"

With that, they all burst into laughter.

WHEN SADIE and Lincoln pulled up to her family home later, Sadie judged the house in a new light. Even though he'd come to her home many times over the years, now Sadie noticed the dilapidated state of the ranch style home. The house could use painting, the blue siding chipped. Her father, the contractor, hadn't updated his own home in years much to her mother's irritation, who found it ironic. This never bothered Sadie because her father worked hard and shouldn't have to come home after a long day to work on his own house. He put most of his home efforts into his vineyard.

"You okay?" Lincoln squeezed her hand. "I should be the nervous one."

She'd never tell Lincoln that her mother's obvious preference for Judson unnerved her. But Lincoln would win her over. Eventually.

"You're not, are you? You've been over here so many times over the years with Beau and Wade."

"Not like this." He leaned over and kissed her tenderly.

"Maybe we should sit here and make out for a while. Just to get you more comfortable." She squeezed his forearms, then tugged on the nape of his neck, bringing him closer where she could gaze into his baby blues.

"I like the sound of that." His eyes shimmered with humor.

But a few minutes later, they were at the front door, holding hands. Lincoln carried a bottle of California wine for her father, knowing how to at least get on *his* good side.

Mom swung open the door, wearing her "Your opinion wasn't in the recipe" apron. "Hello, there."

"Hi, Mrs. Stephens," Lincoln said, holding out his bottle of wine.

"Thank you. Mr. Stephens will be thrilled." She waved them in, and Sadie led the way to the dining room. "We're already sitting down to dinner."

At the entrance to the room, Sadie stopped so suddenly that Lincoln bumped into her. Judson Grant sat at the table.

"Sadie, how lovely to see you." He stood, but froze when he noticed Lincoln and gave him a shaky nod. "H-hello."

"Judson," Lincoln said.

"Hi, Judson." Sadie searched for something smart and witty to say. "Um…"

"I take it everyone here knows each other?" Mom breezed in. "Sadie, you sit here next to Judson. Don't look at me like that. I invited *Dr.* Grant because he's new in town and looked hungry."

"I didn't—" Judson began. "I mean—"

"I'm sitting next to Lincoln," Sadie said in no uncertain terms.

"Yes, of course," Mom said, waving her hand in their direction. "I thought you'd sit between Lincoln and Judson."

"Perfect," Sadie muttered under her breath.

This unfortunately reminded her far too much of the time when Sadie was sixteen and her mother invited two boys over for dinner that she believed were both adequate prospects to take Sadie to the junior prom. Never mind that Sadie didn't want to go with either one of them.

As usual, Dad joined them at the table last, and he did a double take at seeing both Lincoln and Judson flanking Sadie. He sent a silent question to his wife, slowly shaking his head.

"Hi, Daddy," Sadie said, sliding him an equally silent SOS.

"Hello, sweetie," Dad said, bending to kiss the top of her head. "Lincoln, great to see you, son. And I guess you must be the doctor."

"Judson Grant, sir."

"I hope you like pot roast," Mom said, joining them.

"Love your pot roast," Lincoln said.

Mom smiled at Lincoln, then directed her attention to Judson. "Lincoln has eaten with us many times. He's a friend of my son, Beau. They practically grew up together. But please tell us about you, Judson. How long have you been a doctor?"

Sadie turned to Judson, who pulled out his pager. "I apologize. I-I've just been paged."

"I didn't hear anything," Mom said.

"It's on silent buzz. I didn't want to interrupt dinner should it go off."

"That's a shame," Mom said. "We haven't even started eating yet."

"Duty calls." He stood and shook her father's hand, then Lincoln's. "I apologize but this happens sometimes. Life of a doctor. You understand."

He patted Sadie's shoulder and then made fast tracks to the front door.

"Nice seeing you," Sadie called out. The poor man.

"I'll be right back," Lincoln said and followed Judson out.

"That's strange," Mom said. "Who could be paging him? I thought he hadn't even set his practice up yet."

"Wanda," Daddy said. "What did you do?"

"Oh, for the love of Pete, you're both looking at me like I've committed a high crime! Is it wrong for Sadie to see all the possibilities open to her?"

"Only when I'm single!"

"I do not see a ring on that finger, young lady." Mom shook a finger. "And a *doctor* could give you a comfortable life. Seems worth considerin'."

Sadie stood. "You insulted both of these men tonight. Lincoln, because you obviously can't accept him as anything but Beau's friend. Poor Judson didn't deserve this, either. Did you see how he ran out of here? He's terrified of Lincoln!"

"Oh, dear. Well, I'll apologize to him. I didn't mean to offend him."

"You'll apologize to Lincoln, too," Daddy said. "If you think there's something wrong with Sadie marrying a rancher, then maybe you think there's something wrong with the man *you* married, as well."

Sadie sucked in a breath. She heard the pain in her father's words and the kick to her stomach was strong enough for her to lose her appetite. "Daddy."

"Don't be ridiculous," Mom said. "Lincoln is a *rodeo* cowboy, too."

"So?" Sadie crossed her arms.

"You don't think I've heard all the stories? I *know* what a buckle bunny is."

"Dear God, Wanda," Daddy said, shaking his head. "Are we having dinner or not?"

"Sorry, dear. Are we taking up too much of your time? Want to go back out to the vineyard and sweet-talk the grapes some more? Go on, we can wait."

Her father sneered. "Why? What did I miss? Got a new item for my honey-do list?"

"Item twenty-one is still waiting. And it's only been five years!"

Sadie resisted covering her ears as the bitter fest went on. She'd never heard her parents argue like this and suddenly she was worried about a lot more than her mother's lame matchmaking attempts.

LINCOLN GOT to Judson just as he'd clicked the door open to his black BMW.

"Sorry about tonight," Lincoln said, offering his hand.

He believed he'd somehow scared Judson and wanted him to realize he wasn't spoiling for a fight. Having solved problems early on in life, Lincoln believed he could fix almost anything. And he wanted to clear things up between him and Judson.

"I'm the one who's sorry." Judson shook. "When Wanda

invited me over for dinner, I thought it would simply be family."

"But you did expect Sadie to be here."

He shrugged. "I wouldn't have minded either way."

"Look, I apologize if I gave you the wrong impression the first night we met." Lincoln tipped his hat and scratched his temple. "Because I've been a little slow on the uptake."

"You?" Judson cocked his head, looking doubtful.

"I'm kind of an idiot when it comes to romance."

"That's hard to believe."

"Believe it. Sex is one thing. Love is quite another. But listen. I have no doubt you're the better bet for Sadie."

"What? No, I—" Judson backed up a step, putting up his hands.

"Seriously. I'm not going to hit you. Obviously, you're a doctor, you're on time, you bring flowers, you call. I'm a rancher, I don't drive a luxury sedan, I'm rarely on time for a date, I forget to call first, and don't bring flowers."

"Gee, don't be so hard on yourself. There must be some reason Sadie chose you."

Lincoln chuckled, moving in for his final statement that would clear the air once and for all.

"Don't worry. I'm not going to give her up. I can work on all that other stuff. It took me a long time to notice her, but I'm not walking away from her easily. No matter what you, her mother, or anyone else thinks about me."

"Sounds like she chose the right man."

When Lincoln walked back inside the house, there remained a strange tension in the air.

"I apologize," Wanda said, turning to Lincoln. "This should have been a dinner with our family, you, and Sadie. I didn't mean to insult you."

"She really didn't, son," Mr. Stephens said. "You're already like part of our family."

"Not a problem. I like Judson. Good man." He squeezed Sadie's hand because she looked more worried than she should be.

If she thought *this* would scare him off, then she had no idea how tough this cowboy could be.

CHAPTER 18

*I*t took a couple of email exchanges for Lincoln to cement plans to meet the man who claimed he could be Daisy's father. Rusty Jones agreed to meet at a diner in San Antonio, far away from prying small town eyes. From time to time over the years, Lincoln frequented the Greasy Spoon with some of his rodeo circuit friends. Rusty should feel right at home.

Lincoln, not so much. He might be just a bit freaked out that he would be meeting an old rodeo cowboy who'd enjoyed buckle bunnies so much he might have an illegitimate child who'd been raised by another man. For now, Lincoln refused to believe that it might be true. He was simply smart to go on a fact-finding mission on behalf of his father. On behalf of Daisy. As an added bonus, if he found out some more information on his mother, no harm done.

For years, he'd been curious about where she'd gone and with whom. Never disloyal enough to Hank to look her up, but nevertheless interested, though after a while no one else cared. Lincoln figured this was because he, as the oldest, remembered her best. Whether or not he shared any information obtained about his mother with the rest of his family, he'd consider later.

The morning was cold, tinged with a heavy hint of a true autumn. Lincoln arrived early, as he'd planned. The smell of bacon, coffee, and hash browns hung thick in the air. The din of dishes clattering and customers chatting were comforting. Routine.

"Hey, cowboy." Opal Ray slapped a menu down. "Breakin' any hearts today?"

"Hope not," he said. "But I am meeting someone."

"Of course you are." She put down another menu, smiling wryly. "Good luck with that. Coffee?"

"Yup."

He winced because she'd witnessed his, for lack of a better word, "dates." She obviously assumed this morning was more of the same. This was his "kiss off" joint. His "it's not you, it's me" place. Far away from Stone Ridge, and in a public area so he could avoid a scene. Not that he ever expected one, but after getting slapped in a parking lot once, he played it safe. He didn't mind the slap, being tough enough to take it. He did care about the hurt associated when a woman took a swing at him.

He'd never intended to hurt anyone and always wanted to let a woman down gently. Easy. Break it off in such a way where she believed it was her idea. So that she understood she deserved better than him because, more often than not, this was the genuine truth. After a while, he'd become a master, though he wasn't proud of that fact.

He'd wanted to change that part of his life, but just a few weeks ago, tired and stressed, he'd almost slid back into old and set patterns. Nearly allowed finding someone temporary to be his cure for the stress building in him. No strings. And then Sadie…happened. His entire life changed. Hadn't seen that coming. But he still wondered whether *he* possessed what it took for a relationship to last. For the marathon behind a real and lasting marriage like his grand-parents had.

A Google search on Rusty showed old photos of him so Lincoln knew what to expect. But even so, he'd have pegged the sixty-five-year-old slightly bowlegged man that ambled inside the diner as the retired Wrangler World Champi-onship rodeo rider. He looked a lot older than Hank, who at fifty-five, already had a full head of white hair.

Lincoln raised a hand to get his attention, and the man strode in his direction and slid in across the booth from him. "Ya must be Lincoln. Thank ya for meetin'."

"Go ahead and order whatever you want," Lincoln said, sliding the menu across the table. "It's on me. We'll sit here for a few minutes. I'm willin' to listen to what you have to say."

"What about Hank?"

"He couldn't make it," Lincoln lied.

"Ah," Rusty said. "Can't say that I blame 'im."

Opal Ray came by and took their orders. Not hungry, Lincoln ordered flapjacks anyway.

Rusty ordered a banquet. Flapjacks, grits, bacon, eggs over easy, sausage, and coffee. Made Lincoln wonder about the last time Rusty ate a full meal. Then again, Lincoln could also put the food away when he didn't have a rock the size of Texas sitting in the pit of his stomach. He didn't want this man to destroy his family, and if he were right about his mother, Rusty could do that. And Daisy would never be the same.

He doubted any of them would be.

"When's the last time you saw my mother?"

"First of all," Rusty said, taking a swig of his coffee. "I want to let ya know this ain't easy for me, neither. Not proud of the life I led. All I cared about was mahself, the rodeo, and mah buckles. Mah wins. In my defense, I didn't have much family to speak of."

Lincoln ignored that and steered the conversation. "Maggie Mae Carver was my mother's name."

Rusty blinked. "I know. The last time I saw her, she claimed she'd left y'all. We had some fun, and she was off again. I thought probably right back to 'er family. You have to understand, the first time we met, I had no idea she was a married woman."

"Yeah. Figured she didn't announce that." Lincoln took a swig of his coffee. "But the second time?"

"Like I said, not proud of that. Ya probably know what the circuit scene is like. You a good lookin' man. Must have to peel 'em off ya."

Lincoln cleared his throat. "Back to my mother."

"It's awkward talkin' to a son about this. This is your *mother*."

"No time to be shy. It's not like I hold her in high regard. And we haven't seen her since she left."

"*Never* again?"

"For all we know, she's no longer among the livin'."

He'd considered it. Maggie Mae wasn't close to her parents, either, leaving her home somewhere in Oklahoma at age fifteen. There would be no other family ties, or anyone who would contact them about her death. The attorney Hank hired for the divorce sent the dissolution papers to an address in Galveston, the last known address for her.

"Lord, hope not." The food arrived and Rusty wasted no time digging in as if this might be his last meal. He spoke between bites. "Would be such a shame. Gorgeous woman, your mother."

"The last time you saw her. Is that when she told you about Daisy?"

Rusty's fork paused midair. "That 'er name? Daisy?"

"Daisy Lee *Carver*." Lincoln put the emphasis where it belonged.

"Look, I don't want anythin' from y'all. Or from her. I just need to know." Rusty took another bite and chewed, seeming to silently assess Lincoln. "Your mother contacted me a few months after the last time I saw her. Said she was divorced now, and that her little daughter could be mine."

Lincoln's gut clenched. He'd been about to take a bite of flapjacks before they got cold. "You mean *she* wasn't even sure?"

Rusty closed his eyes and pinched the bridge of his nose. "That's why I wanted to talk to Hank, man to man. This ain't somethin' a son should hear about his own mother."

Irritation and anger pressed through him. Had he been informed by a woman that he could be the father of her child, he'd have insisted on a DNA test. He'd have to know *immediately*. No way a child of his would be wandering the world not knowing his real father.

"And you waited all these years to look us up?"

"Yeah," he said, shoulders slumped. He patted his mouth with the paper napkin. "I didn't settle down till my fifties. I quit the circuit and went to work for my brother as an auto mechanic in Dallas. Been leadin' a quiet life. Never had a wife, no kids. And mostly, I tried not to think about the girl. Figured she was better off with the man that she believed was her father."

"Hank *is* her father. And you're right about that. She's better off so why find us now? Do you need something?"

Rusty didn't look too healthy. Maybe Hank was right about his intentions.

"I'm sure I deserve that," Rusty said with a scowl. "But no. Don't need anythin' from y'all. Might even have somethin' to leave to *her* someday."

"She doesn't want for anything. Our family owns a cattle ranch and we do okay. Daisy's an auto mechanic."

Rusty smiled. "Is that right?"

Now that Lincoln figured he wouldn't hear much more about his mother, or at least anything he'd want to hear, negotiations could begin. It didn't escape Lincoln that if Rusty found Hank, he could also find Daisy. No point in trying to hide her. Rusty wouldn't need any of them to approach her once he located her and he could proceed to upend her entire world. Therefore, Lincoln should be reasonable. Appeal to the man's sense of decency, and hope he had some.

"Here's what I think," Lincoln began. "I might have felt differently if you'd come around a long time ago, but now... look, no good can come from this. Just learning that there's any question about her paternity would be harmful enough for Daisy. We'd have to go through the entire ordeal even though there's clearly a fifty-fifty chance she could still be Hank's."

"What are you sayin'?"

"I'm sayin' that I'd like you to walk away. Forget about Daisy. Listen, she's *not* your daughter."

"We don't know that. She's an auto mechanic, just like me."

"But even if biology were to tie you, she's very close to our father. Learning this would destroy her, when there might not be any need."

"I see."

"Am I makin' sense to you?"

Rusty chuckled, shaking his head. "Feel like I'm lookin' at myself, thirty years ago. You think you have all the answers. I did, too. I was a cocky sum'a bitch. Only cared 'bout the buckles and the bunnies. Havin' myself a grand ol' time.

Never thought I'd have need to settle down with one woman. What for, when there were so many?"

They were both quiet for a moment, Lincoln hoping to God Rusty was wrong. He wanted to believe that he was more like Hank, who devoted himself to his family. But at the moment he feared there were too many similarities with Rusty than he cared to consider.

"Can I at least see her? She don't have to know who I am. But I don't know how many years I have left."

"Why? Are you sick?"

"Nope but won't live forever."

Lincoln bristled, his gut churning. A memory slid through him of waiting in the chute straddling an eager Lucky, waiting for his turn. He could beat the time. Or lose. In the end, it was always a gamble. A risk.

There was only one way he'd agree to Rusty seeing Daisy and he hoped Rusty could see the sense in it.

"From a distance," Lincoln said carefully. Slowly. "One look. If that's all you want, to see her, you'll agree. This way, she isn't hurt. You get what you want, and we protect her."

"I ain't all that picky. Maybe that would be for the best."

After the meeting, Lincoln drove straight to Daisy's place of work. He wouldn't have admitted it but hearing about Rusty's auto profession unnerved him. Daisy had been interested in mechanics from a young age, always working on Jackson's matchbox cars with her plastic tools when other girls played with dolls. She did some of that, too, on occasion. One side of Daisy was decidedly feminine, and another side made her just one of the guys.

He found her in one of the auto bays, filling out some paperwork. She strode over to him, her mechanic jumpsuit swimming on her, her name tag reading simply, "Daisy – mechanic."

"Hey there." She smiled at him with radiant eyes. "What are you doin' here? Need help with the tractor again?"

"Nah," he said. "Had to drive to San Antonio, so thought I'd stop in and buy you a coffee or somethin'."

"Wow, big spender." She walked to the car bay and climbed out of her jumpsuit. Under it she wore plain jeans and a T-shirt. "Lou, I'm goin' on that break you owe me."

They walked across the street to a coffee shop, making small talk. Or she did, while he remained quiet, flashing back on the little girl that cried for her mother and eventually one day stopped asking about her. She'd become Hank's shadow after that. Whenever anyone mentioned that Daisy was practically the image of her mother, she left the room. She'd suffered enough being abandoned by her mother to find out that maybe she'd also been abandoned by her "real" father.

Still, maybe he *should* let her know there could be a question about her paternity. Maybe he had no right to protect her from this. If Rusty was her biological father, he a medical history she should know.

Lincoln should have asked Rusty for a medical history! Just in case. But no, this wouldn't be an issue. Besides, Daisy was healthy, and she'd likely remain that way. And if she liked working on cars, that couldn't be in the DNA. She'd been *nurtured* to like cars, spending time around Hank, who'd been ridiculously proud of everything she did.

"Earth to Lincoln?" Daisy asked.

She'd apparently just ordered her drink, probably a milkshake with some coffee in it.

"Just a drip coffee," he said, and paid for their drinks.

Daisy led the way to a table. "So. You and Sadie."

"What?"

"Snap out of it." She snapped her fingers in front of his nose. "Tell me what's on your mind because I can almost hear you thinkin'."

"Nothin'," he lied.

"I just asked about you and Sadie and you stared right through me. Don't tell me y'all broke up already. Eve dumpin' Jackson was awkward, at least Jackson left town. You and Sadie are goin' to keep on runnin' into each other." She stirred her drink with the straw. "Oh, Lord. *Please* don't break up with her. I can't take any more drama."

"I'm *not* goin' to break up with her. What makes you think she won't break up with me?"

"Um, history?" She made a slurping sound with her drink. "Sadie's loved you forever."

"Change of subject," he announced, unwilling to discuss Sadie.

"Have you seen Wade lately? How's he doin'? How's his mother?"

"She went through another cancer treatment and seems to be doin' much better. He's been helpin' over at the new school from time to time."

They talked a little more about his best friend, giving Lincoln a much-needed shift from thoughts of Daisy's paternity. Because no amount of thinking would fix this.

He'd already made a decision, and now he would stand by it.

CHAPTER 19

*a*fter Derek showed up drunk, Jimmy Ray regressed, so Sadie made efforts to quietly praise him for his good behavior. Some days, this was a stretch. She reached for compliments, sometimes thanking him for the behavior she'd expect from any student.

Thank you for giving Ellie the jump rope when she asked.

I sure love the way you've been turning in your homework every day.

Look, your shoes are on your feet, exactly where they belong!

Today, she sat next to him as he struggled with his math sheet, counting on his fingers and biting his tongue as he wrote down the answer.

"Hey there."

He glanced up but went back to his worksheet. "I'm bein' good."

"I know, honey." She ruffled his hair. "I never got to talk to you after that day you ran off to find your dad. When Lincoln found you?"

He nodded. "I couldn't find my dad."

"It must be so hard not seeing your dad every day like you're used to."

He wrote an eight with two circles, one on top of the other. The wrong answer.

"Grown-up stuff can be tough to understand," Sadie said sincerely.

She couldn't understand when, how, and why her mother suddenly become so bitter toward her father. The entire memory of her childhood was tilted on its side as she quietly wondered how long Mom had been unhappy. Or maybe this was just something else she'd failed to notice. Were they simply keeping their problems quiet or did *Beau* know there were problems? Who else knew?

Did they even *have* problems, or was it just a bad night?

"Both of your parents love you very much," Sadie said quietly.

Yes, Sadie. Your parents love you very much.

"I know." He tipped his pencil over to erase his incorrect answer.

Good, Jimmy Ray. Good. Thinking it over, getting it right.

"Do you know if there's anything you ever need to talk about, you can come to me?"

"Yep."

She'd been about to get up and check on another student's work when Jimmy Ray piped up.

"I saw my dad."

That caught Sadie's attention. A shiver of fear slid down her spine. "You did?"

"He can't come home right now. He will later."

"Miss Sadie, I need help." Ellie stood at Sadie's elbow, holding her worksheet in her chubby little hands.

Sadie went to help Ellie with her spelling, intent on getting back to that conversation with Jimmy Ray. But by the time Bobby Joe stole Billy's snack, Ellie and Sue Ellen argued whether you could make the color purple from red and blue or red and green, and Scott needed his shoes tied again, the school day ended.

As she locked up the portable, Sadie waved to the men on the crew today, who happened to be Beau and one of the Henderson brothers. If she were to judge by outer appearances, the new school would be ready soon. Of course, she wasn't allowed inside. She hoped they hadn't found something else wrong with the building because she didn't want to stay in the small portable for much longer. The kids needed more room and so did she.

She walked across the parking lot and stood until Beau noticed her. He walked over to her.

"Hey, sis. I don't know when we'll be done but should be soon. Keep in mind some of our volunteer crew has simply 'dabbled' in construction." He held up air quotes. "I've had to re-do some of the work to be up to code."

"Fine, that's not why I'm here."

He squinted. "Yeah? You ask every time I see you."

"When's the last time you saw Mom and Dad?"

"Hmm." He scratched his jaw. "Guess when we were at dinner last?"

"How did your stripper date go, by the way?"

He grinned. "What makes you think she's a stripper?"

"Puh-leeze!" She crossed her arms and jutted out her hip.

"What's with you? A little pissy today?"

"Look, I just wanted to ask, you know..." She hesitated on saying that Mom and Dad were having "issues." Beau would think her over-reacting anyway. "Um, there was an argument at dinner the other night."

"The doctor thing? Go easy on Mom. She didn't mean anything by it. I think she's having a hard time sliding Lincoln into the boyfriend role. She'll get there. Can't expect everybody to be as open and non-judgmental as I am." He opened his arms as if he was the greatest guy in the world.

She rolled her eyes. "No, that's not it. There was an argument. Kind of a big one."

Beau quirked both brows. "About what?"

So, it wasn't just Sadie. Their parents literally *never* argued. At least not in front of their kids. They'd seemingly had the perfect marriage. She'd always wished for a marriage like theirs.

"I would say it was about stupid stuff, like stuff Dad needs to fix that he hasn't gotten around to, but…they were *mean*."

"Are you sure?"

"Yes, Beau. I've never heard them like that before. Mom being spiteful. Angry. Same with Daddy. You don't know anything about this?"

"No!" He tossed his hands up.

She narrowed her eyes. "Would you…would you tell me if they were having problems?"

"If I knew, yes. I'd get *you* to fix it. You think I know how to help them?"

Sadie sighed. "No, of course not. You're hopeless."

"Listen. Whatever's goin' on is their business. I'm sure they'll fix it if it needs fixin'."

"What about Dad? Does he still act normal around you?"

"If you mean has he come in to work crying, and wanting to talk about his relationship problems, then the answer is no."

"Give me a break. I'm trying to figure out how I can help."

"You can't. Maybe they need counselin', but they sure don't need you butting into their private business."

"How can you say that? These are our parents!"

She didn't need to remind Beau that their parents were perfect for each other and always had been. Daddy used to bring Mom flowers every night, not just on special occasions. He always remembered her birthday, their anniversary, all of the important dates. The first time they went on a date, the first time they kissed, their engagement, and marriage. A lot for a man to remember. Mom used to joke that her friend's husbands couldn't even remember their wife's birthdays much less everything else.

They used to kiss and hold hands while they sat and watched TV every night after dinner. Come to think of it, she couldn't remember the last time she'd seen them behave that way.

SADIE DIDN'T SEE Lincoln for most of the week because he'd gone to a cattle auction with Hank. On Thursday after work, she called her mother and made plans to meet her.

"Come on in, sugar," Mom called out when Sadie let herself in her childhood home after a quick knock.

She found her mother in the kitchen wearing her apron, stirring a huge pot of her jam. "Last of the peaches for the season."

Sadie thought of Pamela Ann picking peaches, her mother canning them, the General Store selling them. The circle of fruit. Setting down her backpack on the table, she went to her mother and squeezed her shoulders. Then she immediately made herself useful, joining the assembly line of mason jars.

"Let me help."

Mom stopped to hand Sadie an apron and watched as she tied it on. "It's gettin' to where I might actually need to hire help."

"That's great. I'm proud of you!"

"Just think. A little operation like mine started in my own kitchen. Who knew? If I could afford to hire some help, invest in marketing, maybe I'd do a lot better." She scoffed. "But your father *hates* the idea."

"What? Why?"

Mom shrugged. "It might mean taking funds away from his precious vineyard. That's where most of our disposable income goes. I keep telling him, yours is a hobby. Mine is a *business*. But the man has no respect for how far I've come."

"I see." Oh boy. Sadie sensed the problem. "Are you okay?"

"Of course. Why wouldn't I be?"

"Well, I mean, you and Daddy had such a big fight at dinner."

She scoffed. "Big fight?"

Sadie chose her words carefully. "You were kind of mean to Daddy."

Mom stopped stirring and went hand on hip. "I should have known you would take his side."

"Side? Mom, there are no *sides*. What are you talkin' about?" Terror sliced through her at something unnamed in her mother's tone. Something cold. Icy.

"Sugar, there's just a lot you don't know. Let's leave it at that."

"But I-I think Daddy's feelings were hurt."

"Because I don't want my daughter to struggle or work unless she wants to?"

"What's goin' on? Do y'all need money? Are you in trouble?"

"Not at all, and you can thank me for that." She added more sugar and stirred viciously.

"What's that supposed to mean?"

"It means that my little jam business has paid plenty of bills for our household. Which helps a great deal since your father has been a sole proprietor for decades. I told him to structure the company into an LLC years ago, but did he listen to me? No, why would he. I'm just a housewife."

Sadie felt her throat tighten, dry up, and threaten to close the pathway to precious oxygen. "You're so angry. You and Daddy never even argued before."

She snorted. "That you know of."

"I just think you should…I mean," Sadie said softly. "Have you talked to him about any of this?"

"Talked? I've talked until I ran out of words. Now, I don't even bother." Mom glanced at Sadie, a flash of regret in her gaze. "I'm sorry to tell you but you asked. He's your father, so I don't think we should talk about this anymore."

Tempted to agree, Sadie nevertheless forged on. Her mother didn't have many girlfriends, similar for many women in Stone Ridge. "It's okay. You might need someone to talk to. I'm here."

"I'm aware you adore your father. That's as it should be."

"You don't need to give me any of the gritty details, but I deserve to know if something is *really* wrong." She sucked in a deep breath. "You know?"

"I'm not going anywhere, if that's what you're worried about."

"And…what about him?"

She snort-laughed. "And leave his precious vineyard? Honestly, I think he loves those grapes more than he loves his own children sometimes."

Sadie believed no such thing, but her father worked hard. As did every father and husband, but like so many in Stone Ridge, his work was physical and at times painful. How many times had she seen him soak his wrists in Epsom Salt at the end of a long day? Did her mother not notice these things anymore? Being their sole support for years meant that he carried the financial load on his own. This meant Sadie's mother could be a stay-at-home mother, all she'd imagined her mother ever wanted to be until now.

"But I thought everything was great. The cruise must have been very romantic," Sadie said. "Right?"

Granted, her mother hadn't made it sound like a great time, but Sadie thought she'd been censoring for her children. Surely there were some, um, romantic things at night. Her mind didn't want to go there. Her brain could never accept more than hand holding.

"The *cruise*." Mom nearly spit the words out. "Trapped on a moving hotel in the middle of the Gulf Coast with a bunch of strangers. Sleeping in a room the size of a hovel with no windows. A dirty swimming pool filled with saltwater. Not my idea of a great time. Besides, it was a wine club thing. Your father wanted to go."

That sounded like a living nightmare for her mother the clean freak. "Maybe you two can think of something you'd like to do next. And you can plan ahead and enjoy it together."

Mom stared at Sadie blankly. "I've no idea what you're talking about."

"Isn't there something you want to do? A trip you want to take?"

"Sugar, there's no time for that. I have orders to fill. My business is booming."

"Didn't you ever dream of going someplace exotic?"

She waved a hand dismissively. "I don't have time for that."

It took everything in Sadie to keep quiet. Her father seemed unhappy, too, and Sadie could tell that much from the other night. Her mother was ignoring the problem. This didn't bode well.

Later that night after leaving her parents' house, Sadie drowned her sorrows in a pint of Cookie Dough ice cream. True, maybe she had nothing to worry about. The only exercise she did these days was jumping to conclusions. Her parents would never split up after all this time. Even now as an adult it would break her heart if her parents divorced. Her mother might be fine and find someone new eventually, should she want to, but her father might be alone for the rest of his life. If there were few single women in their town, there were even less single middle-aged women.

"Okay, you're getting carried away, Sadie Marie!" She threw away her empty pint and phoned Eve, who dropped by within five seconds with another one.

She held it out. "Is this bad news?"

"The worst." Sadie carried the pint of Cherry Garcia into the kitchen and got out two bowls.

"Oh my God, I'm so sorry, honey," Eve said kindly. "But you know what they say. Plenty of peaches on a peach tree."

Sadie froze and almost laughed. Almost. "No. It's not bad news about me and *Lincoln*."

"Oh, whew!" Eve made a mock show of wiping her brow and sat at the kitchen table.

"Why? What have you heard?"

"Are you kidding me right now? You can't let doubt creep in every time someone even asks you a question. You're upset. I took a guess." She shrugged.

"You're sure you haven't heard anything more about Jolette Marie?"

Sadie had already filled Eve in on how she'd embarrassed herself at the Shady Grind. And as usual, Eve saw that as being more about Jolette Marie's problem.

"Nothing."

"And you would tell me?"

"Tell you what?"

"If you hear that Lincoln is seeing her behind my back."

"Oh my God. Sadie. You can't keep doing this!"

Frustration bubbled up. "Eve, you don't know what this is like. No one ever cheated on *you*."

She crossed her arms. "But I've seen cheating, and I know what it looks like. And of course, I would tell you. Immediately. You're my best friend."

Sadie scooped ice cream into the bowls, trying to distract herself. Eve had a point. Sadie should get over herself and put the past in her rear view. No way would she ever miss the signs again. Nor was she associated with the same kind of friends anymore. People who cared more about where they could find the next party.

Sadie handed Eve a full bowl of ice cream which she happily accepted. "Why are we drowning our sorrows in Ben & Jerry's if everything is fine in paradise?"

"My parents."

Eve quirked a brow. "The happiest and longest marriage in Stone Ridge other than Beulah and Lloyd Hayes?"

Sadie felt the salty sting of tears prick her eyes. "I don't think so."

Eve's parents were divorced, but for so long now that no one even talked about it anymore. Like so many, Brenda and Ricardo Iglesias married young. Both were originally from Stone Ridge, and Brenda went to school with Hank. They'd been close friends, and Hank seamlessly passed on that friendship to Brenda's only child. When Ricardo left and Eve was ten, Hank found Brenda a job on the Truehart Ranch as a cook and maid.

"I'm sorry," Sadie said. "I know divorce happens, but I never thought my parents..."

Eve's dropped her spoon and it clanged in the bowl. "They're getting *divorced?*"

"Oh, no, no. I hope not, but something is going on and they're really not happy."

"Wow. They hide it so well."

Sadie snorted, finding that too ironic. "Don't they?"

"But that doesn't mean—"

"I'm just glad I wasn't the *only* one who didn't see this coming."

"This is something you couldn't have seen coming. No one knows what goes on behind closed doors. If they're hitting a rocky patch in their marriage, maybe they just need to figure it out. But I'll bet they will."

"You're right. I'm overreacting."

But a tug of suspicion couldn't let it go.

CHAPTER 20

The next day after school, Sadie again missed a chance to speak to Pamela Ann, so when she got home, she phoned. "Just checking in. Jimmy Ray is doing great in class. How's he at home?"

"Fine except he keeps pushing me on bedtime. But I'm so wrecked by seven it's all I can do to keep my dagum eyes open."

"I know what you mean."

"Listen to me. What am I sayin'? You have fifteen Jimmy Rays every day. Are you exhausted *every* night?"

Sadie might never tell a soul, but every night she worried over her students. She'd never have believed that her heart would expand to love and appreciate each student. At night she'd lie in bed and thoughts would run to Bobby Joe and his obsession with food. She hoped that wouldn't later become a lifelong problem, so she'd brought healthy snacks like celery sticks, apple slices, and granola.

Ellie bit her nails to the quick which just might be a sign of her over-achiever's spirit. And though she didn't have training to diagnose it, Sadie feared that Jimmy Ray might be dyslexic on top of everything else. He took pride in his work, but his reading comprehension remained poor. Until she knew for certain, she wouldn't share her worries with Pamela Ann.

"It's different for me. I have a short day and I have the evenings to recover. Other than grading homework and planning lessons."

She also wanted to organize a field trip and thought that the Carver Ranch would be perfect. Then again, they also had the peach orchards. Sadie hadn't decided on one, and the entire matter of arranging such a thing, with all the legalities and permission slips required, overwhelmed her.

"Sounds like being a teacher is a little like being a mother. You take your job home with you."

"Any word on Derek?"

"No." Pamela Ann's voice lowered, and the sound of the TV in the background faded. "But while I have you, I wanted to tell you something kind of personal and I hope you don't mind."

This might be where Pamela Ann confessed that she'd been trying to work things out with Derek. Sadie wanted to support the family been reunited. It would make Jimmy Ray so happy for his parents to stay together.

"I've become very friendly with Dr. Judson."

Oh, boy. What happened to marriage and a lifetime of commitment? Sadie bit her tongue in half. She had no right to judge Pamela Ann after all she'd been through with Derek.

He'd cheated, after all, or at the least been *suspected* of cheating.

"H-how close?"

"I thought you weren't interested in him."

"Oh, I'm not. I'm with Lincoln and we're exclusive."

"That's what I thought. It looks like he might decide to stay in town. Lillian talked to him and is working with

Beulah to raise funds for a clinic. He was so good with Jimmy Ray. But don't worry, I'm still married, and he knows it. I'm so impressed with him and his plans for the future. He's got every detail ironed out for the rest of his life."

"And you *like* that?"

"Who wouldn't? It's safety, security. I'm a single mother now, so I need to think of those things. I'm not interested in dating a lot. Once I'm free, that is."

"Judson is certainly a kind man," Sadie said carefully while she desperately tried to think of a reason Derek would be the better candidate.

All the reasons seemed shallow.

You have a child together.

You have a history.

There must be something you still love about him.

"I'm not exactly hurrying into anything. I just...you know, he makes me *wish* I were free. We're friends right now but I think he's interested. It shocks me."

"Why should it? You're a great person!"

"Well, um, thanks. That's sweet of you. But I've dated one man my entire life. I met him when I was eighteen and I sure don't look the way I did back then. I'm about twenty pounds heavier for one. But the worst thing about me is that I never finished high school. I'm picking peaches! And a doctor, a *doctor*, is interested in me."

"I'm really happy for you."

But Sadie wasn't happy at all as a stone lodged itself in her throat. Jimmy Ray would hate this. He wanted his parents to stay together, as any child would.

"I worried you'd feel a claim on him since he dated you first. You know how it is around here."

One date with a doctor and it would follow her the rest of her life, apparently.

Sadie sighed. "I don't know if you could technically say I

dated him. We went on one dinner date. I didn't even kiss him."

"You know how it is. Some women in our little town think they're entitled to more than one man. Since there are so many."

Sadie immediately thought of Jolette Marie, but there were other women like her. She bristled at the thought.

"I've always been a one-man woman."

Though in the past not everyone returned the favor.

Later that night, Sadie prepared next week's lessons and then changed into her favorite nightgown: an old and comfy tee that fell to just below her thighs. Time to relax. Unwind. She considered asking Eve over to watch a rom-com, but the poor girl worked so hard between early mornings at the ranch and her job at the clinic. Last night she'd fallen asleep on Sadie's couch while she went on and on about her parents. Sadie didn't bother waking her up until morning, simply covering her with a blanket and going to bed herself.

After hearing a knock on her door, Sadie figured Eve had read Sadie's mind and she threw open the door.

There stood Lincoln, dressed from head to toe in black. He'd rolled up the long-sleeved button down displaying muscular forearms. Even his Stetson was midnight black. His jaw and chin were dusted with a light and scruffy look. He looked like every woman's fantasy of a sexy cowboy.

Her jaw dropped. "I thought you weren't getting back until tomorrow."

His gaze raked from her eyes to her bare feet. He bit his lower lip, teeth grazing across in a way which made her womb contract. "Damn."

Self-consciously, she glanced down at her tee. "I didn't expect you."

He rushed her like a linebacker going for a tackle and she squealed in delight. He would have knocked her over, but his strong hands lifted her into his arms. His hands slid down to her bottom, lowering her to his lips for a kiss which quickly turned wild.

"Lord, I missed you, baby."

After two days, it was good to hear those words. Almost like I love you, and she'd take it. Yes, she would.

When he put her down, she tugged on his hand and led him to the couch. "How did it go?"

He pulled off his Stetson and dragged a hand through his thick hair. She'd seen many cowboys remove that hat and have nothing to show for it. But it was almost a shame to cover Lincoln's hair with a hat.

"Lots of money in cattle."

"I've heard." She smiled and took his callused hand, her fingers making little circles in the palm of his hand.

"What's been happenin' around here?"

"In two days? Gee, let's see. Judson asked me to marry him and I said no. He then asked Eve who also said no," she teased.

"Don't even joke about that."

"Actually, I talked to Pamela Ann and she said she's interested in Judson." Sadie sighed. "I guess she has little hope for reconciliation."

"Hope she waits for the divorce to go through."

And just like that, though she didn't see it coming, Sadie felt the salty sting of tears. She pushed them back with the pads of her fingers.

Lincoln pulled her into his lap. "Hey. Hey, what's wrong?"

She buried her face in his warm neck. "I'm sorry. I didn't mean to get so emotional."

"No, there's no sorry. Tell me what's wrong." His hand slid up and down her spine in a comforting move.

"My parents. They both seem really unhappy and are

having problems. I know it's their business, whatever happens. But I'm worried."

This didn't seem to shock Lincoln the way Sadie expected it might. "Hm."

She pulled back to take a long look at him. No, she wasn't imagining this. Lincoln almost...expected this.

"You're not surprised."

"Not really."

"Why *not*? Eve was shocked. My parents are one of the happiest couples in town."

"I...sensed some tension." He cleared his throat and shifted his weight as though uncomfortable discussing this. "Your mother...she doesn't look at him like she can't wait to get her hands on him. And...it's the same for him."

Lincoln and his blasted honesty. *Watch out for what you wish for*. But Sadie swallowed hard at the truth behind that statement. She hadn't wanted to see it for herself. There were many reasons why a husband and wife might pull away from each other at different times. An argument, perhaps. Some other stressor like finances.

"Lincoln, they've been married for almost thirty-five *years*."

He shrugged and his hands slid up and down her leg in a soothing rhythm. "So?"

"So," Sadie began, aware she was desperately thinking of a reason that a husband and wife who were still in love might not be obvious about it. "Maybe...maybe they're just tired of each other."

Lincoln quirked a brow. "Does that happen when you're in love?"

She chewed at her lower lip. No, that didn't happen when two people were in love. She couldn't possibly picture, for instance, getting tired of Lincoln. Ever.

"No," she said miserably. "It doesn't."

Hand on the nape of her neck, he pulled her close. "Thirty years from now, I assure you I'll still hustle to get back from a cattle run just to see you."

Sadie's heart gave a powerful tug. She pressed her forehead to his. "What about in forty years?"

He chuckled, the sound low, deep and scratchy. "If I can still move, I'll pick you up like this."

Carrying her in his arms, he moved toward the bed where he dropped her. "And if my fingers aren't too old and arthritic, I'll take my shirt off like this. Or maybe you'll have to do it for me."

She came up on her knees and began to unbutton his shirt. "I don't mind doing this even before your fingers are arthritic."

He slid her a wicked smile as the soft cotton shirt slid off his shoulders, revealing gorgeous sinewy muscles and his light smattering of chest hairs. His body covered hers, pinning her down but carefully keeping his weight off.

"I'm not familiar with this, you know."

"You could have fooled me."

He snorted. "No. I'm not used to having to see someone. Anyone. Like my day isn't complete until I do."

Sadie's breath caught and her arms circled his neck. "Don't look now, Lincoln, but it sounds like you're making plans."

He met her gaze, his deep blue eyes open and warm. "What if I am?"

"I'm taking it one day at a time, Linc, just like we said. But I love you. I think I've loved you for half my life."

He brought her hand to his lips and brushed a kiss across her knuckles. "Tell me again."

"I love you, Lincoln."

"And as usual, you're a hell of a lot smarter than I am. I'm still playing catch up. But baby, know that I've never felt this way before."

Her heart swelled and nearly burst in love and affection for this man who turned out to be everything she could have hoped for and more. He was *everything*.

And he would never let her down.

SADIE WOKE THE NEXT MORNING, spooning with Lincoln. This time was markedly different from the first. They were both naked, for one thing, their clothes strewn around the bed. Different enough alone, but the sex that followed last night would go down in the history books. Her history book, anyway. Although she doubted their five future children would want to read about how their father nearly melted all her bones.

Now, Sadie don't get carried away. We will have however many children we have. We will marry, or not marry.

One thing for certain: we will make each other happy for the rest of our lives. Marriage, children, or not.

But she still wanted the children. One or five, that didn't matter. As long as they were *his* children. They would be beautiful, both inside and out. Just like their father.

A memory came to her clear and swift. She turned to face Lincoln. His eyes were closed, one arm still flung over her waist.

"What?" He opened one eye, one corner of his mouth tipping up in a smile.

"You're awake."

"The sun is up and I'm a rancher. What do you think? I'm just waiting for you to wake up."

"Aw, that's so sweet." She caressed his jawline. "Hey, do you remember when Jackson, Eve, and I got drunk after the senior party and you drove us home?"

"Vaguely. But I have saved my brother's ass so many times I lost count."

That night may not have been important to him, but for her, she'd never forgotten.

"I'd never been drunk before that night. Jackson and Eve piled in your truck, but I ran to the bushes. Do you remember why?"

"I can guess." He smirked.

"Some of the kids waiting outside made fun of me. They were laughing, saying that as a lowly junior I couldn't hold my drink. Calling me disgusting. And you yelled at them to mind their own business and go back inside. Then you held my hair back while I continued to make a lasting impression on you." She met his eyes, so deep and blue. "You told me the next time to pace myself and you held my hand and walked me to your truck. I think I officially fell in love that night."

"I remember," he said, tucking a hair behind her ear. "I should have told you that underage drinking is a crime, but I was a little too jaded for that. And that's not the memory I have of you."

"Thank God, because that wasn't my finest moment."

"I remember you coming up to the house to talk to Mima and Hank about Eve. To get them to try to understand her point of view. We were all so angry, but you had enough courage to come and talk to us, for Eve. She couldn't face us. Even you didn't know what kind of reception you'd get. I know I wasn't thrilled to see you. None of us were. I might have been a little scary. But you didn't back down. You wanted to help Eve because that's the kind of friend you are."

"You *were* scary. But I always thought that deep inside you were nothing but a big teddy bear."

"That's me." Then he rolled on top of her, pinning her, growling like a bear.

He went after her neck, tickling, making her squeal. She

dissolved into peals of laughter and only calmed down when he kissed her, shutting her up.

"Can you stay for breakfast?"

"Sure can. After this week, Hank owes me. And next weekend, I'm stuck on the ranch. Today, I'm yours."

A rare treat. "You mean I have you all morning?"

"Why? What are you going to do with me?"

"Oh, so much."

They made love again, taking a shower together afterwards. Sadie got out first, wanting to start breakfast. She toweled off while Lincoln sang "Friends in Low Places" decidedly off-key.

"The acoustics are great in here. How do I sound? Could I make a record?" He chuckled.

"Leave the singing to Jackson."

"Aw."

She shut the door to the bathroom, smiling so hard her cheeks hurt, and hurriedly got dressed. Pulling out her cast-iron pan and the chopping board, she sliced bacon and chopped potatoes. Working fast, she grabbed the carton of eggs and set it on the counter. Lincoln's phone buzzed twice from where it sat nearby.

She glanced at it but did a double take at the message from an unknown number:

See you then. Can't wait.

Looking closer, she saw that this was in reply to Lincoln's text which read:

I'll meet you in Kerrville at ten-thirty next Saturday.

Sadie dropped the phone like live ammunition. She shouldn't have snooped! Didn't Lincoln say he'd be stuck on the ranch all weekend? Why didn't he mention he'd be in Kerrville on Saturday? It could be innocent, but if so, why was the number not listed in the caller ID as one of his contacts? Who or what was the big secret? Why couldn't he tell her? A cold stab of fear sliced through her. Lincoln wouldn't do this. No. He *never* lied to her. There was an explanation for this. It could be perfectly innocent, right?

Lincoln emerged from the bathroom with nothing but a towel around his waist. "Dayum that smells good."

Going back to the cooking, she focused on something she could control. These eggs. She cracked one after another, the process always the same. The white or brown shell would crack, and a yellow yolk and its white would come out. She appreciated the constancy of cooking and baking. The comfort of watching the simplest of ingredients come together each and every time. Unless you messed with the recipe.

Fully clothed now, Lincoln came behind her and wrapped his arms around her waist. He kissed her neck and her body, who hadn't yet engaged from her mind, responded as it always did. She leaned into him, tilting her head to give him better access.

She *could* ask about this message. But she'd have to admit that she looked, and besides, this would also give him a chance to lie to her. If he lied, she would know. The lie would cut deeper. That would slay her.

She could ignore the message and be exactly who she used to be. Squash down any problems or doubts and forge on. Because if she asked, she might not like the answer. She could admit that to herself now. She'd known on some level that her so-called friends were keeping secrets from her. There were little smirks and smiles and jokes she didn't quite get. Looking back, it all made sense.

It became easier to ignore the painful truth. To hide from the discomfort until she couldn't any longer. Maybe someday she would call and thank the so-called friend who'd been the first to confess the indiscretion. If not, Sadie might be living in Australia right now, happily ignorant, until the day when her world cracked open with the truth.

Not this time.

Maybe she didn't have the right, but damn it all, maybe she did. Sadie turned off the stove with a flick of her wrist, picked up Lincoln's phone, and handed it to him.

"You got a text while you were in the shower. Who are you meeting with in Kerrville?"

There. She'd asked. She was strong enough to hear the truth.

Just slice open a vein and bleed.

Yes, thank you, Daddy. Loving someone is messy, but she wouldn't trade this feeling, this sweet and tender ache for Lincoln. Not for all the safety in the world. Lincoln paused for a second, in which Sadie swore she heard the sound of her own heartbeat. But he didn't look away or avoid her eyes.

"I'm sorry." He met her gaze head on. "I didn't want to get you involved in this mess."

"W-what mess?"

He shoved a hand through his damp hair. "It's Daisy."

Okay, okay. She could handle this. If he'd kept anything from Sadie, it was for Daisy's protection. "What's wrong?"

"You've heard all the rumors about how Hank might not be her real father."

"That's nasty talk from jealous men. No one really believes that."

"I didn't want to believe it and I still don't. But a man who claims he might be her father contacted Hank. And he wants to see her."

Sadie's hand flew up over her mouth. This would kill Daisy. She was so close to Hank and having been abandoned by her mother, this could be a game changer. Her entire life would be upended. She wouldn't know where she belonged. Or to whom.

She went into his arms. "Why didn't you tell me?"

"I almost did last night, but we were talking about your parents." He stroked her back. "You were too upset to hear this latest family drama."

"Oh, Linc, I feel terrible. You should always be able to talk to me about anything that's botherin' you."

"I've got it all under control. I'm meeting the man Saturday and drivin' him to Daisy's auto shop. He just wants to see her and agreed to do this from a distance. It's going to have to be enough. I believe I've convinced him that no good can come from a paternity test which will cause too much pain and may wind up not matterin' anyway."

"Because she might still be Hank's daughter."

He nodded. "I don't know. Am I doin' the right thing keepin' this from her?"

"Yes."

He was doing what he'd always done. Protecting his family. Sadie was familiar with truths that mattered and with those that didn't. To bet her future on a man who couldn't ever be faithful? *This* was a fundamental truth that mattered. But to tell a woman that the man who'd raised her, and was her father in every sense of the world, had only a fifty percent chance of being her biological father?

"I don't see what good can come from that."

"What about medical history, that sort of thing?"

Sadie worried a nail between her teeth. "You can ask him, if it comes to that. See if there's anything significant."

"Wish she looked like Hank, but she looks just like *her*."

No need to ask who he meant. "But how did he even know about Daisy?"

"Maggie told him. Called him up after she left us, told him that he might have a little girl."

Sadie drew in a sharp breath. "Oh, God."

"Her last gift to us."

"Does he know where she could be now?"

"He never heard from her again."

Poor Lincoln. He'd been carrying this weight around, not knowing how best to protect Daisy. He took care of everyone, but no one took care of him.

Until her.

CHAPTER 21

A week later, Lincoln drove to Rusty's motel in Kerrville at the appointed time, Sadie's support and belief the only thing moving him forward.

All week, she'd taken care of him, assured him he was doing the right thing keeping this from Daisy. In whispered words late at night, she told him she loved him over and over again. During one of those sweet and erotic nights, he'd nearly told her he loved her a dozen times. But something held him back, something deep and dark that kept him from believing he deserved Sadie. If he had to put a name to it, he'd call that darkness Maggie Mae Carver.

And this could all go sideways on him. If not today, then in the future. Maybe he should forget the whole thing. Call Rusty and explain he'd gotten hung up with some ranch task. Lord knew there was a long list. When on their two-day trip to the auction Lincoln told Hank about the talk with Rusty, and the plans they'd made, it was as if a bomb went off.

"You did *what*? When? Why?" Hank had yelled.

"I told you I'd take care of this. This man won't be botherin' you anymore after this weekend."

"How can you be sure? *Now* he knows her name."

"If he found you, he can find your children," Lincoln yelled back.

"It would have taken him a little longer, at least."

"And then what? What if he just goes straight to Daisy? He could do that, too. You've ignored this long enough."

Eventually Hank's mood was visibly improved by the current price of a head of cattle. They'd sold enough heads to pay for the next year's operations.

Lincoln still wondered whether he was doing the right thing for Daisy. He didn't like the dishonesty. The secrecy. Hank certainly liked the idea of ignoring Rusty, but that wouldn't have lasted long. If left up to his father, he'd have continued to ignore the repeated emails while the fear ate away at his gut. The drinking would have become worse and eventually it would have spilled over into the rest of their lives. Lincoln was no different than his father in one way. The worry and stress consumed him. But he had Sadie.

As he drove, his thoughts turned to her again, that soft and tender place she'd become for him. Her sweetness tugged on his heart until he gave up the fight. Now, he was particularly vulnerable. He'd seen it time and time again, even if this made the first time for him. Men who were in love had so much to lose. They made knee-jerk mistakes out of fear. It was Sadie who helped him decide the risk of telling Daisy wasn't worth the rip it might tear through his family. The family that he believed now, one day, would include Sadie.

Sadie, his wife. Someday. No hurry. He was still getting used to the idea that he loved her and if she would have him, this would happen. Marriage. He'd marry Eve's *best friend*. Jackson, the only one in the family who, understandably, *still* hadn't forgiven Eve. He would just have to get over himself.

Rusty stood outside the motel, leaning against a post like it was difficult to stand without the assistance. No doubt.

"Howdy," Rusty said as he climbed into Lincoln's truck.

Lincoln gave him a moment to get comfortable and adjust his seat belt before he pulled out of the motel parking lot and headed toward the auto shop.

"Ready for this? Are we still in agreement?"

"Yup."

The plan was to park a distance from the shop so that Daisy wouldn't see and recognize his truck. Rusty would sit with Lincoln and watch Daisy at a safe distance. Lincoln would answer any questions he could, if they came up. He also planned to ask Rusty about any medical history, just in case.

The late morning sun shined bright in the sky, the temperatures already warming up the day. Seeing the auto shop, Lincoln pulled to the side of the road and parked.

"This is it." He turned and didn't see Daisy. "She usually takes a break at this time."

"Could she be under a car?" Rusty chuckled. "Maybe we didn't think this through."

Lincoln began to wonder how solid his plan was, when Daisy crossed the street holding a couple of coffees in her hands.

"That's her," Rusty said. "Pete's sake, she's the *image* of your mother."

While Lincoln knew this to be true, it sure would have helped now if she looked even a little bit like Hank. He'd love the certainty.

Now, Daisy smiled as she handed a coffee over to someone, but then she disappeared into the shop.

"I can't see much from here," Rusty said.

"That's all you need to see. You've seen her. She looks like our mother." Lincoln sucked in a breath and turned the key in the ignition. "Ask yourself if it really matters *who* her father is."

Rusty studied him as if he wondered whether Lincoln had been hit in the head one too many times. Without another word, he opened the door, and climbed out of the truck.

"Hey!" Lincoln reached for his shirt to grab him, but the little guy was wily and quick for an old man.

What should he do now? Haul the man back into his truck? Lincoln should have *never* trusted a bareback rider. Those dudes were crazy. Destructive. If he followed Rusty now, Daisy would see Lincoln. He couldn't afford her to make the connection. He'd just have to sit here, helpless, and hope he wasn't about to watch Daisy's life implode right before his eyes.

Because if that happened, he'd climb out of the truck and so help him, knock an old man into next week. But by then, the damage would have been done.

Lincoln watched as Rusty approached the auto shop and disappeared inside. His fists tightened around the steering wheel and he heard the sound of his heart thudding in his ears. A similar sensation happened every time he sat in the chute.

He'd taken a chance and this time it might blow up in his face. He wasn't a fan of losing.

The need to hear the sound of his brother's voice hit him with the force of a sledgehammer. And what else could he do now anyway, sitting in the cab of his truck, completely helpless? Fury ripped through him. He was sick of people who didn't honor their word.

Like his mother.

As if leaving wasn't enough damage, she'd phoned Rusty and planted a seed of doubt.

And speaking of damage, Lincoln had avoided something else for too long. He'd avoided Eve's name with Jackson because every time he mentioned her in passing, something went cold and dark inside his brother. But Jackson would have to accept Eve would be a big part of Lincoln's life, through Sadie. He wouldn't like it, but Jackson would have to live with it.

Having been loyal to his brother for years, Lincoln would think of himself first for once. Because he would not give up Sadie, not even for his brother.

He'd keep this latest debacle with Daisy quiet. Lincoln usually kept uncomfortable situations from his brother. They all did. He lived in Nashville and toured all over the country. And sure, Lincoln felt protective of the little brother that hadn't been abandoned once, but twice.

"Hey, brother," Jackson said, the sound of sleep thick in his voice. "What's up?"

"Lots," Lincoln said. "Cause for an update."

"Oh, yeah? Must mean huge things because you never have an update. One thing you can say about Stone Ridge is 'same day, same shit.'"

Lincoln cleared his throat. "Here's the thing. Turns out, I'm seeing Sadie."

Dead silence on the other line of the phone. "Sadie? Sadie *Stephens*?"

"Yep."

"What the hell! Is it serious?"

"I don't know. Probably...yes."

It had to be love when he couldn't stop thinking about her. When he wanted to see her, and if more than a day passed, he wanted to jump out of his skin. She'd become his best friend in a short time, and he depended on her. Needed her.

More silence. "Shit, Lincoln. You couldn't find anyone else? Why Sadie?"

Lincoln took a deep and measured breath and ran a hand

through his hair. He loved his younger brother, but damn it, high time for him to grow up.

"Because it's not all about you. Hell, I'm sorry Eve left you, and I was pissed for years about it. But you got married, you moved on, and she never has. You're doin' fine. *Better* than fine. And Eve...well, she's okay."

Yet another truth Lincoln would keep from Jackson. Lincoln didn't know what happened to Eve, but he guessed something tragic. No one would tell him, and he wasn't one to pry. She'd come home from grad school hearing impaired. She'd been in an accident and wound up in the hospital for weeks. Nearly lost her life. There was something a bit lost about her ever since, as she tried to adjust into life back home and find her footing again. Sadie was her only friend for a while, and then Mima forgave her, shocking their family.

"The Lord calls on us to forgive," she'd said to Hank and Lincoln, after announcing that Eve would be their new horse groomer. "I've talked to Pastor June about this and I know I'm in the right."

After that, she refused to hear another word about it. Conversation over. Hank, who'd never once sided against Eve, was relieved. Daisy didn't seem to care too much one way or another. Only Lincoln didn't appreciate the prospect of letting Eve back into their lives as if nothing ever happened. But damn, they lived in a small town, and he couldn't stay mad at a woman for too long. Even if she'd crushed his brother's heart.

More silence from Jackson and then he spoke slowly. "Do you love her?"

"Either that or I'm havin' a heart attack every day."

He snorted. "I never thought I'd see it happen."

"You and me both."

"But you sound kind of agitated about it," Jackson mused.

He didn't know the half of it. No one else had either come in or out of the auto shop while he waited. Lincoln wanted to kill Rusty with his bare hands.

He cleared his throat. So many half-truths. He'd never been comfortable with them.

"Well, I'm not used to it, I guess. I don't know *how* to sound."

"You could have any woman you wanted. Someone from another town. Wish you'd found anyone else."

"I wish for a whole lot of things, brother, that I'm probably never goin' to get."

Were someone granting wishes, he'd want a normal family. One in which his mother hadn't been a buckle bunny that abandoned her family. And also, that this old cowboy didn't find Hank. Lastly, Lincoln wished he'd never offered to take care of this. Maybe ignoring the man *would* have been the better plan.

"A long time ago, someone told me you don't get to choose who you fall for," Lincoln said. "And I didn't plan on this. On her. Just…she took me by surprise."

"It's a great song lyric." Jackson groaned. "Guess I did say that."

"God knows you wouldn't have fallen for Eve because Hank loved her and would have chosen her *for you* if he could." Lincoln chuckled.

"Hell no, that's the reason I wanted to *hate* her."

"Didn't work out that way."

"Guess not. At least not until later. And she earned that hate."

"But Sadie didn't."

"Guess I don't have a problem with Sadie. It's her choice in best friends. That's my problem."

"Well, don't make it mine." At that moment, both Rusty and Daisy wandered out to the front of the shop. "Gotta go."

The two of them were laughing, Daisy's hands in the pockets of her work jumpsuit as she tossed her hair back. Then Rusty waved to her, and Daisy went back into the shop. It seemed that whatever he'd said to her, it hadn't changed her life.

Rusty strolled back to the truck and climbed inside.

"What the *hell* was that, old man?" Lincoln wanted to push him out of the truck and let him find his own damn way home.

"Hot dang, that was somethin' else," Rusty said, unapologetically. "I haven't felt that rush of adrenaline in years. Thought you'd come and drag me back to the truck. Expected any second to be lassoed, dragged away, and tied up like cattle."

"You must like takin' risks. I was maybe two seconds away from doing just that."

"Hell, yeah, I miss it. Don't you? The thrill of the rodeo? Wonderin' whether you're goin' to live or die?"

Lincoln realized quite suddenly that he didn't miss that feeling at all. He spoke between gritted teeth. "What did you say to my sister?"

"Nothin'. We talked pistons and engines, stuff I'm bettin' you don't know a lick about."

"You talked to her about *cars*?" Lincoln narrowed his eyes.

"Hell, yeah. I wanted to quiz her. See if she knows her stuff. Told her that I'm interviewin' mechanics and wanted to see what her opinions were on what could be wrong with my truck." He made a whistling sound. "Whowee, that little girl knows engines."

"I could have told you that."

"Well, it ain't the same now, is it?" He took a long and measured look at Lincoln. "I'm stickin' to our deal. Didn't tell her a thing."

"Good to see you still honor at least *part* of your word."

"It's not for you, or Hank. It's not even for her." Rusty stared ahead. "Truth is, Hank's not alone. I wouldn't want to find out that she *isn't* mine." He adjusted his Stetson. "Truth is, if she's mine, by God she's the best thing I ever done. And I'd much rather never find out for sure because at least there's still a chance this way."

A trickle of fear slid down Lincoln's spine. This man might be popping in and out of their lives and Lincoln would have to be the point man. He would also take the risk that Daisy might never speak to him again if she heard he'd played God with her life and choices.

"You do have a point. My father's willin' to believe the same." He started his truck. "What about medical history? Anything significant we should know, just in case?"

"I'm healthy as a dagum horse. If it weren't for my body breakin' down on me from too much rodeoing I'd be fine."

"No diabetes? High blood pressure? Heart disease?"

"Well, now, son, ya gotta die of somethin'."

Lincoln shook his head. "I'm going to take that as a yes."

"Got high blood pressure. But I'm sixty-five. Tell me one old man mah age who doesn't have high blood pressure. I take mah pills."

Lincoln dropped Rusty off, nodded goodbye, and drove away, his truck wheels kicking up enough dust to leave Rusty standing in a hazy brown cloud.

CHAPTER 22

The life-altering mistake Lincoln had made crushed in on him. He couldn't trust Rusty to keep his word. That much he'd demonstrated today. Any day, week, or year, Daisy would hear from Rusty. And she might hate Lincoln for trying to protect her.

She'd fail to understand why he, who hated lies, kept this from her.

Lincoln drove around hill country for what felt like hours, mulling it all over, and the disaster he'd made out of everything. Then he headed to the Shady Grind to get properly tanked. When he arrived it was already afternoon, just past lunch, and Lenny and Brad were the only two there after the lunch rush. He immediately decided he couldn't get sauced with these two geniuses around. They might need rescuing.

"Hey there, Linc." Priscilla said. "The usual?"

"Yep," he said and removed his Stetson.

The Henderson brothers strutted in a little later and talked him into a couple of games of pool, and after beating them, he went back to nursing his beer.

Jolette Marie took a stool next to him. "Uh-oh. Trouble in paradise?"

"Not at all."

Sadie was the one bright light left in his world even if he clearly didn't deserve her.

"Really? Then what are you doin' here all alone lookin' like you lost your best friend? Did she insist on settin' a weddin' date?"

"For your information, she hasn't."

"Okay, so I'm wrong. Hey, if you want to get out of here, I'll cheer you up. I swear I won't tell her a thing. It will be our little secret."

He glared at her, full of both pity, and anger. "If you weren't a woman, I'd smack you. Have a little self-respect and give up on me already."

She hopped off. "Fine! Your loss. Just remember that you're exactly like me. You might tell yourself that you're playing house with Sadie right now, but it won't work. I tried that, you know, three times. It never worked because like you, I can't be tied down."

He didn't want to believe that, but some part of him responded, as if he recognized a fundamental truth. Because one thing was increasingly clear to Lincoln. He was a whole lot more like his messed-up mother than his father. Like her, he didn't particularly like the neediness of children, even if lately the idea of Sadie's children took on a whole other meaning.

Like his mother, he'd never warmed to the idea of being tied down. Like her, he'd made his way through the rodeo circuit, not caring who he hurt in the process.

Finally, in an act so much like her that it shocked him, he'd probably hurt Hank, and failed to protect Daisy.

. . .

LINCOLN DIDN'T COME over later that day as Sadie thought he might. She wanted to hear all about his meeting with the old rodeo cowboy. Nothing could have gone terribly wrong or she would have heard something, so she assumed he'd gone back to the ranch. She'd hear from Lincoln soon. She opened up her laptop, prayed to the Wi-Fi gods, and engaged in a little retail therapy. She bought another dress, but also another pair of Wranglers, because she would be spending plenty of time on a cattle ranch. Probably the rest of her life. She'd learn to love mucking a stall, or if not love, at least tolerate.

Her heart squeezed in a full and sweet happiness completely unfamiliar to her. She loved Lincoln like she'd never loved anyone else. A desperate and intense love but also a soft and delicious feeling that she craved more each day.

When she didn't hear from Lincoln by dinner time, she considered texting him, but reception was almost non-existent on his ranch. She figured he must have worked later than normal to make up for his trip to Kerrville.

Feeling happier than she had in years, Sadie cheerfully dressed. White dress, pink boots. She went next door to find Eve. She'd been ignoring her best friend for the past few weeks and it was high time to correct that.

Eve appeared at the door dressed in yoga pants, her hair pulled back in a ponytail. "Hey."

"It's time."

Eve narrowed her eyes and appraised Sadie's "party" clothes. "Time for what?"

"Time for you to get over Jackson."

"Yeah, right," Eve scoffed. "I'm already over him. Remember who left who at the altar."

Sadie quirked a brow. "Remember who was there when you cried yourself to sleep that night."

Eve walked inside and left the door open for Sadie to follow her in. "I can't go out tonight. I told you. I've got a kitten."

"Don't you think you can get away for a couple of hours? Let's go to the Shady Grind, for old time's sake. Who knows? You might meet someone tonight."

"I told you, I'm not ready for that." She plopped down on the couch where Sadie noted a nearly empty bag of Salt and Vinegar chips.

"And I heard you. Look, you don't have to meet anyone. But I could use some company tonight."

"Where's Lincoln?"

"He had a meeting in Kerrville this morning," Sadie said, unwilling to betray Lincoln's confidence. "I'm guessing he has a lot of chores to catch up on."

Eve smiled. "Look at you, all confident and self-assured. No doubts. The old Sadie would have tracked him down, expecting to find him cheatin' on you."

A curl of love wound itself around her heart and she almost couldn't speak for a moment. "He makes me feel...safe."

Eve's eyes were suddenly misty. "I remember that feeling."

Sadie sat beside Eve on the couch. Time for some hard truths.

"Lincoln told me something the other night. He said Jackson is completely over you, and that you should move on, too."

Eve blinked. "You think I don't *know* that?"

"I'm sorry, honey."

"*When* I move on, not whether, that will be entirely up to me."

"Sure, I get it." Sadie took Eve's hand and removed the bag of chips from her grip. "But until that happens will you at

269

least hang out with me tonight? We can just drink a cold beer, sit, and chat."

"We can do that here."

"But we do *that* all the time. A change of scenery would be nice, right? The last time we were there celebratin', didn't you have fun?"

Eve snorted. "Two men tried to get me to go home with them."

"You can't blame them for tryin'. You're gorgeous, Eve. And one of the last young and eligible women left in town."

"And that's why I stay away from the Shady Grind!"

"Eve, I'm worried about you," Sadie said, getting to the heart of the matter. "It isn't that I want you to start dating someone. But I do want you to stop hiding in this cabin. Okay?"

"I'm not hiding."

"Please." Sadie batted her eyelashes and smiled, clasping her hands, prayer-like. "Girls' night out."

Eventually, Sadie wore Eve down though she fought every step of the way.

"The only way I'm doin' this is my way. I'm not getting all dolled up. No makeup, so take me or leave me. And I'm wearing my Wranglers. Also, I'm drivin' in case I want to leave early and you insist on stayin'. Lincoln will probably show up anyway and y'all will want to stay longer."

"What about *Girls' Night* do you not understand?"

Thirty minutes later, they were on their way to the Shady Grind. Eve parked near her clinic, and they walked the short distance. The clear, warm night surrounded them, the pulsating sound of Garth Brooks shattering the natural silence of their small town.

"Hiya, girls."

Sean Henderson held the door open for them, waving them in with a grin. He took a long look at Eve's backside.

Sadie couldn't help but notice. Not that Eve gave two hoots. She barely smiled at the man as she thanked him for holding the door.

Not for the first time Sadie worried that Eve would never find anyone she loved like she'd loved Jackson. But her friend was only twenty-seven and couldn't just give up. Sadie wouldn't let her.

Priscilla seemed nowhere in sight tonight, and a handsome man stood behind the bar filling orders. Nothing like Lincoln, of course, but easy on the eyes nonetheless.

"Wow," Sadie said, elbowing Eve. "Take a look at him, will you?"

Eve glanced. "Oh, yeah. That's Levi. He's visiting his cousins. Apparently, he's good with horses."

"You two would have a lot in common."

Eve shrugged as Sadie led them to two empty stools at one end of the bar. Okay, Sadie would stop trying to play matchmaker now. It wasn't going to happen. At least not tonight.

"Hey, ladies," Levi said when he finally made his way down to them. "What can I get ya?"

"Two beers," Sadie said with a smile.

"Domestic?" His grin went wide, and yes, he checked Eve out.

Not a shock. Every man with a pulse checked her out.

"Of course," Sadie said and when he went off to get them, she elbowed Eve. "You were a lot cheerier last time we were here. What's up?"

Levi served their beers and Eve didn't even spare him a glance. "I don't mind going out when it's about you. But now, you have Lincoln."

"So, you're done, is that it?"

"Sadie, no offense, but I have a full life building my practice. I have a lot of student debt to pay off and I'm focused on my career. Not *all* of us want to get married and spit out a bunch of children, you know."

Ouch. "Well. That's fair. But as I told you, we're not here to find you a man."

"Okay, then."

She nudged her chin to Levi. "You don't have to be mean to him."

"Um, yes, I do." Eve swiveled on her stool. "Otherwise, he gets the wrong idea and that's not fair to anyone."

"You're right. Sorry." Sadie raised her bottle and clinked with Eve. "Here's to ignoring all of the men."

"I'll drink to that," Eve said with a small smirk.

Sadie laughed, turned, and at that moment noticed Lincoln sitting on the other end of the bar. Alone. Stetson tipped, head lowered, hands clasped around a bottle of beer.

A bit surprising to find him here when she didn't hear from him all day, but he had every right to go out alone just as she did. Just because they were a couple didn't mean they were joined at the hip.

Yeah, she was *that* cool.

"Oh, look," Eve said, following Sadie's gaze. "It's Linc. Well, I'm calling it a night."

Sadie put her hand on Eve's. "Nice try but you didn't even finish your beer."

"Even better." She grabbed her purse and stood. "Call me if y'all need a ride. I'm the designated driver."

Sadie tried to stop her by grabbing her elbow, but Eve went out the door so fast you'd think she'd left something cooking on the stove. Well, nothing to do but move closer to Lincoln and check in on the love of her life.

"Hey," she said, taking a seat next to him when the stool became available.

He turned to her, eyes a bit shadowed by the brim of his

hat. Even so, there would be no mistaking the posture of his body. The grim set of his full mouth.

"Hey, there."

A little spike of fear and warning seized her, coming in hot, like an old enemy. "I take it things didn't go well today?"

"I'm here because I don't want to think about that, Sadie."

Well, that was an answer in itself.

"I'm on a mission to get Eve to move on from Jackson. But she's already gone home," Sadie said, giving him said subject change. "Will you give me a ride home later? If you've been drinkin' too much, she said she'll come back to get us. She's sober as a nun tonight."

"I'm fine." Lincoln stood. "Let's go."

"We don't have to go home right now."

But he was already helping her off the stool and guiding her toward the front door. His movements were sharp, angry. In the truck, Sadie could not stand the quiet for another second. There were bad, funky moods, and there was *this*. A quiet so loud that it roared in her ears.

"We really don't have to go."

"Why not."

"My lord, Lincoln, you're acting like I caught you in the middle of somethin' you shouldn't be doin' and now you want to hurry up and get out of here."

"Funny." He shot her a patient look but said nothing more as he turned on the road, appearing as cheerful as someone headed to a lethal injection.

She didn't want to pry but something was very wrong. "What happened today with Rusty?"

"Don't worry about it." When he pulled in front of her cabin and made no move to get out, she didn't, either.

"Aren't you coming inside?"

"Not tonight. I've got an early mornin'."

But he always had early mornings and that usually didn't

stop him. He didn't say "baby," didn't give her a kiss, didn't tuck a hair behind her ear. Didn't hold her hand.

"Did I do somethin' wrong?"

"Of course not." He made it sound like a stupid idea.

Right. "*Something* is wrong."

"I just need to get a good night's sleep tonight."

A sickening thought occurred to her. "Is there someone else? Someone you need to get back to?"

The words came out before she could stop them.

He slid her a look, as if she'd stabbed him in the eye. "No."

"Okay, I'm sorry. I didn't think so, but you literally never tell me that you love me. What am I supposed to think when you're now this distant and won't even talk to me? I'm not a mind reader!"

"Sadie." Lincoln ran a hand down his face. "I can't take this right now."

"Can't take what?"

"This pressure to tell you that I love you, to make all these stupid declarations that don't mean anything."

A cold trickle of fear stabbed her. "Th-that don't *mean* anything?"

"Look, my mother told me she loved me every day of my life and she still left. Just didn't come home one day. She loved us so much that she cheated on our father. So, what happened to all that love? Maybe they were just *words*. I think we just say them to each other to feel safe."

"Don't say that. I love you, Lincoln. I always have. I don't need you to say it back until you're ready."

"Maybe not, but you of all women deserve that, and I can't give it to you. I don't think I'm capable." A genuine sadness laced his words.

"Yes, you are. You love me, I *know* that you do."

"I can't even say the words out loud. Doesn't that tell you something?"

Those words sliced straight through her, cutting swiftly, and with absolute precision. She half expected to find blood spurting from her chest. "Oh, God. Lincoln."

He looked so sad, so miserable, his deep blue eyes guarded. Shut down. He gripped the steering wheel. "Maybe...maybe we rushed into this."

"Yeah?" Her heart hurt with a dull and deep ache. "What do you want to do?"

"I think we need to take a step back. Maybe we need a break."

Well, she'd asked for honesty. How wonderful to get exactly what she'd wanted. Yay.

"You should see someone else." He took her hand and squeezed it. "I'm not going to, but you should. Because you could do a lot better than me."

The words wrenched a sob from somewhere deep inside her soul. "No. I'll never do better than you. Never."

"Just try, Sadie. Please try, because I don't want to hurt you any more than I already have." He hung his head.

Her heart, raw and tender, split right down the middle. She squeezed his hand back. "Yeah. Okay."

Then he walked her to the cabin as he'd done so many times over the past few weeks. The mood shifted, entirely different as the night air hung between them oppressively. She fought to walk calmly and with her head held high. She'd been hurt before, after all, and survived. Though it was nothing like this raw ache that filled her now.

"Goodnight," she said, unlocking the cabin door.

She refused to say goodbye. This *wasn't* goodbye. She'd see him from time to time, though not nearly as often. Though maybe, if this ache didn't ease with time, she'd have to consider leaving town. Because a person couldn't hurt this much every day and survive.

"Goodnight. I'm sorry," he said, his blue eyes so very sad

and defeated, then walked back to his truck and drove off into the dark night.

Inside her cabin, her back against the closed door, Sadie slid all the way to the ground before she let out the first mournful sob.

Once again, she didn't see this coming.

CHAPTER 23

*C*rying would not be on the menu. No sir. She wouldn't be *that* girl. But the next morning, when she woke to the sound of whipping wind whistling through the lakeside trees, she wondered how she'd survive. Once before, she'd felt the pain of loss accompanied by a healthy dose of betrayal. Yet even then there wasn't an ache like a huge gaping hole in her chest that would never heal.

She rubbed her swollen eyes and tried not to think of what lay ahead. Maybe she'd have to see Jolette Marie's knowing smile, when Lincoln eventually went back to the kind of relationship he could handle. One with zero expectations. No love.

She showered, dressed, and considered her options. Maybe she should adopt a puppy, or a kitten. Eve certainly would help find the right one. Someone who needed her. Daddy would relax his pet rules for his only daughter. She'd have to promise to repair any damage to the cabin. The children could help her name the dog. She would put all their names in a suggestion box, then pick the one she preferred. It would be a nice exercise in both creativity and penmanship.

Her children. They'd get her through this.

Since Eve would be at the Carver ranch all morning doing her grooming job on the horses, hanging out with her was not an option until later. Even then, Sadie worried Eve would just bring Sadie further down. Eve wasn't exactly brimming with hope for a brighter tomorrow last night. This latest news might send her over the edge.

Oh, sigh. So, she'd head on over to her parents' house to possibly talk some sense into her clueless dear old daddy. It took her a few days, but she'd finally seen her mother's point. Her father, her hero, the man she'd set as the standard for all men who came after, was...not perfect. And God bless her mother, who'd never allowed Sadie to believe he was anything less than that.

She hoped to be the same type of mother someday, leaving her children out of any grievances against her future husband...whoever he might be.

The thought brought a renewed ache.

She found her father in the shed by the vineyard, wearing his trusty overalls, holding a pair of trimming shears. The small space smelled of wood and fresh cut grass, and brought up a memory and a pang for her childhood.

"Hello, sweetie." He set the shears down.

She folded into his arms, but despite her heavy spirit, she'd decided not to claim her father's sympathy. Not today. Today was about Mom.

But he must have sensed something, because he patted her back. "Um. You okay?"

"Oh, sure."

He led her out of the shed, arm around her shoulders. "Good. Make darn sure Lincoln treats you right. I wouldn't want to have to kill him."

"Oh, he's one of the most honest men I've ever met."

Painfully so.

"Good man." Dad tipped back on his heels. "I always liked him. Your mother isn't here now. Will you come back for dinner?"

"Not tonight, Daddy." She linked her arm in his and they walked toward his baby, er, his vineyard.

Interesting how her parents grew apart when they discovered their passions after their empty nest. She'd always expected them to grow closer together, to appreciate the privacy, and spend even more time with each other. Spend more nights together, holding hands while watching a movie.

"Are you and Mom okay?"

He sighed and patted her arm. "Depends on what you mean by okay."

Not exactly promising there. "Are you still happy? In love?"

"Well, of course! I love your mother. Why, can't you tell?"

"It's not whether I can tell or not. I wonder if *she* knows."

"When a man works all the time so that his wife can have everything she needs, well, she should *know*."

She shouldn't be shocked that her father wasn't romantic. He'd been far too practical all his life. She sat on a wood bench her father had repurposed from one of the old church pews and placed at the head of the Chardonnay row of grapes. Today was clear and crisp, the sweet scent of grapes lingering in the air all around them.

"It's just that I think Mom doesn't feel…appreciated. You know? I think her business has become very important to her."

"That's just a hobby."

Oh, dear. How on earth did her wonderful father miss this? Probably too caught up in his grapes.

She cleared her throat. "No, Daddy. *Yours* is a hobby. Hers is a business now. With a lot of potential."

He plunked down beside her, staring like she'd suggested the earth was flat. "The *jam?*"

"Yes, Daddy," Sadie said patiently. "She's doing well, or haven't you noticed?"

"She sells to friends and the General Store. I figured she was just breakin' even."

"She's doin' better than that. But maybe if she invested in a marketing plan, who knows, right? Now, it's simply word of mouth and organic sales. And Daddy, she said she's been paying some of your bills with her business profits."

"She helped with our property taxes last year. That was nice, sure."

"I don't think that Mom feels like you appreciate her contribution."

"Of course, I do! What kind of nonsense is that?"

"It's the way she *feels*. Not nonsense." Dear Lord. Her poor, poor sainted mother. "And I'm talking about her business."

"She told you this? Why wouldn't she tell me?"

"You know what? I'll bet she has, Daddy. Have you been listening?"

"To her talk about the business?" He scratched his temple. "She goes on and on about it some nights. It seems all she's ever interested in anymore. I guess maybe sometimes I tune her out. For God's sake, she's canning, like she always has. I'm supposed to get all excited about this?"

"Maybe at least as excited as you are about your grapes?"

Her father jerked back like she'd slapped him, and Sadie regretted the harsh words. But she'd had a hell of a night. She was flipping tired of men. Yes, even *Daddy*.

"I don't know, but I think at some point you guys stopped really talking to each other."

"We went on a cruise, which I thought she'd enjoy."

"Hm. Well, someone recently told me love was easy. All

you need to do is open up a vein and bleed." She met her father's gaze and quirked a brow. "Have you been bleeding lately?"

"I did say that, didn't I?" he chuckled, rubbing his chin. "What the heck was I thinkin'?"

"That love isn't easy and sometimes it means you're going to hurt a little." *Or, you know, a lot.* She shrugged. "No matter how much it hurts, it's worth loving. And it helps if you open up and give that someone you love the deepest parts of yourself. That's the bleeding part."

He ruffled her hair. "My daughter is so wise. Beyond her years."

Later, Sadie drove to the Kerrville Public Library and checked out ten books centered around enhancing elementary school education. Crafts, math and science, language, and how to work with special needs. Just for kicks, and she told herself simply because of where she lived, she checked out a book on the rodeo.

On her way out, she caught a sweet couple finding some privacy in a little nook behind a bookcase. They were in a clinch, gazing at each other like they were the only two people in the world. The man leaned in close, smiled and tucked a hair behind the woman's ear. Like Lincoln used to do. She'd always seen the gesture as tender and loving. Her heart stung with a deep ache. If he didn't love her, he'd certainly faked it well.

I can't even say the words. That must mean something.

On the other hand, some, like Lincoln's mother, threw those words around easily. She recalled a certain charming Australian who'd said them to her on their second date. He didn't mean a word. For Lincoln, those words carried such weight and meant so much that when he said them to a woman, they would mean something. They would mean forever.

And he didn't want forever with Sadie.

Unfortunately, she couldn't tell herself she'd survived worse, because, oh, no she hadn't. She quickly drove back to Lupine Lake, and seeing Eve's truck, headed straight to her cabin.

Eve opened the door holding her kitten. "Meow," the kitty said.

Sadie smiled and gave her head a little rub. "Hey, I wondered if you wanted to—"

"No, I'm not goin' out again. That's final. I'm not interested."

"Not that. I thought tonight maybe we could watch a movie, or play a board game, or do each other's hair, or—"

Sadie suddenly couldn't stop the sobs that wrenched from her. Before she could stop herself, she'd let loose with a cry that to her own ears sounded like that of a wounded animal.

"Oh my Lord, honey, why are you crying?" Eve pulled Sadie inside. "Don't try to talk."

Good thing because Sadie *couldn't* talk. She couldn't catch her breath.

Eve walked her to the couch, gave her a little push, and then set the kitten in her lap. He meowed again and rubbed against her. Sadie tried to say something, but the words didn't find room between her sobs. Her throat tight, she simply petted him and damned if that didn't help. No idea why.

"Wiggle will make you feel better." Eve patted Sadie's shoulder. "That's his specialty. Does this have anything to do with a certain cowboy?"

Sadie nodded.

"Oh boy. Those...those...damn cowboys!" And then Eve simply sat next to Sadie, quietly rubbing her back, and letting her drop every last blessed tear.

After a few minutes, Sadie's sobs wound down, and when the crying became hiccups, Sadie explained.

"He…wants…me…to…find…someone…else,"   Sadie managed to get out.

"What an idiot. And I thought Lincoln was the smart one."

Sadie buried her face in Wiggle's soft, smooth fur and took a deep breath. "I really thought he loved me. Sometimes, I swore that I saw it in his eyes. But maybe I saw what I wanted to see. Eve, what's wrong with me?"

"Nothing's wrong with you! You just haven't found a man who deserves you yet."

"I thought I had."

"It happens. We're wrong about love sometimes. I remember on my weddin' day, wonderin' if I loved Jackson too much. Whether he loved me enough."

"I'm sorry if this brings up bad memories. I didn't mean to do that to you."

"Look at you, worried about *me* even when you're in pain."

"I guess neither one of us is going to wind up with a Carver man."

"Their loss."

Despite the fact that Sadie didn't believe this, might never believe it, she still nodded.

"What do you want to do first?" Eve brightened. "Hair or nails?"

NOVEMBER BREEZED IN, and Sadie made it through the first week. But the Veteran's Day weekend lasted an entire year. Sadie spent most of it sleeping, never having been quite so tired in her entire life. On the last day of the three-day weekend that would not end, she went by her parents' house to pick up jams to deliver to the General Store for her mother, who looked a little happier, at least.

She stepped out of her truck, but thought she saw Lincoln walk across the street. Quickly ducking back inside, she bonked her head on the steering wheel.

"Ow!" She rubbed her poor head and from the safety of her truck, slowly rose, and glanced across the street.

No. Not Lincoln. It was that other handsome man, Levi something or the other, headed to the Shady Grind. Relief flooded through her, even if she realized she'd never be able to avoid Lincoln completely. But later, much later, she'd be able to handle seeing him again. Just not now.

It had now been almost two weeks, and yet no one seemed to know about their breakup. She'd give them no more than a couple more days. By Sadie's calculations, any minute now someone would figure it out and spread the word.

"Hello, Sadie."

Sadie turned to see Judson standing behind her. "Oh, hey there."

"Can I help you with those?" He nudged his chin toward her truck bed and the boxes of her mother's jam.

"I sure appreciate that." She picked one up and he took two others.

"I'm heading back to Dallas tomorrow."

"We'll miss you around here. Are you comin' back?"

"Sure will. I love the scenery here." He eyed her carefully, giving her a shy smile.

Now see, why couldn't she fall for a man like Judson? Handsome, kind, great manners, liked her, and she'd bet *he'd* be able to fall in love.

"I hope you come back."

"Yeah?" He gave her a hopeful smile, as if she'd just agreed to his marriage proposal.

"Pamela Ann seems to really like you."

His smile deflated a bit, but he nodded. "I don't make it a practice to date married women."

"And we appreciate you for that." She heaved the box inside the storefront. "But you never know what could happen."

"Exactly. And I'm a patient man when I see what I want," he said, setting down his own two boxes and giving her a long look. "Are you okay? Suffering from allergies? Your eyes are very red."

Self-conscious, she rubbed them. Really should have at least put on a little makeup today to disguise the effects of her weekend-long crying jag. But she found she didn't much care what she looked like.

"Yeah. Terrible this time of year."

"You should really see someone about that."

"I will, thanks." At that moment, Sadie caught Lillian making her way down the produce aisle in her direction. "I'd love to stay and chat, but I have to go!"

"Okay, Sadie. I'll write to you. Or call you."

"Sure." And with that, she ran out of the store.

CHAPTER 24

On Friday, Sadie clapped her hands together at the end of another week. Given the long weekend, this week felt too short. "Okay, boys and girls. Have fun this weekend and be sure to get your parents to read to you. Remember, read, read, read."

Pretty much all she'd be doing this weekend. At least there were books and she could escape into a perfect romantic world. She would clean her cabin from top to bottom and take up Eve on her offer to visit the nearby animal shelters on a search for the perfect pet. The children were already very excited about having input in naming it.

Sadie hitched in a strangled breath. Yeah, she'd be fine.

The parents arrived to pick up their children, Pamela Ann right on time. She'd likely never be late again. Sadie went back in the classroom to clean up and grab her backpack.

She hadn't seen or heard from Lincoln all week. Her heart was shattered but differently this time. No betrayal from someone she trusted. Just a hard, dull ache that might never go away. She'd wanted honesty, well, she got it, from a man who couldn't say those simple three little words back to her.

Either he'd never be able to love anyone, or maybe he just couldn't love *her*.

She didn't know which one of these two would hurt the most.

Word was now all over town that Sadie and Lincoln were no longer an item. Lovely. She didn't talk about it much, not to anyone but Eve. Judson called from Dallas and wanted to take her to dinner, but Sadie turned him down. Tonight, Eve planned to come over with a gallon of Rocky Road and a stash of romance novels. They were both going to get lost inside the pages of a perfect fantasy world where everyone got a happily ever after.

Well. No point in delaying the inevitable. Her students were gone. She straightened up a few odds and ends and turned to go.

"Sadie."

She turned because the voice carried a ring of hostility. Instinctively, Sadie knew she'd face Derek.

"They've a-already left."

"I know." He brandished a knife.

"Are you kidding me?" Sadie's voice shook and not long after the rest of her body joined in. "How is this going to help anything? You want to *hurt* me?"

"I don't want to hurt you," he said with almost scary calm. "But I do need you to come with me."

"W-what? W-why?" Sadie pictured all types of less than happy scenarios in which she wound up on the wrong side of that blade. "Where are we going?"

"Just walk with me." He pointed her toward the door and walked closely behind her.

She felt the tip of his knife as it bit into her lower back. "This isn't the smartest thing you've ever done."

"That's where you're wrong. I figured out the schedule and Lincoln isn't working on the new building today. I have a plan and it's going to work."

Word obviously hadn't reached Derek that Lincoln wouldn't much care anymore *who* she left with. But there were other men working today, Lenny and his brother-in-law, Brad. She caught their eye as she walked like a robot down the portable's steps.

"Miss Sadie?" Lenny called out. "You okay?"

"Shut up, Lenny," Derek called out. "Mind your business."

"What the hell ya doin' there, Derek? Have you lost your mind? Cause I'll help you find it!" Lenny shouted after them.

Derek shoved Sadie into his truck from the driver's side, holding tight to her arm.

"Please," Sadie said. "Let's think this through. Jimmy Ray needs you to stay out of trouble so you two can be together again."

"Thanks to you, I might never get to see my son again."

"No, I'm sure that's not true."

"Well, if you're sure, this is going to go real easy." Derek started up the truck and drove out of the lot.

Behind them, Sadie saw Lenny and Brad jump into Lenny's truck and follow. A trickle of dread pulsed through her. This could get ugly. By the time they were on the road heading out of downtown, there were three cars following them.

"Damn it!" Derek pounded the steering wheel. "Can't anyone in this town mind their own?"

"Listen, I know you don't want to hurt me. But this isn't the way. I don't know how I can help you, but I'll certainly talk to Pamela Ann if that's what you want."

Suddenly, he revved the engine and accelerated. "That's exactly what you're going to do. As soon as I lose these guys."

The sudden jolt of speed made Sadie nauseous. Or maybe the fact that Derek hauled her out of the classroom with a knife. His desperation, she imagined. She didn't want him to get hurt, but if he thought she wouldn't fight back, he'd chosen the wrong teacher.

All of her life men had protected her, taken care of her. First her father, then her brother, and if either of them missed their chance, there were all the men of Stone Ridge. No wonder she'd gone to college and slid right into a relationship with a man who wanted to love and take care of her, as long as she'd ignore his many indiscretions. Well, she didn't need a man, even those currently following them, all with the best of intentions. She'd take care of this herself thank you very much.

She believed Derek wouldn't hurt her, unless he did so *accidentally*. And that could very well happen if he continued at this rate of speed.

"Slow *down*," she said, as he blew through a stop sign. "You're going to hurt us both."

"I don't care what happens to me anymore."

Oh, God, no. Don't say that. She swallowed hard.

"Jimmy Ray cares." She hoped that would sink in as Derek executed a turn that made the truck spin on what felt like two wheels.

He headed to Lupine Lake.

"When we get to your cabin, you're going to call Pamela Ann and tell her you made a mistake."

"*What* mistake?"

"Introducing her to that high falutin' doctor in town."

"What? No, no, I didn't. He's left town. Derek, she's not dating anyone. She's still your wife."

"Ha! I'm supposed to believe that? She thinks I cheated on her, so this is how she's payin' me back. Well, it won't work. Maybe I'll have you call that slimy doctor, too. Tell him to find his own damn woman!" He hit the steering wheel.

"He was just tryin' to be a friend to Pamela Ann. He doesn't want to date her."

"Likely story."

"You do know that Jimmy Ray went after you and got lost, don't you? Judson checked him over that night, because he's a *doctor*. And that's all there is to this."

Derek screeched to a halt and pulled into the frontage road leading to her cabin. Parking, he jumped out of the car and pulled Sadie across the seat, nearly yanking her arm out by the socket.

"You're *hurtin'* me."

"Oh, I'm sorry, didn't mean to." For a moment, it seemed Derek regained his senses, and he walked her swiftly to her cabin, pulling her along a bit more gently. "Let's go inside and you can call Pamela Ann."

Sadie unlocked the front door. She didn't have a plan but for now she would simply indulge Derek.

She went right to the phone, not wasting any time. "What if she isn't home?"

"Then we wait until she is."

"But what if she won't listen to me? I'm not the authority on her."

"You're the teacher!" Derek yelled. "I don't know if you realize this, but every parent respects you. She'll listen to you."

"And I'm sure she'd listen to you, too, if you talked, instead of ordered."

"Dial." Derek sat on the sofa and splayed his legs, holding the knife steady.

Sadie dialed and no one picked up. "No answer."

Derek glanced at his wristwatch. "Try again in ten minutes."

"Are we going to do this all night? Why don't you just go home, and I'll keep tryin' to call her."

"Nice try. If I leave here, you'll call to tell her what I've done, how crazy I am, and that she should never give me another chance."

Apparently, it hadn't occurred to Derek that she could always do that later. Or that Pamela Ann wouldn't be impressed by the way he'd treated Sadie or inclined to give him a second chance.

"I promise that I won't do that."

She heard several vehicle doors slam outside one right after the other, and then Lenny's voice just outside her cabin.

"Now son, don't be a shit for brains. C'mon outside and stop actin' like you done lost all your marbles."

"Go away." Derek opened the curtain and Sadie could see that there were three trucks outside. "Sadie is fine and no one's goin' to get hurt."

"Gonna need proof of life," Lenny said.

"Oh, for crap's sake! Sadie, tell them you're okay."

"I'm okay, guys," she said loudly enough to be heard. "He just wants me to call his wife."

"Gee, son, you sure like to put on the drama," Lenny continued. "Kidnapping our schoolteacher to get her to make a *phone call*?"

"I didn't kidnap anyone!" Derek shouted, but for the first time since she'd seen him, he looked uncertain. A trickle of sweat formed on his brow and he rubbed his knee.

Someone rattled on the doorknob of the locked door.

"Guys, he didn't kidnap me," she shouted, earning her a surprised look from Derek. She spoke a little more softly to him. "I don't want you to get in trouble. But, really? I think this qualifies."

"Aw, damn." He wiped his brow, put down the knife, and gestured to the phone. "Try again."

Still no answer. She shook her head and hung up. "Derek, what happened between you two? Want to talk about it?"

"What are you, a psychologist?"

"No, but I'm a great listener. Why don't you try me?"

"What do you think happened?" he said roughly. "I lost my job. Then I was no good to her at all. Anyone could tell that Pamela Ann regretted marrying me a long time ago, but losing my job just made it worse."

"*And* the drinking."

He nodded. "Yeah, sure. The drinking. Which started after I lost my job, and when she stopped…when she stopped touching me."

"I can see why that would hurt your feelings."

He winced, as if having feelings was not something he could admit.

"There were a lot of men after Pamela Ann when we met. She could have married any one of them. She married me because she got pregnant. Too bad, because it was the last time I did the right thing. Jimmy Ray is the best thing that ever happened to me."

"And he adores you."

"But Pamela Ann doesn't. Not anymore. If she ever did." He shook his head sadly, looking defeated.

Her heart filled with sympathy for poor Derek. He looked so lost. He just needed a little bit of guidance to get on track, just like his son did. To know that someone in this town would take his side. Sure, he'd gone about it the wrong way, but he needed her to help him. And after the scene at the school when he'd shown up tanked, he hadn't imagined she'd do him any favors. He would have been right.

Sadie took a deep breath. As it happened, she'd recently gained a ton of experience when it came to matters of the heart.

"I know how you feel because this happened to me, too."

"What happened?"

"I love someone who doesn't love me back."

Derek scratched his temple and narrowed his eyes. "Lincoln?"

She nodded. "But you know what? I don't regret our time together for a minute. Whether or not someone loves you back, you can still love them. Sometimes it has to be from a healthy distance."

"I don't like *that* idea."

"No one does. But Derek, I'm going to ask you something and listen carefully. How much do you love Pamela Ann?"

"Well, a lot, I guess."

"Someone that I love, and respect, recently told me that love isn't all that hard. All you have to do is open up a vein and bleed."

He blinked. "That sounds pretty hard."

"It's a different kind of difficult, isn't it? But if you love Pamela Ann, and you really want her back, you're going to have to clean up your act. Then you're going to have to open up that vein and bleed. Tell her how you feel. Everything that you told me here today. It might hurt, but on the other hand it also might be the most wonderful and freeing thing you've ever done."

Again, someone yanked on the doorknob. This time it sounded like Riggs Henderson. "Open up! You *want* me to call 911? Might take a while but they'll send out a county deputy. You'll want them to get here before Lincoln does."

"Shit fire!" Derek said.

And of course, Lincoln *would* show up. Not because he loved her, but because he was a solid man of Stone Ridge, born and bred. When the community needed him, he'd be there. Someone obviously alerted the phone tree just like on the first day of school. Now, they were coming to rescue her from a depressed husband and father who probably drank a few more cold beers than he should. And she appreciated it very much that everyone cared what happened to her, but *she* would take control of this situation.

"What are your demands?" This from Lenny, who'd

apparently read the hostage situation manual in the last few minutes.

"I don't have any demands because this isn't a dagum hostage situation!" Derek shouted, peering through the curtains.

"Then why won't you open the door so we can all discuss this like rational men?" Riggs pressed.

"Because this is none of y'all's business!"

While this exchange went on, Sadie kept pushing buttons on the phone over and over again, and finally, thank you Jesus, Pamela Ann picked up the phone.

"Hello?"

"Derek! I've got her on the phone."

He moved away from the window toward Sadie and the phone, tucking the knife in his back pocket.

"Derek is there with you?" Pamela Ann hissed. "What is *he* doin' there?"

"Well, honey, that's a long story. I'm going to let Derek tell you all about it." She handed him the phone.

He stepped back, tossed his hands up. "You tell her for me. I don't know what to say."

Sadie continued to hold the phone out. "Yes, you do. Just tell her what's in your heart. Everything you told me. How you're hurtin'. That you don't think you deserve her. And what you're willin' to do to be able to come back home."

Derek took the phone and with a deep sigh put it to his ear. "Pamela Ann, baby. *Please* listen to me."

And Sadie heard the man who wanted his family back finally make his case.

CHAPTER 25

"Well, Albert, I've failed," Lillian said.

"Tried to warn you. You're terrible at this matchmaking thing," Albert said from where he sat perched on the kitchen counter. At this point, she could see him anytime of the day and didn't have to sit down to write to him. Good thing because her arthritis was getting worse, not better.

She'd seen poor, sweet, Sadie at the General Store last week dropping off some of her Mama's jam. Her eyes were red-rimmed and she hadn't worn a lick of makeup, her hair in a braid, making her appear far younger. Looked like she didn't give a hoot what she looked like. That's when she'd understood.

Her Lincoln failed to recognize that everything he'd ever wanted and needed existed in the form of Miss Sadie Stephens.

"It *would* have worked. Somethin' just went wrong. I blame Maggie Mae. That woman left those children of hers a hurtin' somethin' fierce. And Lincoln, worst of all three. He blames himself. It's goin' to take a miracle, or at least some pretty fast thinkin' on my part."

"Well, get to thinkin', then."

"What do you think I've been doin', old man?"

The phone rang and Lillian picked it up.

"Hello, Lillian. I've activated the phone tree," said Beulah Hayes. "Tell Lincoln and Hank to get on over to Lupine Lake. Sadie's cabin. Stupid Derek kidnapped Sadie and has dragged her over to her cabin."

"What on earth?" Lillian clutched her chest and she didn't do that often.

Even Albert blinked in surprise.

"Stupid is as stupid does," Beulah said, as if discussing the weather. "Will you tell your men?"

"Yes, I'll tell them! When did this happen? How many men are on their way?"

"Quite a few. Ol' Derek don't stand a chance. Lenny was the one who called. He and his brother-in-law saw it happen."

"He *kidnapped* her?"

"That's what he said. Right out of the schoolhouse in broad daylight. Boy don't have the sense to come in out of the rain."

"Maybe you should call the law. This sounds serious." For once the men of Stone Ridge would need assistance.

"By the time they get here, we'll have taken care of this on our own."

But Lillian couldn't be sure.

"Oh, lawd." She hung up the phone and felt the salty sting of tears. "Albert, I think I may be comin' to be with you soon."

He snorted. "Woman, you're goin' to outlive 'em all."

Sadie! Kidnapped. What if that horrible man hurt her? And Lincoln, her poor lamb. He'd feel responsible, Lillian felt certain, even if he'd *nothing* to do with this. The way he'd been for most of his young life, sweeping up problems, taking on all of the family baggage.

She shuffled out the door fast as she could, in other words not fast at all, hopped in her truck, and drove up the hill. Once she could walk between their properties. Way back when she wasn't seventy-five with arthritis in her hips. She saw Lincoln and Hank in the field. Hank drove the truck with the apparatus that deposited feed for the cattle every few hundred yards. Lincoln stood at a gate filled with cattle, locking it.

He looked up at the sound of her truck and sprinted over. "What's up?"

"Something horrible! Sadie has been kidnapped by Derek."

Even under the shadow of his Stetson, Lillian saw all the color drain out of his face.

"You and Hank have got to get on over to Lupine Lake, lickedy-split!"

Lincoln ran in the direction of his truck.

"Wait. Go tell your father," Lillian called out.

"You tell him. I don't have any time to wait for him." With that he peeled down the hill, kicking up dust.

"Lord, let him get there in time," Lillian prayed.

LINCOLN GRIPPED the wheel and drove viciously toward Lupine Lake. Of all the many thoughts of Sadie in the past two long weeks without her, not one of them were about her safety. But he *should* have remembered Derek. *Should* have remembered that he posed a threat. Shit for brains Derek thought taking the schoolteacher would somehow help his case with Pamela Ann.

Jesus, the things men did for love. Crazy, stupid, insane things.

Like backing down and "needing to take a step back" and "a break," code for "I'm scared spitless of what I feel for you."

The day after he'd broken it off with Sadie, Lincoln thought he might actually die. Just drop dead in the middle of the day. His chest stayed perpetually tight, his breathing short and shallow. Had he been an older man, he'd have self-diagnosed the onset of a heart attack. That's how his grandfather had died, after all. Walking toward the barn one day and simply collapsing. He'd already been gone by the time Lincoln reached his side.

A quick, clean, natural, and swift death.

But this pain, this ache, felt *unnatural*. He'd thought he'd get past this after a few days. Didn't happen. Sadie remained his first thought every morning and his last one at night. He'd missed just seeing her face, and the way she looked at him, like he was everything. During the days, he kept busy. He stayed away from town, preferring solitude. Even when he physically wore himself out he still couldn't get her off his mind. Her wide hazel eyes always studied him with such earnest, deep, and unconditional love. The utter sadness in her shimmering eyes when he'd broken it off. The resignation. She didn't cry in front of him, didn't scream, didn't hurl accusations. Too bad because he could have handled that. But she'd simply accepted his words with a quiet strength.

She was stronger than he'd ever be.

And if Derek so much as laid a hand on a single one of her hairs, Lincoln might wind up in prison for a very long time. When he pulled in front of Sadie's cabin, there were men standing around, shooting the shit, doing nothing. Riggs was here which usually meant results, so this didn't make any sense.

"What the hell is goin' on here?" Lincoln asked, joining the rest of them.

"He kidnapped Sadie." Lenny pointed to the door.

"Now, calm down." Riggs approached Lincoln hands held out to stop him.

"I'm not goin' to calm down!"

"He ain't hurtin' her," Lenny said. "Just wants her to make a phone call."

"That's ridiculous. And you *believed* him? Who does that?" Lincoln banged on the front door. "Open up!"

"We tried that," Lenny said, not helpfully.

Then someone seemed to be talking behind Lincoln, possibly Riggs, saying something about cooler heads prevailing or some other such nonsense. That perhaps he needed to let them handle this. He barely heard the words, because his body buzzed with unbridled energy and raw fear. Lincoln thought he understood fear. The first time a horse threw him. The terror at not being able to find his brother for several hours the night he'd been jilted by Eve. The time Daisy didn't come home after a date.

But there was nothing like the fear of losing someone you loved more than your own life, when you could stop it. Lincoln knocked the door down with one swift kick, bringing him face to face with everything inside.

"Holy Beelzebub!" Derek shouted, and then hid behind Sadie, who simply stared from him to the door, back to him again.

"Want to tell me what you're doin' kidnapping Sadie?" Lincoln yelled. "And don't hide behind her."

"He didn't kidnap me." Sadie tilted her chin. "I came with him and I'm perfectly fine."

"Liar," Lenny said. "I saw it happen."

The rest of the men crowded the splintered frame. Pieces of the former door lay scattered on the ground.

"Regardless," Sadie said. "I'm handling this."

"You're handling this? You're *handling* this?" Lincoln asked stupidly. "Do you get kidnapped every day now?"

"Of course, I don't. But Derek and I managed to *talk* and work out our issues. Unlike *some* people."

Yeah, he got it. He was an ass for staying away. She'd sent him a not-so coded message.

He pointed between Sadie and Derek. "You mean the issue of him *kidnappin'* you?"

Derek stepped out from behind Sadie, hands up. "Please don't kill me. I just wanted her to talk to Pamela Ann for me."

Sadie crossed her arms. "Some men want to work *out* their problems. Instead of walking away."

"I thought he *did* walk away." Lincoln jutted his chin toward Derek.

"Pamela Ann kicked me out, Lincoln."

"Whatever."

Derek tossed his hands up. "I don't want her datin' some doctor! Can you blame me? If she just gives me half a chance, I'll make her...proud of me again."

The tender and gentle expression dialed all over Sadie's face would have been enough to tell him she'd fallen for Derek's dog and pony show.

But if that weren't enough, she put a hand to her heart. "You can do it, Derek."

Sadie, trying to save the world again.

God, he loved her.

"I want *him* to get out of here." Lincoln gestured to Derek.

"He's stayin' put," Sadie said.

"No, he's leavin'."

"He doesn't *have* to!"

Derek, whose head was jerking back and forth between them like viewing a ping pong match, spoke up. "Sadie? I want to go."

She rolled her eyes. "Fine, then."

He ran out of the cabin.

"Good choice," Lincoln said to his retreating back.

"You can go now, too," Sadie said, nodding toward the door. "I'll get Daddy to fix that and send you the bill."

"I'll be the one to fix that door and I'm not goin' anywhere until you listen to me."

She slid a look at the open entryway. The November breeze blew a few leaves inside. Lincoln followed her gaze to see Lenny, Riggs, and the rest, openly staring. Didn't even bother looking away.

"I told y'all I didn't *need* your help. Thank you, anyway, I know you meant well, but y'all can go now." She shooed them away with one hand.

They turned almost as a cohesive unit, but Lincoln stayed rooted to his spot. "Still not goin' anywhere."

"Oh, you are so maddening! From the day you took me to the hospital, I told you, I don't *want* to be another burden to you. Another person you feel like you need to look out for. Protect. I can take care of *myself*, Lincoln Carver." She stomped her foot and turned her back.

"I never doubted it."

"Then why are you *still* here?"

He shrugged. "Maybe I want to take care of you *anyway*. Is that a crime?"

"But *why*?"

The words he'd never said out loud to anyone other than his grandmother, brother, and sister wanted to come out in a sudden rush. But he wouldn't say them to her back. They were too important, and he realized before he said them, that they would change his life. Forever. But he felt ready now, ready for all that came with that fierce commitment. Because of her and the way she'd loved him first.

He took two steps toward her and turned her around to

face him. Gripping her shoulders tightly, ready to beg, he said, "Because I love you."

She froze, arms at her side, eyes rounded. "W-what did you just say?"

"I love you, and don't sound so surprised. You already know this. I love you, Sadie. I have loved you since the day you fell, and I thought I'd killed you. I love how brave you are. I love that you don't give up on anyone. Not even on me."

Her hand flew up over her mouth, then slowly lowered. "I thought maybe I'd been wrong."

"You're *not* wrong. You have great instincts about people and even if it's extremely frustrating and sometimes dangerous, I love that you want to help everyone in the world." He tugged her into his arms. "I love the way you look at me, making me think that I'm everything you'll ever need. It's pretty addictive. I didn't even know I wanted that, until you showed me."

With that she wound her hands around his neck, and he lifted her to him. She wrapped her legs around his hips.

Her breath hitched. "You said I'd be better off without you. That could never be true."

"I hope not, or I'm tellin' you, I'm sunk like a rock. I won't be good to anyone if you ever leave me."

Her eyes filled with tears and she buried her face in his neck. "Oh…Lincoln. I do love you."

"Thank God. Can I be your man again?"

She kissed him, sweetly and tenderly, giving him the answer he'd wanted.

EPILOGUE

Six months later

The month of April rushed in, clear and beautiful, and the repairs to the new school were complete. Beulah had scheduled an "unveiling" this weekend so the entire town could come and witness the project they'd all supported.

Sadie arrived early one morning, because Beulah wanted her to see the building before anyone else did. Excitement rushed through her, because both Lincoln and the rest of the crew had carefully kept her from seeing their recent progress.

Last night, before bed, she'd tried to tease a small hint out of Lincoln. Had they completely replaced the wood floor? Rumors said with such extensive work, they may as well have bulldozed the building and started over.

"One hint? Please? I'll do that thing I do with my tongue."

"Sorry, baby, you'll have to see right along with everyone else." But he'd looked strangely shy, giving her a small smile and avoiding her eyes.

The past few months cemented their love and commitment to each other. That same night, Lincoln had repaired her broken down door. A shame he'd lost his temper, but hey, sometimes love required breaking down a door.

Suddenly it seemed that no one said Sadie's name without soon after saying Lincoln's, and vice versa. Jolette Marie came to accept she didn't have a prayer of coming between them and had moved on months ago.

Her mother quietly came to accept that Sadie would never choose another man, no matter how much money he made, or how many letters followed his last name. Speaking of Judson, he wasn't seeing anyone, too busy trying to set up the clinic in town. He'd been going back and forth between Stone Ridge and Dallas. Pamela Ann and Derek were back together, Derek enrolled in a twelve-step program, Pamela Ann's condition. He'd found work with Sadie's father, on her referral, of course. She would have thought of that earlier, but Derek's commitment to recovery was key. Jimmy Ray? He was happier and better behaved than ever.

Sadie's parents were making their marriage work. Her father invested funds from his company's budget, as a "loan" to expand her mother's business. When they'd invited Lincoln and Sadie over for a family dinner to announce the unveiling of the renamed "Wanda's Wicked Jam" marketing plan, her mother beamed with joy. She'd smiled at her husband like she'd met him for the first time. Sadie hoped that one day, they'd get back to where they used to be. Baby steps.

But she understood that not everyone could love a man the way she did. Not with breathless, heart-pounding adoration. And that was okay. She might love him too much some days, in fact, but there was little she could do about that. Sometimes the thought would spring of how different her life would have been if she'd wound up moving to Australia and never coming home. Thank God for blessings which didn't seem like ones at the time. Through a great deal of pain and growth, she'd wound up with the right man. The one she'd loved since she was a teenager.

Sadie walked over to the new school and opened the unlocked door, immediately inhaling the fresh scent of oak wood and dried paint.

She took a step back at the sight before her. A brand-new building, all right, but something else grabbed her attention immediately. Her Lincoln stood in the middle of the room, Ellie hugging his leg, while the rest of her students surrounded him. All wore smiles.

"Hi, guys. What's this?"

Their little heads turned up to the tall man. He wore his gray Stetson, a crisp white button down rolled to his elbows, and his Wranglers. And that wicked dimpled smile that made her body go limp. In one swift move, he dropped to one knee and unfurled a pink poster board. On it, written in the scrawl of children's handwriting, were the words:

Would you marry me?

Someone wrote a backwards "e," so adorable, and she would never forget this moment. Ever.

Ellie came out from behind Lincoln. "Are you goin' to marry him, Miss Sadie, or what?"

Tears slid down her cheeks, and she stood with a hand clamped over her mouth. Dropping to her knees, she joined Lincoln just as he pulled a ring box out of his pocket.

"Oh, and also, there's a ring," Ellie said.

Indeed, a shiny new ring, a diamond oval with a band of two strands of gold twisted together. Far larger, shinier, and more beautiful than she could have ever dreamed.

"Yes, yes, yes!" she said, louder each time, with her "outside" voice.

"Yay!" Jimmy Ray said, leading the claps and cheers. "Woohoo!"

He then proceeded to do his little victory dance, which Sadie allowed him to do every day at the beginning of recess. His parents were back together, but this boy still had plenty of energy.

"Remember when he lassoed you, Miss Sadie? Remember?" asked Bobby Joe. "Huh?"

"I sure do."

"You fell and hit your head," Ellie said. "I saw it happen."

"We all did," Jimmy Ray protested. "And it was my idea."

"How did you manage this?" Sadie asked, her hands wrapped around Lincoln's neck.

"The kids asked to help me when I told them that I wanted to surprise you. Oh, and also, they put me through the ringer. Worse than your father, honestly. Interrogated me and wanted to make sure I'd take good care of you. And I will. For the rest of my life." He took her hand, brushed a kiss across her knuckles.

"We'll take care of each other. Always."

ABOUT THE AUTHOR

Born in Tuscaloosa, Alabama Heatherly lost her accent by the time she was two. Her grandmother, Mima, kept both the accent and spirit of the southern woman alive for decades.

After leaving Alabama, Heatherly lived with her family in Puerto Rico and Maryland before being transplanted kicking and screaming to the California Bay Area. She now loves it here, she swears. Except the traffic.